Tales You Wouldn't Tell Your Mother

Recollections of a Maybe Truthy Skivvy Honcho in Korea

Tales You Wouldn't Tell Your Mother

Recollections of a Maybe Truthy Skivvy Honcho in Korea

Robert E. McCoy

Paperback ISBN: 978-1-63490-853-5
Hardcover ISBN: 978-1-63490-854-2

Library of Congress Cataloguing in Publication Data
McCoy, Robert E.
Tales You Wouldn't Tell Your Mother by Robert E. McCoy
FICTION | War & Military
    HUMOR | General
Library of Congress Control Number: 2015914923

Published by BookLocker.com, Inc., Bradenton, Florida, U.S.A.

Printed on acid-free paper.

This is a work of fiction based upon authentic historical events. All characters are the product of the author's imagination. Any resemblance to actual persons, living or dead, is purely and strictly coincidental.

BookLocker.com, Inc.
2015

First Edition

"Enlisted men are stupid, but extremely cunning and sly,
and bear considerable watching."

attributed to
U.S. Army Officers Field Guides
of the late 1800s

Table of Contents

Dedication

This book was written with great respect for the members of the P'yŏngt'aek Business Women's Association (PBWA), with purposeful care taken that "Business Women" is written in two words. Most readers will have no clue as to the purpose of this organization and I have made no effort to add any clarity on that, but nearly all will likely figure out its intent from these *Tales*. Regardless, the PBWA members have earned my compassionate admiration and respect for having dealt with their circumstances in life by assuming a strong sense of dignity and self-worth, and for displaying a *joie de vivre* beyond what any Westerner could possibly imagine, despite the setting in which they were required to exist.

Prologue

It was drizzling rather insistently – not quite a full rain – in the dark early morning hours in mid August 1964 when I finally landed at Yokota Air Base in Japan after a long and uncomfortable flight from California. The seats did not recline and they faced the rear for safety reasons on the Air Force C-135, the military version of the Boeing 707 commercial airliner. The meager passenger accommodations were located inside the cargo hold where it had been cold and noisy. Now, I was a bit groggy from not getting enough restful sleep, but I knew that my journey was nearly over.

On the ground, the monsoons were making their presence known, and the low clouds and misty surroundings were captivatingly surreal. Tendrils of fog wound themselves among the tall conifers along the sides of the narrow two-lane road that led from the airport terminal to my intended assignment just a few miles away. Lights were beginning to come on in the small thatched-roof wooden houses visible from the narrow highway that already had traffic. It was a shock to be riding on the "wrong" side of the road, and even more disconcerting to look down from the bus window into the deep concrete ditch right next to the narrow-shouldered road. Japan was certainly different from the States.

Truth be told, I was both ecstatic and dismayed to be in Japan. It was exciting to be in a foreign country and to finally arrive at my first operational assignment in the Air Force. I had just concluded two years of intensive academic and then military training in the Korean language and culture. After all that, I should have been in Korea. Instead, I was assigned to bloody Japan.

Everyone told me that getting Japan was better duty: it was more modern and more open to Westerners, plus married guys could have their families with them. Then there was the siren call of Tokyo and its fabled Ginza, sort of like the Strip in Las Vegas! Well, be that as it may, I thought, why in hell study about Korea only to wind up in another country?

It was a strange series of events that caused me to be in Japan. I was supposed to be assigned to Korea along with my language school classmates, but I had requested a delay after all my training in the States in order to take care of some pressing personal business. I was granted a deferment for a few weeks, only to have the Air Force personnel office screw up and lose track of me. This was back in the day when humans did a lot of the paper work without benefit of computers, and the military paper jockeys were always overwhelmed. After waiting several weeks, I requested an update on my status since I did not get my assignment and travel orders at the expected time, only to learn that I had no assignment at all. Finally, when everything got sorted out and my travel orders came through, I was going to Japan instead. Geezus!

To make matters worse, I was an unexpected arrival at my new assignment. It seems that the unit to which I had been assigned was an airborne squadron that had only recently been relocated from Korea to Japan. Somebody at Headquarters must have assumed that the extra time I had spent taking care of personal business during my deferment in the States had actually been devoted to the additional training required for airborne linguists. Well, you know what the military says about assume: "Just look at the word. It makes an 'ass' out of 'u' and 'me.' Do! Not! Assume!" What a bunch of dumb asses!

In any case, there had been no announcement of my

impending arrival until the very last minute. Fortunately, individual finance and personnel records back then were sealed up in packets to be hand-carried by airmen as they moved from one assignment to the next. Even though I had arrived relatively unannounced, I had all the necessary field records with me and things got squared away within a few days. But I still had no idea how a lack of airborne training was going to work out for me at an airborne unit.

There were other surprises in store for me – starting almost immediately. I had landed at Yokota Air Base because it was the only military runway in the immediate vicinity that was capable of handling large jets. That should have been great, for Yokota was my base of assignment. But no, due to budget restrictions, the Air Force had not been able to build a passenger terminal there, even though large military cargo and transport jets had been landing at Yokota for years. If anybody ever tells you that the military can move fast, you can chalk him up as a lying asshole. So now, under the glowering eyes of military guards since passengers had not yet cleared Japanese Customs, we were herded aboard military buses to be taken to the Tachikawa Air Base passenger terminal where that was handled, even though it was roughly ten miles away. While it was still dark, the day was becoming long already.

Once there, I had to surrender all of my U.S. currency. I soon learned that military personnel in Japan – Korea and Taiwan, too – were not allowed to have real U.S. paper money, instead being required to use Military Payment Certificates. Using MPCs was intended to prevent black marketing on the local economy and to stop illegal trafficking in U.S. dollars by communist sympathizers in Asia. Yeah, well, I would certainly ask someone about this when I had the chance. Awful damned strange!

Each denomination of MPC bill had a different color and came in a different size, the largest being the twenty-dollar certificate. All, however, were smaller than a standard U.S. note. The fronts of each were intricately engraved, usually with the face of some female beauty, with the backs featuring meticulously rendered famous battlegrounds or impressive military equipment.

Due to their colorful nature, everyone usually referred to them as funny money or Monopoly money. I was told to shut up and not complain by the gruff military cop guarding the currency exchange area. At least the military in Japan could use real coins, whereas the U.S. military in Korea had to use MPC for everything down to the nickel. Only the penny was exempt. Geezus, who wants to walk around with a wad of almost worthless paper coins in his pocket?

By the time all of us passengers had cleared Japanese Customs, changed our money, and collected our baggage, it was beginning to show daylight. Takeoff from the States had been delayed for several hours due to some unspecified mechanical reason, and once airborne I discovered that the aircraft had few of the amenities common on civilian airliners. It made for a lousy flight. We had landed in the middle of the night and now it was already day. I had been traveling for nearly 24 hours and I was exhausted, ready for some Zs, so I was grateful that my sponsor met me as soon as I got off the bus at Yokota.

Upon arriving at a new base, every airman has a sponsor who shows the new person where to go for all the logistical things such as quarters and chow, the finance and personnel offices, laundry facilities and mail room, and so on. Most sponsors also augmented that duty by introducing the new guy to the more interesting stuff such as the Base Exchange, the appropriate on-base military Club, and the USO Center – as well as the various offerings of interest that were available off base.

My sponsor Harry did an outstanding job, particularly regarding the latter. I took an immediate liking to Harry, as he seemed to be an eccentric kind of guy always looking for a way to have fun or make a score. That he turned out to be a bit of a devious character did not alter my appreciation of his nonconformist spirit at all, and I suppose that it was only karma that Harry would figure prominently in many of my Asian escapades.

The first instance occurred only a few days after Harry got me squared away on base and situated at work, when he took me to a Japanese show house off base near another village some distance away. The place seemed to be just a normal American-style theater that had nice fold-down cushioned seats and padded armrests. The only difference was that a short and narrow catwalk extended a few feet out from the center of the stage into the audience. I thought I was about to see a Japanese movie or stage performance, and since I spoke absolutely no Japanese, I was wondering why Harry would take me here. He told me to be patient as we took seats in the very back row, just in time for the curtain to go up.

A scratchy recording of a Japanese song began to play as a Japanese lady in full geisha costume and stage makeup came out from behind the curtain to perform a classical Japanese dance. The unusual and colorful costume coupled with the dancer's highly ritualized movements were interesting, I thought, but I really had no appreciation for the art form at the time. Then a second record began to play, more Western in composition, heavy on the beat with a brassy melody. The young geisha appeared again, but this time to perform a tantalizing strip.

Completely naked at the conclusion, she posed very briefly in the demure posture of a woman caught coming out of her bath before scurrying off stage.

The third song was bump and grind with very little subtlety and not a whole lot of dancing. It was then I became aware of an undercurrent of animal-like noises emanating from the audience, nearly all of whom were well-dressed, middle-aged Japanese men. Before the song ended, the naked woman proudly strutted down the catwalk to squat down at its very end with her legs canted wide open. She invited the men to examine her most intimate parts, and they did so with gusto. One man got in so close between her thighs that his wire-framed glasses were bent in the barely controlled melee that ensued.

This three-record set continued with other women for more than an hour, by the end of which I knew that I was in a different world. Harry noticed my astonishment and remarked that what we had just seen was what Japanese "salarymen" typically do on a payday night. He further explained that, if this sort of thing appealed to me, this particular show was for Japanese only, but that similar entertainment was available near our base in a part of town that catered to the American military. Harry chuckled, however, saying that I really ought to experience Korea, for the "attractions" there were cheaper – as well as being far more "fulfilling." Well, no shit, being a healthy young man and believing that I knew enough about the Korean culture and language, I heartily agreed as I mentally began to make plans for a leave of absence to Korea as soon as I could manage it. Little did I know what was in store for me as my career-long involvement with Korea would soon begin.

And so begins the series of adventures that I narrate here as *"Tales You Wouldn't Tell Your Mother,"* absolutely and positively without any exaggeration or censorship whatsoever and as truthfully as one old skivvy honcho can manage. I would not lie. Well, maybe just a little, but really not much – I swear by the three holy Hans.

Chapter One: First Night in the Ville

It was only two months after my arrival, in the middle of October 1964 and I was able to go on leave for a few days, finally getting to Korea. My barracks buddy Buck was coming along to act as my guide there. I had met Buck at language school back in the States where he had been in the Korean language class several months ahead of me. Upon completing his course of study, he had been assigned to Korea and had eventually qualified for airborne duty. When the flying part of the unit in Korea was transferred to Japan in early 1964, he naturally went with it. Consequently, Buck had been at Yokota for only a few months when I unexpectedly arrived.

Buck was the only person I knew when I reached at my first overseas assignment, and I had been glad to see him. He took me under his wing regarding my duties and it was during one of our conversations about Korea during a break at work that Buck insisted, "For chrissakes, man, just take a week off and go there!" He said that he would be more than happy to accompany me if I wanted someone to show me the ropes. I accepted his offer, although I knew that the real reason for Buck wanting to go along was that he missed Korea.

Buck had taken me to the part of town just outside Yokota Air Base where airmen went to drink and perhaps strike a deal for sex with Japanese bar girls. Japan disgusted Buck because the Japanese women always demanded that guys first buy them outrageously priced and watered down drinks on which they earned hefty commissions. It was a business model that served both the bars and their resident bar girls quite well. Airmen did not think much of the setup, though, for more often than not, all they got for having spent a great deal of money for drinks was getting "back-doored." A bar girl would sit with an airman until he ran out of money or it was closing time. If it was a case of no more money, the bar girl just moved on to some other airman equally unwise about "investing" his money. If it was closing time, the bar girl would often disappear via the barroom back door, leaving the poor guy with a handful of empty promises. Buck insisted that, as far as he was concerned, Korea was the place where things were as they were supposed to be. I was about to learn that not all Asian countries are the same.

The flight from Japan was uneventful if slow on an old DC-6 four-engine propeller airplane still in use by the Air Force, but I decided to put the time to good use. Like most guys in the military, I had quickly learned to nap whenever the opportunity presented itself. Besides, looking at the clouds or trying to see the East Sea from 18,000 feet is interesting for only a few moments. I also wanted to be rested when we got to Korea.

Looking out as we started our descent to land at Kimpo Airfield near Seoul, I saw many differences from the area around Yokota Air Base in Japan. Korea seemed to be mostly mountains and rice paddies. There were few cities or towns visible and hardly any roads that I could discern. Hmm, perhaps Korea is a bit primitive, I thought. I was in for surprise after surprise, and it wasn't about the size or number of Korean cities versus Japanese ones.

The first surprise was the weather. Whereas in the Kanto Plains area of Japan it was still mild, October in Korea was already damned chilly, particularly when the wind was up. I was not adequately dressed for the cold and breezy day. As I was agitating about freezing my ass off, Buck advised me to not get my piss-box all foamed up, that we would get plenty of "anti-freeze" as soon as we got to the Ville. The Ville is a military term used to refer to the camp town villages that had sprouted up around U.S. Air Force bases and U.S. Army posts throughout Korea after the Korean War.

Since we had not yet left the U.S. side of the airport, we did not have to clear through Korean customs yet. That was supposed to come later at our destination, Osan Air Base. Our first task was to get there from Kimpo. I wondered aloud about taking a Korean bus, but Buck vetoed that, saying that it would take too bloody long, and it would be an uncomfortable trip.

Although the direct distance between Kimpo and Osan is less than 45 miles, the Korean bus would have to go through Seoul, the large capital city of South Korea, to get to the highway that ran from Seoul in the north to the port of Pusan on the southeast coast, passing on the way through the Ville next to Osan. Getting to that two-lane paved road would not be an easy task in itself – and then the bus would stop at every town and village along the way. There would be no reserved seating and we would likely have to endure squawking chickens or squealing piglets and their messes on the way to and from various farmers markets. Who wants to put up with barnyard shit? I said I'd wait.

Buck was able to locate an American pilot itching for an excuse to get out of Seoul and log some flight hours. The short flight to Osan was just what he was looking for. We climbed eagerly into an L-19 light observation plane, the Army version of a Cessna Bird Dog, and were airborne after using hardly any of the runway.

I soon learned why aviators are grounded when taking certain medications. As luck would have it, I had severely sprained my ankle in a game of semi-touch football the day before I was to leave for Korea. The doctor at the Yokota

Emergency Room had given me some pain meds to get me through the trip when I had informed him with a straight face that my trip was official business, not a leave of absence. I was not about to miss Korea just because some damned bastard got a little rough playing football. After only minutes of being buffeted by the winds, the gyrations of the small plane on top of the meds had me feeling queasy. Fortunately, the trip was only a half-hour or so.

We landed and were directed to the Korean Customs area. My small bag was opened for inspection and the South Korean customs official eventually pulled out a cellophane bag of Japanese noodles. Looking suspiciously first at them and then at me, he irritably demanded to know why I would insult the Great Republic of Korea by bringing in Japanese noodles. I was instantly pissed because I knew how those noodles had gotten into my bag and I also knew that the penalty for contraband would be stiff. Black marketing in Korea was a serious problem that was dealt with in a serious way. I just hoped that noodles were not on the list of prohibited items.

I managed to explain that I did not know whether Korea had noodles and that I just enjoyed the Japanese ones so much that I did not want to do without them during my short visit. The Korean official merely snorted and shoved the noodles roughly back into my bag. It was then that I noticed a tear in the cellophane along the seam of the package. However, I put my temper on hold as we exited the terminal and made our way onto Osan Air Base proper.

Dusk was approaching and we had to hurry if we wanted to eat cheaply at the chow hall and arrange for sleeping accommodations in the squadron barracks. When we got to the squadron area, Buck soon located some friends that he hadn't seen for several months and we were quickly pointed to two empty bunks where we could crash when we were not getting stupid drunk or laid in the Ville. We hustled on to the chow hall where, for 45 cents each, we had a passable supper served to us by Korean waitresses who also functioned as bus girls.

Then it was time to go the Airmen's Club. Buck wanted to meet a certain waitress working there in whom he had been interested. I too wanted to meet her since it was for that very same waitress that my sponsor Harry had stashed the bag of noodles into my bag. I was curious as to why someone would send Japanese noodles to Korea when there was a plentiful supply of Korean noodles already there. I was about to learn the conclusion of the story involving Korean Customs.

Inside the club, Buck selected a table off to one side of the main room. Within moments, a young Korean waitress came over, ready to take our order. She was not the one Buck was after, and after sniffing her nose loudly in disgust, she went to find the one he was looking for. The requested waitress arrived after a bit and Buck introduce her to me as Sun-ja. She almost immediately inquired as to whether Harry had sent anything with me for her. I was surprised by the abruptness of the question, but I handed her the paper sack that contained Harry's bag of Japanese noodles. Using the sack as a receptacle, Sun-ja ripped the cellophane and dumped the noodles out to retrieve a small lady's makeup kit that had been stashed within my noodles.

Holy hoosegow! Had the Korean Customs officer discovered that, my ass would have been immediately arrested and hauled off to a Korean jail until who knows when. That would have been a serious situation. I was beginning to feel the hot burn of anger at the danger Harry had exposed me to and Buck recognized that I needed something to get over the close call. He magnanimously sprang for the first round of drinks, an expenditure of just half a dollar.

Sun-ja was ecstatic with the cosmetics kit. Korean women working on base made good wages compared with those working off base, but they didn't make enough to spend wastefully. Then there was the problem of where in Korea to find the stuff in the first place, certainly not in the Ville. Those smuggled cosmetics would enhance her already considerable beauty. Sun-ja was quite tall for a Korean and, although a bit thin for my taste, it was easy to understand why both Buck and Harry would be after her. Sun-ja made it clear that she was definitely available – if there was a wedding ring and a ticket to the States in the deal. The problem was that Buck didn't make enough money to suit her, and Harry was already married to Sun-ja's former co-worker. So Sun-ja would be friends with them both – and keep on looking for her shining knight in U.S. Air Force armor.

Contraband delivered and stiff drinks nicely tamping down a decent meal, Buck declared that it was time to hit the Ville. Since Buck was one of the guys who had been in Korea before the airborne unit had moved to Japan, his experience in the Ville would be invaluable to me if I wanted to avoid being seen as an inexperienced new guy. I didn't want to be seen as a "jeep" as the experienced Ville rats called new arrivals, and I damned sure didn't want to be picked out as a "green bean" by the business women of the Ville. The origins of these two terms have been lost in time, but suffice it to say, they were both used as derogatory labels that no new guy wanted to wear.

After converting some of our MPC into Korean won, we hailed a taxi and headed for the main gate of the base. The way to the gate was paved and well maintained inside the base. Just outside the gate, however, the road became heavily cratered with large holes filled with ugly brown water, runoff from the recent rains. Vendors of numerous Korean delicacies hovered with their carts just outside the gate, and even though there were few streetlights as such, the way was adequately lit by the lights of shops and restaurants on each side of the road.

We left the taxi at the gate and pushed through the crowd to start down the only paved thoroughfare in the Ville toward one of the off-base clubs. Not far after we left the base, we ducked down a narrow and twisting alley that was slippery with mud and other things that I knew were not clods of dirt but foul-looking material that I really did not want to identify. After just a minute or two of treacherous slogging through a viscous mess that reminded me of loose stool, we could hear the music of the Aragon Club even though we were still several yards away from the entrance.

Its unassuming exterior concealed what lay inside. The inside was nothing more than a high ceilinged cavern, not quite the size of a basketball court, partially filled with wobbly tables and rickety chairs arranged around a dance floor. A huge sheet of Plexiglas protected an elevated platform at the rear where a Korean DJ was operating two professional grade turntables that he fed from shelves of vinyl records. The volume from a theater-class sound system was seriously loud.

A bar lined nearly one entire wall and an auxiliary setup stood in a corner of the opposite wall ready for when more drink service was needed. Overhead was a mirrored ball that was more than a decade ahead of its time for disco music. Any U.S. fire marshal or public health official would have had shit fits over the numerous conditions not up to the most basic codes:

electrical, plumbing, lighting, and general sanitation to name only a few of the obvious areas. No one cared, certainly not the young Korean women there, and certainly not the airmen that came to dance with those women.

Had my optic nerves not been holding them in, my eyes would have popped out of my skull. Here was every shape of woman imaginable! There were tall ones, short ones, thin ones, plump ones, and every combination in between. They were dressed and made up to look their best, and most were effective to at least some degree in their endeavors to attract the attention of the American customers. Although by American standards, makeup was not overly done for going to a party, it was enough in Korea to set the women apart from normal society. Another difference from the average Korean woman was that most of the women in the Aragon Club had skirts that ended above the knees and blouses that were either low-cut or clung to their breasts. It was an out-and-out smorgasbord of Korean femininity!

I quickly discovered that Korea had two types of beer: barely acceptable and not quite. The brands were OB (referred to as Old Belch, although the initials really stood for Oriental Brewery) and Crown. Crown tasted like it was laced with horse piss – some said it was actually formaldehyde, quoting an old newspaper report in Seoul. Nobody ever knew which it was, and nobody ever really gave a rat's ass about it because if a bar ran out of OB, everybody there just switched to Crown. After all, since whisky was not available in the clubs off base, beer was beer and airmen were airmen. Geezus, it wasn't rocket science, you just drank whatever poison was served, and you were happy to get buzzed.

The stated function of the off base clubs was to give

American military personnel a welcoming place to drink and dance off base in Korea, and many airmen took great advantage of that throughout their year-long tours. However, the real purpose of the clubs was to provide a place where U.S. military personnel and Korean business women could meet and enjoy the Western music by which the guys could demonstrate their best mating dances. The men came there to find their ladies for the night and the ladies were there to make a living from the men. The clubs made their money by selling beer – lots of it – to the airmen and by collecting membership fees from the business women for the privilege of using the clubs as their "show rooms." From all perspectives, nearly everyone was quite successful by the end of most evenings.

Buck agreed to take me on a tour of the remaining clubs before shacking up for the night. In addition to the Aragon, there were the Stereo, the Five Spot, the A-Frame, and the Paradise Clubs, the last one being some distance from the main part of the Ville. Only hard-core die-hards went there. Buck was an active member of the HCDH Association, so we went through the chilly Korean night in search of whatever and whoever awaited us at the Paradise Club.

We did well in our quest at the Paradise, even though I had by then become somewhat fuzzy headed from the beer teaming up with the prescription med for my sprained ankle. Although I didn't recall much of the later part of the evening, I certainly had been successful, for I woke up the next morning with a slightly achy head, and a sour gut – but a well-satisfied johnson, all in the company of a cheerful young lady who wanted to know, among other things, how much money I made and when I would be back to see her.

I hastened to make my exit after fumbling a bullshit excuse

about duty rosters not yet being posted and therefore being unable to give a return date. Finally out the door, there was yet another problem: I was completely and utterly lost. Fortunately, I have a good sense of direction. I knew from the base map that the highway ran generally north and south and that the base was just directly west of the intersection where the highway meets the spur road from the Ville to the main gate. The Paradise Club was well east of that on a dirt path that I remembered had started from the A-Frame Club. I struck out in what I thought was the correct direction and the sun shining through the clouds soon confirmed my choice.

I managed to get back to the base, make it to the correct barracks, and collapse into what I hoped was the proper bunk. Holy hangover! The gods must have looked with favor upon me since I had survived my first bawdy night in the Ville.

Chapter Two: A Life Lesson Learned Late

Buck was an old hand at hardy partying and he was the first to arise. Showing no evidence of the previous night's escapades, he roused me from an unsettled slumber all too soon. Despite my hung-over protesting, Buck hustled me through the normal morning rituals, and we headed off to the Snack Bar for some grub. It was too late for the less expensive chow hall and neither of us felt like the longer walk to the Airmen's Club.

After our late breakfast, Buck went off in search of friends he had left when he had been reassigned to Japan and, feeling much better after some decent chow, I decided to look up some of my former classmates that had gone to Korea on their normal assignment schedules. Buck and I agreed to meet in the squadron lounge later that afternoon.

Getting in touch with my old classmates wasn't easy. First, everyone works shifts in our line of work at Osan. The rotation was three days of swing shifts followed by 24 hours off, three days of midnight shifts and then 24 hours off, three days of day shifts and finally a 72-hour break in duty, also referred to as the "big break."

It was a perfect military solution for providing 24/7 staffing of positions that operated around the clock. While one of the flights was on Swings, another would be on Mids, yet another would be on Days, and the fourth flight would be on big break. After each three-day period, everyone would rotate to the next shift. This forced the readjustment of circadian rhythms every 72 to 96 hours and caused some guys to be constantly tired or grumpy.

Further, shift work created a tendency among airmen to make friends and hang out only with those working the same schedule. In fact, workers on the same shift were almost always billeted together in the same barracks wing so as to cause minimal disruption of their sleeping schedule.

A class system was an inevitable byproduct of shift work. The guys working shifts sometimes envied senior staff that had jobs with duty only during normal day hours and only on weekdays. Occasionally, the envy turned to jealousy and a day job guy was labeled a Day Lady or Day Pussy, depending upon whether the person under discussion was respected or not.

None of my former classmates had a day job. All were on shifts, which meant that half of them would be either working or sleeping at any given time. One quarter would be on big break, therefore most likely to be in the Ville or Seoul – certainly not to be seen in the barracks. The other twenty-five percent might be around in the squadron area somewhere.

The only classmate I could find was Doug, a tall lanky guy with a sometimes revolting sense of decorum. He seemed glad to see me and we agreed to carouse the Ville the next evening. By the time Doug and I caught each other up on what the other had been doing during the several months since we had last seen each other, it was time for me to rendezvous with Buck in the squadron day room.

Buck excitedly informed me that we had been invited to have dinner with Mr. Lee, Buck's former houseboy. Houseboys – actually more like communal manservants – are one of the perks of being stationed in Asia. To make a tour in a country such as Korea more palatable, the brass decided that local citizens could be hired to perform some of the more mundane chores that befall all airmen living in barracks.

Everyone involved was in favor of this. Commanders were rewarded with better barracks inspections and more meticulously dressed troops. The airmen themselves were of course delighted to not have to make their beds, shine their shoes, or wash and iron their clothes. The houseboys did all the facilities cleaning and lawn maintenance as well. There were waiting lists of Korean men and women hungry for jobs that were much cushier and better paying than what was available off base.

Houseboys were paid $2 twice a month by each person living in the barracks wing served by that houseboy. At roughly 15 airmen per wing, that yielded as much as $60 a month, an unheard of salary for a Korean blue collar laborer. As for Korean taxes, well, that was an issue between the houseboys and the South Korean government, for the airmen certainly didn't care a rat's ass worth about South Korean government revenues.

Mr. Lee was a good worker who was well liked by his customers. Over the months when Buck had bunked in Mr. Lee's wing, he and Buck had developed a close relationship. Even so, to be invited to a Korean's house for dinner was an honor. Mr. Lee took care to make me feel welcome along with Buck as he explained that his house was not fancy.

He was right. The house consisted of only two rooms, one of which was the main room of about 12 feet square. The other was considerably smaller. The kitchen was in a separate enclosure, more like a shed, attached to the house but at ground level. Smoke – and heat – from the kitchen fire exited through a chimney that first snaked through a flue just under the floor of the house. Koreans have had this kind of central heating for centuries, long before Westerners embraced the concept.

Two low tables were pushed together in the main room and Mr. Lee's family had gathered about them. Room was made for Buck and me. I was very interested in sampling the various dishes, as the aromas were exotic and tantalizing. Koreans generally didn't have a big meat dish with their meals. That method of getting protein was too expensive. For Buck and me, however, ox-tail stew had been prepared. It wasn't bad and I easily ate most of it. I learned by observation, though, that diners are expected to consume even the gristle between the tail joints; however I just could not get that down.

Kimchee, the ever-present fermented cabbage side dish so loved by Koreans, was pungently present. I tried it and immediately felt the heat from the red peppers on my tongue. A generous mouthful of rice suggested by my chuckling host soon eased the discomfort and we continued to enjoy the food. There was not much conversation, though. It seems that when Koreans eat, they focus on doing just that. Speaking was limited to asking for a dish to be passed closer. As the table was being cleared, Buck and Mr. Lee caught up on affairs. I mostly tried to follow along but my language skills were not nearly as good as I once thought.

Houseboys report for work very early in the day, and soon it was time for Buck and me to leave so that the family could retire for the night. In retrospect, I was not sure that I adequately thanked Mr. Lee and his family for their generous hospitality, but it had been a great introduction to Korean family life.

On the way back to the base, I told Buck that I was ready for another night in the Ville but he said that we ought to pace ourselves in consideration of the meager financial resources of our low rank. Buck might have been a hard-core die-hard Ville rat, but he was no dummy about money. I earned a little over $200 a month, not exactly a princely sum, and I could hardly afford to booze it up every night. Besides, Doug and I were going to run the Ville the next night, stopping at all the clubs from one end of town to the other, minus the distant Paradise Club.

The next day, I was really anxious to get to the Ville. Doug, however, insisted on a bit of preparation. We first needed a good greasy meal to handle the alcohol, he opined, so off we went to the chow hall.

Eventually we got to the Ville and began making the rounds of the off base clubs and began to set up our expected successes. Doug, I found, did not choose his women well. He was impressed more by flash and appearance than by personality. I thought that he was making his move on a lady who was not having a good day. Given Doug's less than amusing demeanor when he was having a bad time of it, the stars seemed to be aligning for a cosmic climax much different from what he was seeking.

Doug and his choice soon left and I concentrated on a young woman with a rather spirited personality. She was cute enough but it was her sense of playfulness that had me. We departed for her place shortly after Doug and his lady left. I found that this young woman was willing to help me with my inadequate grasp of Korean. A bit to my surprise, I discovered that we could joke and she willingly devised some Korean phrases to match the common military expressions so often heard on base, one example being "dip shit." We even discussed serious topics, such as the color of a fart – yellow, as even a fool knows, she confidently stated. So naturally, I got her address with the promise to write when I was back in Japan.

Back on base later the next day, Doug and I were discussing the previous night's events while sitting in the day room. In mid-afternoon, it was deserted and I thought that we would not be overheard. It wasn't the subject matter I was concerned about, it was Doug and his anger at how he had been screwed over by the lady he had been with. Damn it, he was embarrassing me with his vindictiveness. He had wanted some lip service to start but she had been disinclined to provide that. That seems to be a part of Korean culture and it's just the way things are. I felt that he was badmouthing her without cause, that his attitude was at least partly, if not mostly, responsible for whatever had gone sideways. I figured that you just couldn't expect people to do what is foreign to their culture, even if they are business women.

Before Doug could explain what it was that had really set him off, I heard the measured steps of military boots with heel cleats coming down the hallway. It was First Sergeant White, the top NCO of the squadron administration section, housed in the same building as the day room. He passed the door to the room and continued on for a few paces toward his office, but then the footsteps paused for a moment. Then I could hear him coming back and I just knew that he was coming to see us. Doug was agitated and his loud angry voice along with the topic of conversation had apparently captured the attention of First Sergeant White.

Indeed in he came, tall and burly First Sergeant White, with a look of displeasure on his face. He stopped right in front of me and demanded to know who I was. He had obviously recognized that I was not a member of his squadron. I identified myself, told him how I came to be in his day room, and silently hoped that he was finished with me. He then addressed Doug, saying that he had recognized his voice, even though Doug had not been visible from the hall.

First Sergeant White then began a speech that I will never forget. He started out with, "Listen up, assholes! You've got a lot to learn about Korea and I'm gonna give you sorry sacks of shit the first lesson. Maybe you'll stay alive long enough to learn the next one."

He proceeded to lecture us on how the ladies we patronized came to be doing what they do for a living in the Ville. This stuff was not covered in any lesson at our language school, and it sure as hell was never mentioned in any military briefing that I attended.

Everyone knew that Korea was a poor country at the time. That was part of its appeal to the American military man: cheap trinkets, cheap booze, and cheap women. As for those cheap women, it seems that unfortunate farmers would often consign their unmarried daughters to roving solicitors looking for young girls to "work in the big city." The promise of a good paying job and the need to reduce costs at home would usually override any qualms that a destitute father might have. In his society, daughters were not as valuable as sons, anyway, for they were an expense with little to no potential for income to help the family.

Of course, First Sergeant White continued, those good paying jobs never materialized and the "aunties" who volunteered to take in these girls on credit until they found that never-to-materialize job would soon turn them out to work in the off base clubs to repay their debt. Often enough, the young women would earn barely enough to get by and never make much progress in paying off what they owed. It could be a vicious circle. The young women needed money for clothes and cosmetics so as to attract clients and make money. Further, living expenses – board and room with the aunties – ate up quite a bit. Any necessary medical or dental care just added to the bill. Then there were the membership fees that the business women had to pay to the clubs for the privilege of working there.

He paused to take a deep breath before resuming. A pretty

woman or one with a charming personality had hopes of attracting an airman who might marry her and return to the States at the end of his tour of duty with a Korean bride. He said that many women never escape the spiral. A few would end up as aunties themselves. Of the others, they end up as old diseased streetwalkers or beggars.

Well, shit, that certainly took the fun out of no strings attached sex with the business women of the clubs! I left the day room that day filled with anger and disgust and guilt and shame, directed mostly at Korean culture and some at Doug, but also a bit at myself. I needed to start seeing people as being people, regardless of what they might do to get by in this world.

Years later during one of my rare assignments Stateside, I attended a social function with an American lady I was dating at the time. We were seated at a large circular table that was populated mainly by unattached women in their late twenties or early thirties. As soon as my date excused herself for the ladies room, two of the women turned their attention to me, flashing brilliant smiles. One asked, "So I hear that you are in the Air Force – are you an officer?" I saw the predatory looks in their eyes as their calculations began. When I replied that I wasn't, I saw their gleams dim back to normal and I recognized them for the ill-concealed gold-diggers that they were.

I wonder how much those American women really differed from Korean business women who, totally without guile asked, "How much money do you make?" It seemed to me that the latter are more honest than the former.

Chapter Three: Tall Tales and Good Times

Somewhat dispirited after the lecture by First Sergeant White, I chose to stay out of the Ville for the last two days of my leave in Korea. Instead, I decided to hang around with some of the old hands, those that had been in Korea for a while and could help me understand the culture better. Most of their stories were interesting, some were absolutely amazing, and all were things that I was glad to hear about.

One incredible story was how Osan Air Base repeatedly lost part of a taxiway to theft. The base runway ran East/West – 09/27 in pilot speak – and at the time, the taxiway that fed the eastern end of the runway was close to the base perimeter fence and not well lit at night for some reason. Runways are made of reinforced and very thick special-grade concrete. Taxiways don't have to take the pounding that runways do when aircraft weighing tens of thousands of pounds slam into them during landings. Consequently, they can be made of cheaper material like asphalt.

Well, the surface of the east end of the taxiway had reached the end of its life and was in the process of being replaced with new asphalt. Air Force investigators had been unable to figure out how – let alone why – many large chunks of newly laid asphalt kept disappearing night after night.

Now, as any high school chemistry lab survivor knows, asphalt burns if heated to the proper temperature. I don't know what that temperature is, and it probably various from asphalt mixture to mixture anyway. But what I do know is that the method used to heat most Korean houses then was up to the task. Those stoves in Korean kitchens burn charcoal blocks that produce a lot of heat.

One night, an elderly Korean worker was leaving the base late one evening and as luck would have it, he staggered just as he was passing the exit checkpoint. When the sentry rushed over to help the man back up on his feet, the old Korean was discovered to be hauling just about a cubic foot of fresh asphalt via the A-frame on his back. The authorities were surprised to learn what the heavy load was, and then astonished to discover how much weight the old man had been toting. I never learned what happened to the old man or what steps were taken to protect the new runway from further asphalt theft. The story in itself, however, was astonishing in that it illustrated just how far hardy Koreans would go to in order to survive.

I also learned from another old hand how some Koreans living near U.S. military bases were able to build their houses. Airmen drink huge amounts of beer when they are free to do so and huge amounts of soft drinks when they aren't. In order to endure transportation across several thousand miles from the States to the remote locations in Korea, most everything was always shipped in cans. Beer was always in cans, soda pop was always in cans, bulk goods for the chow halls and on-base clubs always came in cans, and even soda crackers came in cans.

In those days, cans were made of steel, not the aluminum cans of later years. Both the bottoms and the tops were crimped and bonded on. Empties littered the bases, particularly behind the lounges and snack shops on base. This would have eventually become a huge trash problem for the military – but some enterprising Korean who worked on base quickly had a brainstorm.

He discovered that there was a great market for those empties in the Ville. This unknown entrepreneur began gathering up all the cans he could haul on his A-frame and took them off base. Others quickly followed suit. Koreans would cut the tops and bottoms off the cans, split the seams that ran down the sides, and straighten the cylindrical parts of the cans into flat metallic rectangles. These small rectangles became the building materials of many roofs and even some exterior walls for more than a few houses in the Ville.

While Koreans were recognized as being very resourceful and inventive, airmen too were creative in developing ways to amuse themselves. Buck told me about a guy named Dell and some of his buddies who were a few of the more imaginative devotees to pushing the envelope with regard to what they could get away with. They found another use for empties by inventing the soda-can bazooka.

Cutting off the tops and bottoms of four or five steel soda cans was the first step of the manufacturing process. One more can had only its top removed and a large hole punctured in its bottom. In the final step, all of the cans were linked together using military-grade duct tape, making sure that the can with the punctured bottom was at one end with the intact bottom facing outward. A tennis ball would be crammed down the mouth of the "bazooka" tube and a liberal amount of lighter fluid would be sprayed into the hole of the bottom can. The tube would be vigorously shaken for several seconds until sloshing sounds were no longer heard. When a match touched off the vaporized fuel, the tennis ball would be propelled out of the tube for many yards accompanied by a hollow boom, sort of like the whump of a mortar being fired.

It is probably fortunate that such military mischief was most often conducted on Mids when senior NCOs or the brass were generally not around. One Mid shift, Dell and his buddies constructed a bazooka at work. One area of their workspace was a long rectangular room with operator consoles against both of the longer walls. A wide aisle down the middle allowed passage between the positions. At one end was an emergency exit to the outside and at the other was an area partitioned off with a plywood wall that had a large Plexiglas window through which the console operators could be monitored. The shift supervisor and his functionaries usually stayed in that area.

When Team Dell created the latest version of their bazooka that night, they decided to test it by aiming it from the far end of the console area toward the plywood just to see if the tennis ball would have enough impact to startle those who sat behind the partition. After clearing everyone from the aisle, the bazooka was ignited. The tennis ball did not disappoint them. Only by sheer luck was the trajectory sufficiently low so as to not hit the Plexiglas. But that was the only bit of fortune that night. Someone must have increased the dose of lighter fluid. Whatever the reason, the tennis ball punched partially through the plywood to leave a big blister of splinters on the far side.

The detonation and the almost immediate impact of the tennis ball gave rise to the loudest exclamation of "What the fuck?!" that had ever been heard. Dell and his buddies were beside themselves with glee. Tears of laughter were on the faces of some – but none of those behind the partition were amused. One junior NCO had actually soiled himself in his panic. Two victims of the prank later confessed that they thought the damned bastard North Koreans had attacked once again.

After the commotion died down, it occurred to someone that government property had been conspicuously damaged. While nobody expected a court martial over it, everyone knew that there could be consequences of some sort. After thinking about it for the rest of the shift, by consensus the mischief-makers decided on "the story." Someone must have spilled a cup of coffee or a soda pop and someone else slipped in the mess while carrying a typewriter and one end of its platen went smashing into the partition wall and this is what caused the indentation on the one side and the eruption of protruding splinters on the other.

I wouldn't have accepted that story for a Ville freebie, but the gullible Operations Officer seemed to have swallowed it whole cloth – or maybe he saw the humor in the situation and wasn't about to make a stink over some relatively minor and easily repaired damage. It was only few days before a repair crew replaced the ruined section of plywood, but in ˙the meantime, whenever a group of guys went by the wounded partition, there were whisperings followed by unexplained outbursts of raucous laughter.

One of my co-workers in Japan named Archie may have been involved in that, although when I asked him about the incident when I got back from leave he claimed with a grin that he was only a witness. After Buck got out of the Air Force, Archie and I began to hang out together. Archie and I wound up being stationed at a number of the same bases together throughout our careers, eventually becoming good friends. I trusted him and I never knew him to lie or outrageously embellish a good story.

Archie had gone to language school a couple of years ahead of me and therefore he had his own set of classmates. As we were getting acquainted after work one day, he told me about an episode in which one his classmates suffered an inglorious comeuppance for violating curfew one night in the Ville. Because the Korean conflict ended in cease-fire and not a peace treaty, the North and South were technically still at war. Due to frequent and bloody border skirmishes that could have heralded another full-scale attack by the North, and in view of communist agents periodically infiltrating the South, a curfew was in effect from midnight until 4 AM in the Ville. Violators could be shot. Those not shot but captured could expect severe punishments. That included any American military personnel, except that the U.S. military, not the South Korean police, would administer any punishment. Consequently, few guys ever risked violating curfew.

Archie's buddy Wally had been off base at the Five Spot and had failed to heed the club warning announcements that midnight approached. The announcement meant that airmen needed to haul their drunken asses back to base or to quickly choose the prettiest young woman available and then speedily retire to her place before 12 AM.

Either Wally's beer goggles weren't working at all or he might not have had enough personality in his wallet that night. Regardless of the cause, Wally made a delayed attempt to get back to base, sneaking through the rice paddies after curfew. There was a full moon that night and if you have had the opportunity to see a full moon on a cloudless night unsullied by city pollution, you know that there is enough light to actually cast shadows.

Wally thought that he had it made. He could easily see to walk along the narrow paths atop the low dikes between the water-filled paddies. But then he was spotted. Ignoring shouts in perfect Korean and fair enough English to stop, Wally began to run along the paths. What he forgot to consider is that the wide spots where two dikes intersect were not always just larger walking surfaces.

Often enough, such widened areas were actually pits into

which Korean farmers dump their night soil, the contents of their chamber pots and shallow outhouse craters. Wally ran straight into the middle of one such pit and sunk to his waist in a thick and putrid liquid that defies further description.

As Wally was recovering from the shock of being in deep doo-doo, two Korean policemen cautiously approached. When they realized it was only a drunken American serviceman, they contemptuously declared, "You go base now, you in enough bad." Wally did not get shot – and he did not suffer at the hands of the military authorities, either. When he got to the main gate of the base, the sentries on duty looked at him from a distance of several feet and told him to not approach any closer – and not to bother fishing for his ID card. They weren't going to get near enough to verify it under any circumstances. Besides, no commie would go through all that in order to penetrate the base through the gate. Better to just let the stupid fool go and to take pity on the poor houseboy that had to clean up his mess.

Back at his barracks, the enormity of his punishment began to dawn on Wally. In those days, all military personnel had to wear uniforms off base. Wally had worn his Class A uniform, which consisted of a blue shirt and tie under a summer-weight blue Air Force tunic with matching trousers. The tunic and trousers, being of wool, required dry cleaning, but there was no way the base cleaners were going to accept such a mess. His uniform was as good as gone. His shoes and tie were also worthless, and although his shirt and underwear were probably washable, whether his houseboy would deal with it was questionable as well. The cost to replace all these items would keep Wally out of the Ville for a long while. I never got to meet Wally but Archie recalled that he never had much interest in discussing the pitfalls of running along rice paddy dikes at night.

After I returned to Japan, I could not get Korea out of my mind. Don't get me wrong; it wasn't just the business women and carousing. I missed the people and the country I had studied about. Koreans seem to more readily accept outsiders into their lives. I also felt that they were more fun to be around, and I wanted to return to Osan as soon as I could.

Some months after my first trip to Korea, I had the chance to take another short leave and I seized it without hesitation. I would be going solo without old hand Buck to guide me around. That was not going to be an issue as I quickly looked into which of my friends were still there. Most had returned to the States by this time, but I made arrangements with Doug, one of the very few classmates of mine still in Korea. I planned my early February 1965 leave in to arrive when Doug would be starting his big break in the duty cycle.

Doug suggested that since it would be in the dead of winter when I arrived, a stay at the Onyang Hot Springs Tourist Hotel would be just the ticket to forget the sub-zero cold, wind, and snow. I thought that was a marvelous idea and then wrote the young lady I had met during my first visit to Korea to see if she would like to accompany me and another couple for a stay there. Mi-ja immediately wrote back her agreement.

Onyang was only 30 miles or so south of Osan, not a great distance, but nearly a one-hour train ride from the closest train station at the time. The entire city was a tourist attraction due to the hot springs that burble out of the ground at well over 120°F. The American military had an arrangement with that hotel, which afforded U.S. military personnel substantial discounts. The hotel was centered within a large walled-in enclave perhaps two city blocks on each side. A significant benefit of staying at this hotel is that, as long as we remained on the hotel grounds, no uniforms would be required. Holy hospitality! What a sweet deal that was going to be.

Doug made the reservations and when I met up with Doug at Osan, we arranged to meet early the next day at the Osan bus station for the ride to the train station up the road. Evidently, Osan was too small to warrant its own station. I had no idea where either station was but Doug assured me that Mi-ja would know where the bus station was and that she would get me where I needed to be at the appointed time.

Getting on that Korean bus early the next day with Mi-ja was a rude awakening. The bus was primitive and it seemed like it had absolutely no heat. I could deal with the chill during the short trip to the train station, but the main problem was the overpowering stench of kimchee, fermented cabbage, that permeated the confined space of the bus. It seems that Koreans eat that stuff even during the breakfast meal. I have since come to enjoy kimchee, but it was a shock to me back then.

It was not pleasant for Mi-ja, either, but for a totally different reason. She had to endure the sidelong glances from the other Korean women on the bus. They did not approve of Korean ladies, business women or not, associating with Americans. Much to her credit, Mi-ja was a stoic and she remained pleasant in her conversation with me. I tried to speak as much Korean as possible so that those who were eavesdropping would understand that I was no ordinary American. I don't think it helped much.

At the train station, I asked for first-class tickets but we were informed that the train we needed did not have that level of service, not even a club car for drinks. Instead, the best we could do was to purchase reserved seats in a car as far back from the coal-fired steam locomotive as possible to reduce our exposure to soot and smoke. The accommodations in the rail car impressed me. Although it was not luxurious, the seatbacks were upholstered on both sides and were hinged in such a way that seatbacks could be flipped from the front to the rear of the seat and still have the same degree of inclination. That way, passengers could choose to ride facing forward or, if traveling with friends, flip the seatback to face others with no loss of comfort. I have never seen that arrangement on trains in the States and I wondered why Americans weren't smart enough to figure out something like that.

After getting our foursome seating arranged, Mi-ja offered everyone some of the snacks she had bought from a train-side huckster for the ride and I ate them even though they were not to my liking. Doug had purchased a beer and some dried squid. I let him and his lady have at it. Although Doug's lady and Mi-ja were polite to one another, I sensed that they were not – and never would be – friends. Oh well, Mi-ja and I weren't tied to them anyway.

We finally arrived at the hotel grounds and what a sight it was! A grand old four story building that had somehow survived two wars, although it was in need of some cosmetic attention. Nonetheless, I thought that we would have a great time. During the summer, the hotel and its surroundings must have been beautiful, what with all the trees, gentle hillocks, and scattered planting beds. During the winter, though, it was just trees with stark naked limbs and mounds of snow. Yet as it was snowing later that evening, it was a beautiful setting, equal to any winter scene I had noted anywhere.

The room we had was adequate if not luxurious, so we unpacked and left for dinner in the hotel restaurant. I was not prepared for the prices and I knew that I would have to be careful in how I spent my funds. Mi-ja must have sensed this and she thankfully did not over-indulge in ordering food. We stuck to simple Korean dishes and had a nice dinner without a ruinous cost.

Doug and his lady appeared to be having troubles. She sullenly ordered a rather pricey meal of beef while Doug asked for dishes similar to Mi-ja's and mine. After eating, we went to the bar, thinking to have a drink or two and see what was going on there, perhaps dancing like in the Osan clubs off base that catered to the American military. There was a small band that played only Korean music. Dancing to those slow songs was nothing like grooving to Rock & Roll; it required mastery of ballroom stuff. Neither Mi-ja nor I had any experience with that although we struggled through a couple of songs.

As I finally conceded defeat, we both gratefully left the dance floor and tried to locate Doug and his lady. Doug was at the bar sitting alone. He said that his lady had gone to find a drugstore for some headache medicine. When she came back, she seemed more composed but she did not speak to any of us. About a half an hour later, she left again. This time when she came back, she was not walking with confidence, her speech was a bit disjointed, and her eyes did not focus quite right.

Not long after that, Doug's lady left a third time, but instead of going to take a pill, she went and took a powder. Doug was beyond angry, barely in control of himself, at having spent all that money for nothing. He stayed at the hotel for the first night but then returned to Osan the next day, leaving in a blue funk. Actually, I was greatly relieved, as I did not want a negative third person around pissing on my good times with Mi-ja. We weren't falling in love, but we seemed to enjoy one another's company, and a sour Doug would have been like a wet blanket.

With him gone, Mi-ja suggested we move to a Korean bed-and-breakfast, which would be much cheaper. That meant I had to wear my uniform again but we still enjoyed the rest of our stay in Onyang and my money supply wasn't completely wiped out.

When we returned to Osan after a great holiday getaway, Mi-ja and I said our good-byes. I think she understood that it was unlikely we would ever see each other again. I was a bit sad about that since she was really a sweet fun person. I never saw Doug again either, but that was just dandy with me.

Chapter Four: Deployment to Korea

Back at Yokota Air Base in Japan, I frequently reminisced about my two leaves to Korea. I wanted to return, but I knew that I needed to concentrate on learning more about my job to overcome my lack of formal airborne training, so reluctantly, that is exactly what I did.

After a year, I was rewarded with a promotion. The extra money from that plus the flight-pay for which I had finally qualified was welcome, and it was nice being accepted as a fully functioning member of my work unit. Military life consisted of flying one or two missions a month and working my desk job on the ground between flights. It was very easy duty at first, simply because the amount of work we had was not that great.

As a result, the was plenty of time for trips around Japan, mainly sight-seeing jaunts into Tokyo, and parties in the barracks or at the homes of the married airmen who had brought their wives over from the States. After that first year, though, the workload began to slowly but steadily increase, and after two years into my assignment, we were starting to feel pressured to keep up with it all. By early 1967, we were being overwhelmed.

I had been working overtime, sometimes putting in double shifts, in order to get all the analyses and reports out on time. The guys that prepared the materials from which I worked were swamped as well. During the previous months, we had picked up additional duty in the form of having go on temporary duty to Vietnam. Although many others from our squadron had been going to Vietnam on temporary duty assignments for some time, they were Chinese, Russian, and Vietnamese linguists – and they were not being inundated with work from the missions being flown out of Yokota. Plus, they had a helluva lot more people to begin with. The added duty in the war zone was a first for Korean linguists, one for which we were not staffed, and the loss of personnel sent there on temporary duty really hurt our ability to handle our already burdensome local workload.

It took way too long for us to get some relief in the form of more linguists. These additional airmen had formerly worked as Korean linguists but they had cross-trained into other languages, mostly to avoid the yearlong assignments without families to Korea. Uncle Sam, for the good of the military and without regard for personal lives, snatched them back to being Korean linguists. Some were happy to return to their old jobs while others weren't. Regardless, the additional help was appreciated and we began to make a little headway in working through the backlog.

Then the unthinkable happened less than two months after I had earned another promotion. The North Koreans seized the U.S. Navy vessel *Pueblo* in January 1968 and all hell broke loose throughout all of Far East Asia. For several days, our unit was ordered to stand down from flying missions while the dithering brass back in the States tried to figure out what to do. It was a true cluster fuck! It seems that no one at the Pacific Theater or national level could figure out what to do in response to something like this. What a bunch of dick-heads! Meanwhile, backlog or no backlog, we were itching to get involved.

Finally, we were authorized to start flying our missions again, but this time it wasn't just a handful of missions a month, we were ordered to fly around the clock. That amounted to 90 missions every month, about ten times what we normally flew, and we did not have the aircrews for that. Everyone greatly exceeded the maximum number of flight hours allowed in a month on a routine basis. Waivers were granted to fly the increased number of missions with the few existing crews we had, and to hell with damned regulations.

For the first couple of days after the resumption of flying, we flew our missions just as before, but with one major change that added to their length. Instead of returning directly to Yokota Air Base in Japan, we landed at Osan Air Base in Korea to drop off our mission materials for the squadron there to process. This made perfect sense because nobody was at Yokota to process the mission materials anyway – everyone at Yokota was busy flying missions.

The guys at Osan were soon overwhelmed by the quantity of stuff we dropped on them after each mission. It was obvious to everyone that this could not continue, and so another major decision came from the States. Instead of dropping stuff off at Osan and returning to Yokota, we were told to prepare for "temporary" deployment to Osan. In early February, and in accordance with a hastily developed schedule, each of our tired crews that took off from Yokota to fly its next mission landed at Osan to stay there for at least six weeks. "Temporary" my ass! Those deployments continued for well over three years.

Osan Air Base was not ready for the influx of troops that responded to the Pueblo Crisis, as the situation became known. The first night that we were there, one of our crews had to sleep in the Order Room on the floor with only blankets and day room chair cushions for beds on the carpeted floors. Within a matter of days, however, there were tents pitched in every conceivable open space to house the overflow. The winter of 1967-1968 was one of the coldest on record and the kerosene space heaters did little to heat those tents. Even beer froze solid if stored on the floor near a tent wall.

Despite those disadvantages, the crews billeted in tents were luckier in at least one respect than those that were forced to share bunks with others in normal barracks. While those airmen slept in heated comfort, many of them also acquired pubic lice from hot-bunking, as shared beds were called, with others whose hygiene was less than desirable. Hot-bunking was a poor solution to the problem of lack of sleeping facilities, for aircrews soon picked up various maladies from the shared bunks that grounded them from flying. It wasn't but a couple of weeks before the brilliant brass realized that this was a severe health hazard. One whole barracks had to be fumigated to rid all the bunks of the various vermin. There was a huge concern that infestations would spread back to the bases from which all the responders had come. With different crews rotating in and out every other week or so, the concern was justified.

Once every six weeks, a crew would get to return to Japan for a week. But during that week home, our airmen were expected to report for duty as if nothing was out of the ordinary. The fact that most of us were working close to 300 hours a month in Korea meant nothing to the Day Pussies and brass at Yokota. The claims of extraordinary work demands simply were not believed.

Most guys would want to hit the sack eight or nine hours before scheduled pre-flight briefings. That would allow them enough time to arise in order to do the "Four Esses" (shit, shave, shower, and shine) and eat before reporting for duty. But despite being tired upon completing a mission, we all knew that it was not wise to go to bed right after flying because most of us would wake up long before time to fly again and we would wind up being tired just as our next flight was to began. So we would nap for a short period soon after a flight – and then feeling somewhat refreshed, we would head for the Ville or the squadron lounge without any concern for what time of day it was.

The Ville loved this. Before the crisis, clubs and other establishments that catered to the American military wouldn't open until late afternoon or early evening. With the thousands of additional personnel that responded to the Pueblo Crisis – not merely our unit - and most of them working around the clock, business in the Ville was often booming as early as 9 in the morning.

Even our squadron lounge started to remain open 24 hours a day. After all, the guys working shifts wanted to shoot pool or otherwise relax, and it didn't matter to them what time of day it was when they got off shift. That led to some interesting situations as Day Pussies began to encounter large numbers of shift workers looking to wind down by full-blown partying that was not normally seen during the day, let alone early in the morning.

Due to my acquired expertise in analysis and reporting, I soon found myself on the ground helping to process the mission materials. In addition to the two of us from Yokota that were qualified for this duty, our unit had been sent several airmen from emergency reaction units scattered throughout the world. We now totaled perhaps a half-dozen guys whose task it was to get out the reports and summaries that were quickly piling up. By virtue of just having been promoted to junior NCO, I was one of two supervisors, and by fate I was the senior of the two.

After a brief consultation with the other supervisor, I decided that we would split into two shifts of seemingly twelve hours each, and after I explained that one of the benefits of working the night shift would be the avoidance of Day Pukes, another loving term for Day Pussies, there were enough volunteers to staff that shift. I volunteered to lead the night shift because there was another benefit to working extended Mid shifts. When it was our turn to be off duty, there would be no crowds anywhere, not at the Club, not at the squadron lounge, not in the Ville. We made a science out of taking advantage of this.

Actually, the way it turned out, the two shifts were closer to ten and a half hours than twelve, but since we were working seven days a week without break, I felt that the brass had no basis for complaint. And even if they did disapprove, what were they going to do – send us to Korea?! We just didn't give a rat's ass. The shift extension was achieved by arriving early, well before the normal Mid shift began, and then leaving on the very last crew van that ferried Mid shift workers back to the barracks area. Riding that last van gave us just enough time to get to the chow hall for a last call breakfast. A military breakfast, at least at Osan, was good grub and we chowed down in preparation for what was to follow.

Once out of the chow hall and after hitting the barracks for a shower and a change of clothes, we all regrouped at the squadron lounge to wait until 9 AM when the gate would open to the Ville. In response to the increased DEFCON – Defense Condition, a state of military combat readiness – the local brass decided that only those that had official business could leave the base before that time. To tell the truth, that delay of less than an hour meant very little to us since we had stimulating ways of entertaining ourselves until then.

Some guys tossed darts or shot pool while downing a beer or two to get a head start on the Ville. For most of us, though, Indian or Thumper was the pastime of choice, one being just a variation of the other. Both required beer and concentration. After a bit, the beer part became easier and the concentration part became harder. In preparation for either activity, chairs and couches were arranged in a rough circle so that participants all faced one another.

If the game was Thumper, then outlandish names to be used during the game were chosen by everyone. If a guy hesitated in selecting his moniker, a particularly insulting label would be chosen for him. The game began with everyone taking a drink of beer, teetotalers not being allowed. Then, to the rhythm of stomping feet or slaps to one's thighs to establish a cadence, the one chosen to go first would announce his game name and immediately call out the name of another. The person being called out had to recognize his game name, repeat it in acknowledgement, and then call out another name, all within a pre-arranged time limit, usually a second or two, which was refereed by the others.

Indian was different only in that, rather than ridiculous names, appropriately bizarre gestures or postures would be chosen. You can imagine some of the rude – or even obscene gestures – that were chosen, no doubt with the intent of livening up the atmosphere. No matter, the results were always the same: incongruous words being shouted out or incomprehensible actions being performed, sooner or later followed by loud protests when someone failed to react in time or used an invalid response.

Both games provided many welcome opportunities for chugs of beer when mistakes were made. In a spirit of friendly competitiveness, most participants saw value in taking simultaneous gulps along with the player that had incurred the penalty drink. On the rare occasion when a long period would elapse between errors, someone could be relied upon to halt the proceedings with a loud demand for everyone to perform a courtesy drink.

Clearly, no one could engage in this sort of activity for long, but generally it was only about a half an hour or so before it was time to hail a sufficient number of taxis for those going to the Ville. Although I have never been a morning person, 9AM never looked so good to me as on those times in Korea after an extended Mid shift.

Life continued like this for several weeks and then stories started to circulate about the unusual events that occurred after some airborne linguists had made their forays into the Ville.

In order to understand any of this, you need to recall that Korea was nearly destroyed first by the Japanese during their brutal occupation of the country, and then by both sides in the Korean War as battles raged up and down the peninsula. Even well into the 1960s, much of South Korea had not risen very far out of the ashes of ruin. The people were poor and had very little in the way of personal goods. Life in much of Korea was a challenge just to survive. Koreans were, however, industrious and ever ready to strike a good deal.

Many of the little treats we Americans took for granted were unknown to Koreans. One example of this was candy, and a case in point was the incident involving the Korean wife of my sponsor Harry. Harry was always getting into trouble but he invariably managed to come out of it better off, or at least no worse, for the experience – except this time.

Shortly after Harry and his Korean wife first arrived at Yokota Air Base in Japan, he had given his wife $100 to buy groceries and household supplies for the month at the Base Commissary and Base Exchange. She returned with more than

$98 in candy and nothing else. She was fairly good at doing math in her head, but she later stated that she had intended to spend the entire $100 on candy and the only reason she had that any money left at all was due to the tendency for stupid American prices to not be in whole dollars.

My coworker Sonny must have heard about that. When he got to Korea, he took a one-pound bag of plain M&Ms to the Ville and was able to spend a night of bliss in the arms of a more than willing young lady. Indeed, she was actually anxious to conclude the deal because she quickly realized that she could parlay that pound of M&Ms into something far greater than her normal fee.

Sonny was probably aware of this, but he didn't mind, for he got what he was after. The next item he tried was a 32-ounce can of orange juice. It worked just as well, although Sonny admitted that the can was bulkier to deal with than a pound of M&Ms. Airmen are nothing if not resourceful and innovative, and it wasn't long before that cumbersome can of OJ was replaced by a small jar of powdered Tang, an orange-flavored drink of the time principally known now for having been used by early American astronauts in space. A catch phrase quickly came about to "Get some poon for your Tang," but somehow I never could see General Foods using that in their advertising.

Bartering with American goods was supposed to be illegal, but there was that huge and tempting black market in the Ville. Despite the ease with which guys were making sweet deals, I was too nervous to see what I could get away with. Instead, I focused upon improving my language skills with the ladies and in trying to avoid the dissatisfaction of engaging in strictly-for-money arrangements. Accordingly, I tried selling the concept of friends with benefits to some of the business women. Often enough, however, that was not what those ladies wanted. Even so, I was frequently fortunate in finding a young lady who appreciated an airman that saw something more in her than being a sexual convenience.

For most Americans, Korean names are difficult to pronounce, and as a result, nearly all of the business women had nicknames in English. One of the ladies at the Stereo Club was known as "Pyramids" for her ample breasts. Pyramids was a difficult woman to fathom. It seemed that she wasn't just out to make money without at least a minimal level of friendship, but neither was she interested in any long-term relationship. She had evidently had in the past some sort of enduring relationship with an airman, but something in that arrangement had not worked out to her benefit and she seemed sour on long-term compacts.

What some of us did not realize at the time was that she had a young infant from that failed relationship and that she was still nursing the child, as most Korean mothers do. One day, a group of us had arrived in the Stereo Club after a warm-up bout in the lounge. None of us were roaring drunk but none of us were stone cold sober, either. Roger, one of the augmentee airmen, walked up to Pyramids and loudly declared that she was the most beautiful woman he had ever seen. She thought he was mocking her and began to let him know how little she appreciated his hurtful remarks. He was able to calm her down by assuring her that he was serious. Pyramids asked him why he would say such a thing, to which Roger replied that, while her face was indeed sufficiently attractive, he had never seen a Korean woman with such an astonishing bust.

All of us burst into laughter and, after considering whether to believe Roger, Pyramids allowed herself a chuckle or two. She explained that she was a nursing mother and that is why her breasts were so full. Roger was quite taken aback. He did not know whether to apologize or to just let it go. After a pause of couple of seconds, Pyramids realized that it was Roger who was now uncomfortable, but she knew just how to get everyone back into party mode.

She pulled down her low-cut halter-top to remove the absorbent padding from her distended nipples. Both of her rather spectacular breasts were fully exposed as she began to gently massage them, directing streams of milk toward Roger's shirt. Roger quickly backed away, and that set the stage. Pyramids ran around the small barroom, aiming her streams of milk at anyone in her path. It all quieted down in less than a minute, and impressive breasts once again mostly concealed from view under her clothing, Pyramids asked in a loud theatrical tone, addressed to no one in particular, "I am pretty, I am Numbah One, yes?" Of course, everyone there including the other young ladies gave her an approving round of applause.

I was able to see another side of Pyramids several months later when we had once again congregated early one morning in the Stereo Club. Lew, an acquaintance of mine – I certainly would not call him a friend – split his pants while doing an insulting parody of how another guy danced. Some guys did not like Lew because of his caustic humor, and we all knew that he could be a belligerent drunk at times. Some of the young ladies avoided him as well. However, recognizing the predicament he was in, Pyramids quietly told Lew to follow her home so she could mend his pants. They both disappeared for perhaps a quarter of an hour and Lew came back with his pants repaired to nearly new condition.

Once again, I was struck by the inescapable fact that business women were human beings. I wanted to never forget that. On my way out, I stopped to thank Pyramids for being kind enough to fix Lew's pants. I was repaid with a strident cry of, "You like Lew, you like boys now?" That really pissed me off and I continued my exit – wearing a scowl. Later, I was able to laugh it off as I realized that she was not about to let me get past her gruff exterior.

Chapter Five: Life on Base

It was now summer of 1968, and all of us were still working long hours and flying too many missions at Osan, those frequent deployments from Japan to Korea continuing. Sleep became a most welcome luxury for most of us. On one occasion, though, I was rudely awakened by a loud commotion accompanied by a tirade of profanity coming from the other end of the barracks wing. The overhead lights came on even though it was still in the middle of the night. Through my sleep-induced daze, I was able to figure out that Cooper – usually we just called him Coop – had made a serious mistake involving a laundry bag that did not belong to him.

Laundry bags are large sturdy cotton bags with pliable rope for drawstrings. They are issued to all airmen during basic training and most of us hang on to them for their intended use of storing dirty clothing. We usually tied our laundry bags to the ends of our bunks. Since the heads of bunks usually abutted the wall, the other ends jutted out toward the aisle that ran down the center of the barracks wing. Having laundry bags at that end made things handy for the houseboys when laundry day arrived.

Coop had come back to the barracks marvelously drunk just before midnight. He quickly crashed into his bed and was almost instantly out for the count. However, he had failed to do the two things that any experienced drinker knows to do before going to bed. The first is to down some anti-hangover potion and the second is to drain the bladder. Coop had evidently been roused from his stupor in the middle of the night by a bladder clamoring for relief.

Most laundry bags are olive drab green, but a big beefy guy named Johnstone – nicknamed "Stoney" for his toned body as well as his name – had an oddball white one tied to the end of his bunk. In the dim light provided by the emergency exit signs at either end of the wing, Coop saw what he thought was an extraordinarily convenient urinal. He staggered to it and began relieving himself all over that white laundry bag.

Stoney came awake to the sound of a liquid splashing onto the floor near the end of his bunk. It was a few moments before Stoney realized what was happening and then he came unglued. Fortunately, the intervention of several other guys prevented a still woozy Coop from getting thoroughly pounded by a steamed up Stoney. The mess on the floor was left for the houseboys to deal with when they came to work in the morning.

Probably due to an interrupted night's rest, I had slept too late that morning for the chow hall. As I headed for the latrine to clean up, I noticed that the mess on the floor from Coop's misadventure had been cleaned up and that Stoney's laundry bag was missing, it and its contents presumably being washed by the houseboys. Once I was presentable, there was still time to get to the NCO Club for breakfast. At the club, I saw Charlie, a co-worker, with another guy whose name I didn't know, and I joined them at their table.

While what I really wanted was a BLT, the prospects for that weren't good since the breakfast menu was still in effect. The waitress crew that morning was supervised by an older Korean woman that somebody way back when had christened "Ruthie." Ruthie was both efficient and cordial, but she was not known for her patience or sense of humor. Charlie and his friend had just beaten me to the club so all of us needed to place our orders.

Before a waitress arrived, I mentioned that I could really go for a BLT, a sandwich item that officially was not available until after the breakfast run. Charlie was one of the augmentees that had been recalled to Korea from another assignment. He had been in Korea before and he knew how to get around seemingly ironclad rules. Just as a waitress came over, Charlie told me to watch and learn how to get what I wanted.

Charlie requested a bacon and egg sandwich to which the young waitress apologetically replied that sandwiches weren't available until after breakfast. Without hesitation, Charlie said that wasn't a problem and to please give him one egg over hard – break the yolk please – with an order of bacon and two slices of white bread toast with butter – but keep each slice in one piece. The waitress wrote all this down dutifully. Understanding fully what had just transpired and believing that the young waitress had fallen into the trap, Charlie's friend and I decided to have the same thing as well.

Soon enough our food arrived and Charlie cautioned that now was the time to be a bit discrete. He quickly built his bacon and egg sandwich while keeping a wary eye out for Ruthie. It was all for naught as Ruthie had been watching us from the kitchen door when the young waitress set our orders before us. Just as we were about to chomp down on what I knew was going to be the best damned breakfast sandwich ever, Ruthie appeared standing hip-shot and arms akimbo next to the table right where a fourth person would have sat.

To say that she was agitated would have been an inadequate description of her demeanor. Ruthie opened her mouth to say something, but then realized that we had done absolutely nothing wrong. Indeed, all of the things that we had ordered were standard *a la carte* items on the breakfast menu. But we had challenged her strict administration of the NCO Club dining room, and that was an affront requiring some sort of response.

For a few seconds, she appeared to be ramping up for an all-out, full-scale verbal assault as she glowered at us. But just as quickly as she had materialized, she strode off, leaving in her wake a litany of Korean curses that were master-level invective. Anyone who thinks that military personnel know how to swear has never heard a pissed-off Ruthie. One of us eventually realized that our poor inexperienced waitress could very well be in for a hard time because Ruthie might be tempted to vent her spleen on any available target. To rectify that as best we could after the fact, the three of us left exorbitant tips.

For the next couple of days, we were not very welcome at the NCO Club when Ruthie was on duty. Eventually she calmed down enough to explain why she was so angry. It seems that some ignorant club members would ask for sandwiches that could not be assembled from the breakfast menu – turkey or roast beef, for example. The poor waitress, and then Ruthie, would have to point out that something like that was not part of the breakfast menu. When that happened, Ruthie and her staff often had to deal with arrogant and ungracious patrons.

I figured out that, if I intended to build a sandwich from the breakfast menu, I needed to sit in an inconspicuous spot, and I should ask the waitress to inform Ruthie about what I was doing. That seemed to resolve the issue, as Ruthie and I developed a friendly relationship over time.

We all need to be reminded at times that kind words and positive attitudes can make great differences in our life experiences. I believe that to be true – but I also know that there are exceptions. Sometimes nothing can make a nice person out of a hard-ass. A case in point was an experience I had at the Osan Snack Bar one evening during one of our early deployments there.

One night in the squadron lounge, a bunch of guys were

clustered around the black and white TV watching something that was of no appeal to me. I hadn't gone to the mailroom yet that day, so I announced that I was going to check my mail, wondering if anyone else needed to do so and walk along with me. Immediately somebody hollered out asking whether I would make a Snack Bar run since it was right next to the post office. I normally don't like being anyone's mule but there was no graceful way out of the request.

My only condition was, since I had been burned before on this kind of errand, that I had to be paid upfront for each and every order before I go. Donny said that he didn't have any money and that he would pay me later. Donny was one of the jerks who had burned me in the past, so I told him my condition specifically applied to assholes like him. I pointed out that he seemed to have money for the beers he was buying and that I was not going to be owed and never get paid.

Donny grudgingly dug a five out of his pocket and shoved it impolitely into my outstretched hand. I told him to watch it or I would deliver his food in the same rough way. I got everyone's order written down before I set out for the five-minute walk. After checking mail – nothing – I got in line at the Snack Bar, which was doing a lot of business at that moment. Nobody was answering the phone and that was probably why the guys in the barracks hadn't just made a telephone order.

When I finally got to the order station, I pulled out the list and went down the several orders. The older Korean guy taking the orders ridiculed me for having to write all that down, saying something about Americans not having much smarts. I decided to show him up by asking him if he had memorized the orders exactly as I had spoken them. He closed his eyes and repeated the orders back to me exactly as I had read them, even getting the various condiments for the different sandwiches dead-on.

I was impressed but I still wasn't pleased that he obviously saw me as a mental defective or a lazy ass. Thinking to knock him down a notch or two and using the Korean term of address for an older person, I asked him, "Uncle, if you are so smart, why are you just taking orders at the Snack Bar?" As soon as the words were out of my mouth, I regretted them, thinking that I had no need to prove myself to this guy. I quickly found out that I had taken pity on the wrong person.

Evidently, Uncle had skipped a couple of lessons in the Dale Carnegie handbook on *How to Win Friends and Influence People*. With absolutely no hesitation, he shot back with a bit of a sneer, "You Americans so stinky rich, I get all I can before you go." That shut me up. With no good reply, I merely moved on to the order pickup station to wait.

An airman behind me said that if the old piss-colored midget had spoken to him like that, he would have reached across the counter to smack the guy. I pointed out that the old Korean guy had heavy callouses on his knuckles, that he was likely quite skilled in some form of Korean martial art, and that he would probably have tied both of our skinny asses together in a bow. But the larger thought in my mind on the way back to the barracks took the form of, "Well, whaddya know, there are assholes in Korea, too!" That should not have been a surprise to me, but it nevertheless was.

The food from the Snack Bar was acceptable when right off the grill, but by the time I got back to the barracks, some of the sandwiches had gotten soggy. Even so, the smell of the bacon on some and the aroma of the French fries made me hungry, but unfortunately the chow hall wasn't open that late. Since my stomach was now informing me that it didn't give a rat's ass what time it was or where it was fed, I decided to go the NCO Club.

On the way over there, I had an idea that would get me in Ruthie's good graces for sure. In the past, I had overheard her talking in Korean with some of the other waitresses about how she really loved mandarin oranges. I knew that Japan grew fantastic tangerines and that the two species were very close, with some people actually saying that they were the same thing. Whatever the case, I thought I would bring Ruthie a small crate of tangerines the next time I returned from Yokota. The investment in good relations would be worth it.

At my next meal at the NCO Club when Ruthie was on duty, I called her over to ask whether the club had any tangerines for dessert. Holy citrus fruit! Ruthie began to rhapsodize about how she wished that were true. Then she looked at me quizzically to ask whether I could get her some the next time I went back to Japan. Well, her frank question caught me a bit off-guard. I had wanted to make the offer, not respond to any request, although the outcome of such a deal would likely be the same.

As I digested her rather forward request, Ruthie slowly began to realize that she had just propositioned me. Many airmen offer goodies from Japan or the States in order to wangle dates with the young ladies working on base, and for Ruthie to ask me outright for something would be seen as a very unsubtle indication of her desire to go on a date with me. She actually blushed and I began to grin widely at the incongruity of the situation. Ruthie was not unattractive, but she was about 10 years older than me. If it were a day when she was not grumpy (already fed up with stupid customers or something), and if I were feeling in need of an adventure, it would have been easy to take her up on such an offer – had it been made in earnest.

As it was, I told her in my best Korean that I knew her intended meaning and to not feel any embarrassment. That I recognized her blunder added to her consternation, but Ruthie calmed down when she realized that I had no designs on her nor was I going to give her a hard time about her rashly expressed wish. I explained that I brought the subject up to see if I could show my appreciation for being able to get breakfast sandwiches without a big fuss when she was working.

So, after they came into season, I brought Ruthie small crates of tangerines on a couple of occasions, much to the amusement of others. To the waitresses that teased me about it, I simply explained why Ruthie and I were friends. To the guys who they were less polite about it, I simply said that Ruthie was one fireball of a woman – and that they ought to ask her out themselves. No one ever did and the jeers eventually stopped, but had anyone ever made a play for Ruthie, I would have laid heavy odds against his surviving the act of just asking.

As for me, I always got the fastest service, often with more generous portions, than other guys, even friends at the same table. If someone complained to Ruthie about the inequity of it, she would snap, "You should be more like him," gesturing abruptly at me while walking away. I'd just shrug and nothing more was ever said.

No one really ever thought that I was doing Ruthie, but some of the guys wanted to get back at me for the benefits of my being her friend. It just so happened that there was a fad at Osan at that time, one akin to the streaking craze that hit the States several years later. This one, as is the case of many military pranks, was quite a bit cruder, a lot more personal, and rather appropriately termed "catching the red-eye."

In one room in the Operations Building, the one with the

aisle between two lines of operator consoles, some of the guys had prepared a deception for me. The story was that one of the operators must have lost the last page of his typewritten work at a console when the technical support crew had kicked him off the position for some PMI – a preventive maintenance inspection.

I left my desk to look for the missing sheet and saw that the console had indeed been shut down with its typewriter gone, all of the electronic gear removed from its front panel, and a large piece of cardboard covering the hole where the gear would have been. As I peered about for the missing sheet of paper, I heard a noise coming from within the console. Thinking mice or something similar, I pried the cardboard away from the hole to be faced with – more accurately, to be reared by – the quite naked and very close buttocks of Roger. Holy hemorrhoids! Mooned at a distance of less than two feet, I had just caught the red-eye. The entire shift erupted into howls of triumphant laughter as a bent-over Roger bellowed from the depths of the console, "Gotcha, you dumb ass! And you can't say I didn't!"

Chapter Six: Did I Love Lucy?

I was surprised to learn that Koreans believe that a baby has attained one year of age after only 100 days following birth. When I thought about it, though, it does make sense since the duration of pregnancy plus 100 days is roughly equivalent to a year. For Koreans, a baby's life begins at conception, not just when the child enters the world at large. For an infant to reach 100 days after birth is cause to rejoice for yet another reason. If a newborn survives for that length of time, it is thought to be healthy enough to continue on through childhood, barring any natural catastrophes or accidents.

I knew from talking with old hands that one-hundred day celebrations are major events. They all said that often a big hall is hired and special dishes are prepared for the extended family and close friends attending the proud event. Gifts for the baby are presented, although cash donations to the parents are not uncommon. Even with cash donations, the cost of such a celebration can be a burden for families that are not well off. They are disastrous for a single mother.

Although single parent households in Korea were exceedingly rare due to social stigma, they were not unheard of among the business women in the Ville. One such person was Lucy who worked as a bartender at the Stereo Club. I knew Lucy from our many conversations when I would sit at the bar. It did not take me long to figure out that Lucy was not in the business of servicing American airmen. I sensed that if a guy expressed a serious interest in her as a person, she might consider dating an American. All in all, she seemed like a normal woman in both demeanor and dress – except for the place where she worked.

She was a lively young lady with a sparkling personality, and

I enjoyed practicing my Korean with her, if only because she was remarkably tolerant of my frequent mistakes. In exchange, she often asked me to dance with her, teaching her the latest American moves to all the new tunes. I was only too happy to oblige because I enjoyed dancing with her. She was a quick learner and she felt damned good in my arms when we slow danced. But because she was not a true business woman – she worked primarily behind the bar – I made no attempt to seduce her. At times, though, I was sorely tempted for she did not shy away being close to me when a slow number was played. The problem was that I had a normal male reaction and even though I made efforts to conceal my arousal from her, she must have known how I felt. She knew I that I was a typical airman in Korea regarding business women, but I felt it would be insulting to be friends with Lucy and then go home with another woman from the club where she worked.

Some months after we began our first year of deployments to Osan, I didn't realize that it had been quite a while since I had encountered Lucy, when all of a sudden she was back in the club one night. She teasingly asked if I had missed her, to which I gallantly replied that I had been heartbroken during her absence. The words came honestly enough even if they were a bit of exaggeration, for although I had been unaware of it, I had indeed missed her and the easy camaraderie that we had developed. I also missed dancing with her. Lucy asked me to speak only in English, which made me think that I was really off in my pronunciation that evening. She explained that not everyone she worked with knew what she was about to tell me and she wanted to keep it a secret.

Lucy informed me in a low voice that she now had a son who would soon be reaching his 100-day milestone. Wow, I thought, that explains why she looks a little plump. Don't get me wrong, I like ladies with some substance – it lets you know that you are in bed with a real woman and not some skin-and-bones thing that cooperates with you. The time that I took to absorb all this must have caused Lucy to think that I disapproved.

With downcast eyes and a bit of sadness in her voice, she explained that the guy she had been going steady with, and whom she thought would marry her, just disappeared. When she had asked the airmen that knew him, they told her that he had returned to the States, obviously without telling her. She felt betrayed by the whole experience, then looking me square in the eye, she asked me in a demanding tone why American men lacked the honesty to tell a woman when their affair was over.

I felt very sorry for her, realizing that she had been handed a truly raw deal. She said it had been a difficult birth and that she had racked up some serious medical bills. My buddy Matt from Yokota sitting next to me had not been eavesdropping, but he had heard enough to figure out that Lucy was an otherwise decent girl in trouble. He gave me a telling look and then pulled out his wallet to dig out an MPC fiver. Instantly understanding what he intended, I took his money and matched it with one from my own billfold. I told Lucy that this was a loan, not a handout, and that she could pay us back whenever it was convenient. She didn't speak as she carefully folded the two bills and stuffed them into her now ample cleavage. As I observed her, I had an erogenous thought as I recalled Pyramids from a few months back. I was actually surprised when she gave each of us a quick peck on the cheek as we left.

A couple of days later, Matt and I were again in the club where Lucy worked. When she spotted us, she left the table where she had been chatting with some redneck-looking guy to ask us if we had any special plans for around 9 PM that evening. When we both shook our heads no, she asked us to meet her at the club entrance just before then, when she would be taking a short break.

Not knowing what to think, Matt and I nursed beers until time to meet Lucy at the door. When she came to the entrance, she motioned us to follow her as she walked up the street a bit and crossed over to a storefront that actually was an office behind which was a Korean rental hall. As we went through the office area into the hall, it dawned on me that this was the 100-day feast for Lucy's son.

Before us was a room perhaps 25 feet long by 15 feet wide. Down the center were several low tables pushed together to form one long one that looked roughly 15 feet in length. On that table were all the Korean dishes that I had learned about in language school plus a host of others that I could not recognize. In the center was a platter that contained the largest smoked fish that I had ever seen. The fish itself must have been at least 24 inches from nose to tail and even dressed out it was a plump one.

Lucy took us around the table to point out the various delicacies and why they were important. It seems that some Korean dishes possess symbolic meanings as well as having flavorful tastes. My eyes were agog at the display of what for Koreans must have been a feast suitable for the gods. Then two things hit me at once.

The first was that Lucy's family might not be attending since she had had a child without benefit of marriage. Even if the sonuvabitch airman had stuck around to marry her, it was possible that her family would disapprove of her having married a foreigner. Koreans are quite adamant about keeping their bloodline pure. And probably none of her friends and associates from the club would be there, either, for they would be busy trying to earn a living from the potential customers at the club. She could wind up being alone, though later her landlady who was now watching her baby would probably join her.

The second thing was that this spread was an extravagance that Lucy felt compelled by Confucian custom to pull off, but it was something that she could ill afford. I was overcome by feelings of sympathy and sadness, almost distress, for there was nothing that I could do for Lucy at this point. Life is sometimes just un-fucking-fair!

She asked Matt and me to sit down on either side at one end of the table. She sat between us at the head of the table, and she reached for our hands as she spoke in Korean something that I later discovered was a blessing used by Christians in Korea. My clue was the soft "Amen" at the end of her words. She filled our plates with items she knew we could eat with enjoyment as Matt and I began to chow down. When we could partake no more, she gathered up our plates for washing later and threw the chopsticks away.

As the three of us left the hall to head back to her club, I was at a loss as to what to do or say regarding Lucy. I knew of course that she was not my problem – hell, the baby wasn't mine. Geezus, she and I had never even been together. Still, for some reason it gnawed at me to the point that I told Matt that I wasn't in the mood for any more fun and games that night. He agreed and together we said goodnight to Lucy and headed for the base.

I wish that I had been the one to think of it since Lucy was more my friend than his, but it was Matt's idea to take up a collection for Lucy and her son. She hadn't told us about the 100-day event, possibly thinking that we would feel obligated to bring some sort of gift even though we were not Korean. Now that we would get a collection going, there would be at least a little cash for Lucy.

Since it was Matt's idea and he had the reputation of being a good family man as well as being somewhat religious, he was the one to put the bite on everyone. I followed him around as he hit up most of the guys from Yokota and a few from the emergency reaction units. One by one, MPC paper got dumped into a bag, mostly a couple of ones at a time but occasionally a fiver also found its way into the pile. At the end of the night, we had $117.

Matt left it to me to make the presentation to Lucy and I knew just how I would do it. It would be easy to explain that, since she had not given us any notice about her son's 100-day celebration, we were unable to prepare for it according to Korean tradition, as we would have wished. Consequently, we would have to make our offering now, a bit after the fact.

Lucy at first was very reluctant to accept the money wrapped in red paper until I explained it exactly as I had rehearsed. Then a strange look crossed her face as she quickly gathered me in her arms to hug me tightly for a good long while. I soon became most uncomfortably aware that there was a pleasingly plump and very attractive young woman pressing herself tightly up against me. Maybe she felt my involuntary reaction or maybe she became self-conscious of her own accord, but she loosened her grip to slowly back away while keeping her eyes locked on mine as her hands continued to hold mine. Her face was pleasant but inscrutable.

We continued to exchange pleasantries when we saw each other at her club, but I sensed that something was now different between us. We never discussed the 100-day party or the collection, and we were still friends with her still willing to help me practice expressing various concepts in Korean. And I continued to dance, even slow dances, with her every time she asked. Everything was exactly as before, except I felt that something was on her mind that she wanted to discuss with me but, for whatever reason, chose not to do so.

After some weeks of seemingly continuing our friendship as before, I came across Lucy on the street during the day, or rather she came across me. It was not one of my best moments. There had been a morning birthday Ville run for one of the guys I knew at work. I hadn't slept well the night before and I had not had much to eat before starting to drink. By mid-day, I was in the bag, simply wasted. One of the guys mentioned that it might be a good idea for me to get my drunken ass back to the base before I got into trouble with any of the Day Pussies, and for once I heeded the advice.

I left the club, not even remembering which one it was, to stagger toward the gate, when out of nowhere someone grabbed my arm to declare that I was in no condition to be in public like this, particularly in the middle of the day. I turned to peer closely and finally focused sufficiently to recognize Lucy. She had a look of concern on her face that I intended to ignore by pressing on toward the gate. With a bit of disgust in her voice, she sternly informed me that I was going in the wrong direction. Oh, well, why not let her escort me to the gate where I could get a taxi back to the barracks and go to bed, I thought.

After what seemed like all afternoon, I found to my surprise that Lucy had walked me to what I discovered was her place. I was in no shape to put up much of an argument, even when she undressed me for her bed pallet. For absolutely no good reason, I was shy in front of her and resisted as best I could but to no real effect. Clothes off and under her quilt, a feeling of comfort soon came over me and I drifted off into a sound sleep. The last thing I remember is telling her that the only reason she brought me home was that she wanted to see me naked. Much later, I recognized the Freudian implications of what I had said. It was me who, in my drunken state of mind, finally admitting that I wanted to see Lucy's naked body. I passed it off as having been only my johnson talking.

A couple of hours later, Lucy roused me and I started to get up. She pushed me back to a sitting position and handed me a small bottle of something labeled in English as Bacchus-D, insisting that I drink it down. She said that all the Korean men drank it when they went out for a night on the town. It tasted faintly like orange juice, but with a zing to it. Then she brought me her chamber pot and told me how to use it while she turned her back. My bladder shyness was overridden by the need for relief. I thanked her for her consideration and started to get up once more. Again, she told me to get more sleep.

When I woke up the next time, it was getting dark. I was feeling quite well because I had caught up on my sleep, the lack of which probably contributing as much to my sorry state as had the alcohol. I quietly got my clothes together and gently slid back her door. Lucy appeared almost right away. She had been sitting in the next room with her landlady when she heard the sliding door.

Lucy put both her hands on my chest to prevent me from going, insisting that I stay there for the night, that she really didn't feel up to going to the club anyway. Besides, she said, we could work on my Korean some more without the interruption of her serving customers. I agreed if she would allow me to take her to dinner. She nixed that, pointing out that she paid board and room here and that included a meal for a guest every now and then. I could eat real Korean food with her.

I didn't feel trapped, and I gathered that she truly did want me to stay, so it finally came to me that there were worse fates in life than spending a night with Lucy. We ate plain fare for supper with only the landlady and Lucy's son there – the several business women living with the landlady would eat after work when they returned from the club. Everything tasted just fine, even the spicy kimchee that I had come to appreciate.

After eating, I did a quick field-style cleanup at the well pump in the yard, brushing my teeth with Lucy's toothpaste on my finger. I washed as much of my upper torso as I could in the cold water without exposing too much of my male body. Finally, I felt like I could be in public once more.

The remaining evening hours passed uneventfully working on my Korean, playing card games, or just talking until time for bed. Lucy seemed to take things matter-of-factly as she modestly but quite unselfconsciously undressed for bed, but I wasn't sure how things would play out here so I felt it best to count on nothing happening. Perhaps it was having slept so well during the afternoon that made it difficult for me to get to right to sleep. Regardless, I remained awake and I shortly became aware that Lucy was making sniffling noises.

I rolled to gently touch her shoulder. The room was faintly lit from lights shining through the translucent oiled paper covering the latticed door of her room, and that allowed me to see that her eyes were open when she turned to look at me. I asked her if it would be better for me to leave but she grabbed my arm and rolled over for me to hold her. Hell, I didn't know what else to do.

It did not take long for me to get the measure of just how

fetching a young woman Lucy truly was and she quickly became aware of my obvious appreciation. She giggled as she held me in her hand and gently squeezed. I felt like a kid about to get into the cookie jar when no one was looking. As I descended between her thighs, I saw that Lucy had a hand covering her lower belly. I gently pulled it away to see that she was hiding an elongated vertical scar, the result of the difficult birth – Caesarian – of her son. That did not deter me as I moved up to deliberately kiss every inch of that scar, then slowly continued my way up her body, pausing for extra attention to her most enticing spots, until I was looking into her eyes. She kissed me with many small and fluttering nibbles as we began to enjoy one another.

The next morning, Lucy was all smiles as she told me that I was under no obligation, but she would like to see me to frequent her club just as before so we could continue our friendship. I was confused by her casualness. I left for the base very uncertain as to exactly what was going on, in light of us now being lovers as well as friends.

Back at the barracks, I figured things out. I had been perplexed because I had expected a bit more of a romantic – or at least appreciative – response from Lucy in the morning and I didn't get that. While I didn't want her to be all clingy or love-struck, I thought she should have said something about how much she enjoyed our time together. My ego was bruised because I didn't get any reward for appreciating Lucy as a normal girl friend rather than as a business woman. I hadn't realized that I had already received the best possible reward: Lucy had responded to me as she would to a lover, not a customer. She had not made anything of our great night together, maybe because she did not want to put me on the spot of having to respond in kind, just in case I did not share her feelings. How utterly stupid of me, for I should have told her how much I had enjoyed our evening together. I was a real dumb ass!

Somehow I got over it to resume meeting Lucy at her club and we settled back into the banter of teasing one another, me working to get better at Korean, and us even dancing slow together. Soon, though, Lucy stopped appearing at the club. After several weeks of not seeing her, I began asking around of the other ladies working there. Eventually, one of them told me that she now had a steady boyfriend and she no longer worked in the club. Well, shit! I was not pleased. I mean, I was happy that Lucy might be able to snag husband, for I had no intentions of settling down with just one woman at this point. But gawd-dammit, I wanted my friend back.

It must have been several months later, in mid 1969, when I next saw Lucy, about the time when some of us from Yokota had managed to secure semi-permanent living spaces in the Osan barracks due to our constant presence there. In some of the barracks, partitions had been built to create two small rooms at the far end of some of the wings, one room on either side of the center aisle. I had one of those rooms that I shared with another guy. Since the two of us worked on nearly opposite schedules, it was like having a private chamber much of the time.

I was in my room napping from not getting enough sleep during the night. One of the houseboys timidly interrupted my rest to announce that there was a young lady just outside the exterior door. Wondering which astute sweet young thing it could be, I cautiously stepped outside into the warm summer sunshine. There was Lucy, smiling widely and looking absolutely stunning in a light blue Western summer dress. I think that my heart actually skipped a beat for some stupid reason.

Ever the suave and polished diplomat, my first questions were about how she got on base and how she was able to find me. She lost a bit of her smile as she replied that it was actually quite simple. The only military personnel that spoke Korean to any degree were from Skivvy-Nine, the uncouth nickname for our unit. She told a taxi driver to take her to the Skivvy-Nine barracks area, and then she just described me to everyone she met walking around until one of them told her where I was.

As for her being on base, she explained that she was now married to an airman and she just wanted to properly say good-bye to me. She coyly stated that he was working and did not know that she was on base. Well, I surmised the reason for her being here at my barracks and it would have been oh-so-easy for me to invite her into my personal quarters. I was certain that she was hoping for some sort of farewell encounter, perhaps trying to repeat our one time together – and I certainly would have enjoyed that. I wanted to tell her that she looked absolutely amazing and that I had really missed her. But ....

Instead, I gave her a big hug and congratulated her with all the sincerity I could muster. She slowly pulled away and looked into my eyes for a very long moment before smiling slightly as she turned to walk away. As she went, she peered back over her shoulder to give me another long look before disappearing around the corner of the barracks.

I did not trust my voice to speak out loud as my throat seemed to be clogged up with phlegm or some such shit. "Good-bye, Lucy, and the best to you always," I silently thought as she disappeared from sight, leaving a large and unexplainable emptiness in my chest. Letting her go was probably the right thing to do; after all, she was married. But if it was the right thing, why did I feel so fuckin' down about it?!

Chapter Seven: Base Shenanigans

Shit was always happening on base, occasionally as a consequence of some piece of brass issuing a spectacularly uninformed order. Usually it was just the product of airmen looking for random ways to entertain themselves. On those rare instances when these two vectors intersected, the results could be truly inspirational.

For example, brand new second lieutenants are arrogantly ignorant and therefore dangerous, a category of officer to be avoided whenever possible. They are a necessary evil, for from that budding level would eventually grow a few officers with integrity and a true capacity for leadership. Normally after some months, butter-bars – so-called due to the color and shape of their rank insignia – come to realize that they are not the salvation of the military world, and that they actually show some intelligence by deferring to the advice of experienced NCOs. Until such realizations hit and a bit of maturity settles in, though, it can be fun to mess with a second lieutenant that is full of himself.

Second Lieutenant Church was just such a butter-bar. Pudgy and unkempt, he seemed to derive great pleasure in micro-managing the lives of airmen who had probably forgotten more about the job than His Exaltedness would ever learn. One day, at the end of a particularly hectic mission, members of our flight crew were being debriefed in the makeshift ready room of the Operations Building.

There was a lot to go over and, even though we were anxious to be off duty, we also wanted to get it right for the benefit of the next crew. A few of us were aware that Church was getting impatient, so just to be perverse, we went into details that were not really necessary but were merely interesting tidbits about the mission. We knew we couldn't draw it out for too long, and eventually we all headed for the crew van for the ride to the barracks area.

Unfortunately – or perhaps accidentally on purpose – somebody had to go back into the building for a few minutes. The rest of us waited in the crew van with Church, knowing that he was about to erupt, and the tension was becoming noticeable. Finally, he bellowed out something about having to use the latrine. Without thinking, out of my mouth came, "Piss? You say you gotta piss? Geezus, I always thought officers went tinkle-tinkle."

Everyone exploded into unrestrained laughter, even the van driver. Even though what I said was not a court martial offense, it should have been noted as an act of disrespect, under normal circumstances requiring some sort of discipline. However, with the whole crew snorting and guffawing like little children, he had to let it go. I understood that I had gotten away with a taunt that Church would not forget, so I made a mental note to avoid him in the future. Fortunately for me, he was soon recalled to our home unit at Yokota in Japan, and shortly thereafter he was reassigned out of there, as well.

Before Church left Osan however, my friend George broadened my affront to include all officers, and he did so in a manner that could not be ignored. Coming back from an exceptional night in the Ville, George was not in his right mind and he even missed the last, midnight bus from the main gate to the Skivvy-Nine barracks area. He also had no money left for a taxi and thus had to walk the long distance from the main gate to our barracks. Along his path was the swimming pool reserved for officers. Recalling everyone's contempt for Church, George hesitated only briefly before concluding that all officers needed a wake-up call, the kind that he would willingly provide.

Quickly scaling the fence surrounding the pool, George divested himself of all clothing before jumping into the deep end. Once in the water and consequently out of sight, he emptied his bowels directly over a recirculation drain. The flow of water completed his intended objective. The next day, a hastily lettered sign outside the Officers Club announced that the pool was shut down indefinitely due to a "contaminated water supply," but that night we celebrated George for his gross misdemeanor with as much beer as he could handle.

Not all lieutenants are jerks, particularly not all mustangs. A mustang is an officer who had some years of military experience as an enlisted person before becoming an officer. I found that mustangs could be divided into three groups: those who used their experiences as enlisted personnel to become better officers, those who wanted to remain "one of the guys" while also enjoying the rank and privileges of being an officer, and those who would lord it over the lowly enlisted level they escaped. The last two types seldom made any rank beyond captain, while a number of the first type progress to much higher levels.

First Lieutenant Snodgrass was a mustang of the first order. A dedicated family man, we knew that he struggled with not succumbing to the temptations of the Ville. It was difficult for any healthy male to resist the enticements of the business women, but Snodgrass was a straight arrow kind of guy. Being a straight arrow meant never deviating from the proper path, no matter what that path might require. Snodgrass did not assume any air of moral superiority regarding this matter, and he never spoke ill of anyone who availed himself of the delights in the

Ville. He also was a great leader in the making.

At one squadron gathering in the Ville, attended by most of us that were not on duty that day and including the squadron commander and the operations officer, Snodgrass got a little tipsy, a most unusual occurrence for a junior officer in the presence of his superiors. We even saw him socializing with one of the young ladies of the club where we held the event. Nevertheless, at the end of the festivities, he dutifully returned to base with his reputation and dignity still intact. Over the next few days, those who worked with him closely dared to tease him gently about his flirtations. Snodgrass readily admitted that he had been gravely tempted but that he was somehow able to resist.

As part of the farewell tradition toward the end of his extended deployment, Snodgrass was given a baseball hat embroidered with the squadron emblem that included a golden arrow stitched on the back, intended to signify having been a straight arrow. However, his arrow had a slight but noticeable waver to it, the meaning of which no one had to explain, and Snodgrass wore that hat for the remainder of his Osan days with good humor.

Despite the conventional wisdom of officers and enlisteds not getting along, nothing could be further from the truth for most of the guys in our line of work. To begin, most of us in our line of work were either linguists or analysts/reporters, and some of us were both. It takes a certain level of intellect to learn another language well enough to bet people's lives on it. For analysts and reporters, a logical mind, the ability quickly discern events, and then to write accurately are prime requirements. We weren't just a bunch of pretty faces with impressive dicks; most of us had some smarts, too.

Even those not directly involved in the job were a cut above normal: Every one of us had undergone an extensive background investigation, and on the surface, we all looked like squeaky clean upstanding young citizens. Consequently, most officers soon learned that nearly every situation wound up being resolved, not by rank, but by knowledge – which the enlisteds most assuredly possessed by virtue of their training and experience.

While airmen like us definitely had well-developed egos, most of us did not look with disfavor upon those not in our field – at least not most of the time. There were exceptions, of course, most often occurring in the Ville. Guys in our line of work always felt as though we were at the top of the list, Number One as the Koreans would say, never Number Ten, at the bottom. Another plus for us was our *esprit de corps*. This was frequently manifested in occasional outbreaks of the long-standing Skivvy-Nine song, sometimes at inappropriate locations or times.

Although the full story behind the name Skivvy-Nine is lost in the dust of history, it likely has at least something to do with the fact that all of our four-digit squadron designators began with the digits "69." For example, the squadron designator for our Yokota unit was 6988, and the one for the Osan unit was originally 6929, later changed 6903 after a command reorganization. That such a number series could even be considered, let alone actually implemented, speaks to the deviant sense of humor rampant in our command. It is highly probable that the meaning of "sixty-nine" was explained at some early point to the young ladies in the Ville.

Regardless of the story behind our squadron designators, what was well established was that Skivvy-Nine members seem to always have been known as skivvy honchos. A holdover word from the Japanese occupation of Korea, honcho denotes leader. Being labeled as skivvy honchos was commonly taken by us to mean that Skivvy-Nine men excelled in the bedroom arts – masters of sex, so to speak. However, it never occurred to any of us that just perhaps the business women of the Ville saw Skivvy-Niners only as being leaders in depravity.

At any rate and as might be expected, all of these dynamics were immortalized in the Skivvy-Nine song, a ribald parody of an old college fight anthem. For lack of a better title, it was simply referred to as Oom Ya Ya, from the peculiar sounds of its chorus, which consisted only of odd sounds that were actually part of the collegiate theme. Originally, it seems that a list of the last names of prominent alumni was used as the chorus, but as time passed, fewer and fewer of the students could remember them. The names were soon replaced by fill-in sounds that came to be used as the title to the Skivvy-Nine song. The chorus is simply

Oom ya ya, Oom ya ya, Oom ya ya, Oom ya ya
Oom ya ya, Oom ya ya, Oom ya ya ya
Oom ya ya, Oom ya ya, Oom ya ya, Oom ya ya
Oom ya ya, Oom ya ya, Oom ya ya ya

The final "ya" of the chorus at the end of the song was usually rendered as a shout, to signify intensity of purpose or just plain exuberance. The song, which Skivvy-Niners so enjoyed performing, was nine bawdy stanzas in length.

Oom Ya Ya

Oh, we're from Korea, the land of the short time;
For whiskey and women we have such a yen.
We work so little, we'd much rather diddle,
We're typical Sixty-Nine Skivvy-Nine men.

Chorus

The NCO losers are Number Ten boozers;
They go to the village again and again.
The airmen politely present themselves rightly,
They're typical Sixty-Nine Skivvy-Nine men.

Chorus

The officers nightly get drunk and unsightly;
The girls in the Ville say they're all Number Ten.
The airmen they're glad to take to their pad,
They're typical Sixty-Nine Skivvy-Nine men.

Chorus

One day in the Ville this broad said to me,
"Hey, GI, you come to my house once again."
I said, "look here, Jo-san, I haven't got much Won,
But you can give it to Sixty-Nine Skivvy-Nine men."

Chorus

We're not even APs, we frown upon KPs;
The 314th squadrons are all Number Ten.
We're not from Supply, we much rather die,
We're typical Sixty-Nine Skivvy-Nine men.

Chorus

The meat's on the table, she's willing and able,
But you must have one thousand five hundred Yen.
But you can get it for nil down there in the Ville,
As long as you're Sixty-Nine Skivvy-Nine men.

Chorus

We go to the village, get drunk and we pillage;
We're rarely back at the base before ten.
By 12 o'clock nightly we're all shacked up tightly,
We're typical Sixty-Nine Skivvy-Nine men.

Chorus

If we leave Korea without gonorrhea,
'Twill be a surprise to all us good men.
Our peckers are tired, so often they're fired,
We're typical Sixty-Nine Skivvy-Nine men.

Chorus

This is the last verse, it couldn't get much worse.
We're saying good-bye but we'll see you again.
The keg's in the cellar for every young feller,
But you must be Sixty-Nine Skivvy-Nine men.

Chorus

Well, just as described in the first stanza of the Skivvy-Nine song, Bert was one of those many guys who had such a yen for whiskey and women. He was constantly in the Ville when he was not flying. Just as constantly, Bert was, quite understandably, running low on cash. Whiskey had recently become available in the Ville, but it was not as cheap as on base, it certainly wasn't as cheap as beer; and business women didn't make a habit of giving their services away – they knew that Americans were always willing to pay.

On one particular deployment to Osan, Bert had arrived with a supply of cash that he already recognized as being insufficient funds, but he was unwilling to take the risks of bartering for poon with M&Ms or Tang. With a new crew change-out just about every week or two, Bert sent a letter requesting additional funds to his wife via the first return crew and hoped that he could stretch his money out somehow until his wife could resupply him. Roughly two weeks later, Bert anxiously met the arriving crew, fully expecting that his wife would have sent him at least a few bucks.

Bert was in for a complete let down, for there was nothing from his wife. He quickly scribbled out another letter to be carried back by the crew that was departing the next day. In the second letter, Bert requested $50 so that he could buy deodorant, razor blades, shaving cream, and other stuff. On the next crew rotation, Bert was overjoyed to see that he had received a care package from his wife. He opened the box and was pleased to see that the package contained toiletries as well as an envelope from his wife. Expecting that the envelope contained a check or some cash, he eagerly tore it open. In a short note, his wife had tersely written that she was sending the necessary toiletries but there would be absolutely no money with which to buy other things. She concluded emphatically, "You get your *'stuff'* at home, buster!"

Pauley was another hard-luck case. It was common knowledge that Pauley had such a highly developed libido that he had given up smoking and drinking solely to conserve precious funds to use in gratifying his baser desires. He even refused to spend money at the base theater or the Snack Bar. Pauley would watch TV in the lounge for free and eat in the chow hall at no out-of-pocket expense, regardless of what was being served.

Even measures such as these were insufficient to his needs, and Pauley often went around complaining of pain and discomfort due to a bad case of blue balls. Someone jokingly suggested that, after hearing this for the umpteenth time, Pauley should present himself at the base clinic for help in dealing with his ailment. The advice was given with the implication that Pauley should try a bit of moderation, that perhaps there was some sort of medication that could lessen his drive to the point where his financial supply could meet his carnal demands and thus lessen the burden on the rest of us in having to listen to his complaints.

Pauley thought that the suggestion had merit, based upon the meaning he took from it, so the very next morning, he eagerly showed up at sick call. An hour or so later, he reported for work and all of us impatiently waited for him to tell us what the doctor had to say.

When Pauley stopped swearing enough to make his point, he throttled back to being just brutally uncomplimentary of the military health system. He did not concur with their conclusion or their reasoning, and he even questioned their medical training. It turned out that, in the collective wisdom of Osan doctors, there was no medical justification for prescribing sex at government expense to mitigate Pauley's condition. Pauley did not get the expected prescription that he could take to the Ville to be filled by business women so that he could enjoy their services and have them bill Uncle Sam for their fees.

In addition to the logic behind the moral or medical reasoning, there was a single, extremely practical, justification for not funding the gratification of military sexual appetites. Holy hard-ons! That would be just too damned expensive.

Nevertheless, given the opportunity, most healthy young men somehow found a way to avoid suffering Pauley's fate. Flight crews stuck for 24 hours in alert trailers near the end of the runway were no exception; however, their solution to their particular predicament was exceptional for a number of reasons.

It was commonly known that Air Force B-52 bomber crews were always on alert at bases in the States, and that there were always fighter pilots on alert ready to scramble at a moment's notice at key bases throughout the world. Some shining brass concluded that we didn't have enough to deal with, that we should spend 24 hours in alert trailers before flying a mission as well.

It wasn't long before our crews were obliged to report to the alert trailers one day in advance of their next flight. To say that these trailers were primitive would be an understatement. There was room for five sets of bunk beds, two sets along each wall with a narrow aisle between them, then a bathroom across the width of the trailer, and finally a small space in the rear containing a final set of bunk beds across the back wall.

The bathroom consisted of a very small shower, one commode, and a sink with mirror. Located where it was in the trailer, the bathroom had doors to close it off, which effectively gave the rear space and its final set of beds a lot of privacy. Normally, the Airborne Mission Supervisor and his second, the Airborne Analyst, would bunk in the rear. However, for the common good, this private area was put to better use on at least one occasion.

Somebody had the idea of installing a business woman in the rear area to mitigate the boredom and other maladies of crews being sequestered in alert trailers for a whole day. The first objective was to find a business woman interested in raking in a large amount of money in short period of time. Eventually, a plan was developed: A buddy from another crew not stuck at the alert trailers would go to the Ville and explain the assignment to select young ladies. After choosing one that, in his opinion, would best fill the bill, he would then sign her onto the base as his guest, deliver her in a taxi to the alert trailers, and then return in a few hours to sign her off base.

Since the shining brass hadn't thought to provide the alert area with any type of security, getting a female guest into the trailer area was not much of an issue. My deployment at that time was primarily ground duty, and I heard all about the escapade later in the very day that it happened. Everything in the plan went off without any glitches. No one ever discussed any of the transaction details, other than to say that money changed hands and that everyone involved – including the young lady herself – ended the day with smiles on their faces, quite satisfied with a job – or jobs – well done.

Chapter Eight: Foolishness in the Ville

I was finally going to actually work with one of the really old hands, one that Archie had long ago told me had mentored him when Archie first got to Osan. His name was Nate and Archie was profuse in touting his abilities on the job. I knew that Archie was highly skilled, so if he considered Nate to be good, then Nate must really be something.

As one of the augmentees that had been recalled to Osan, Nate was not happy. In addition, I soon learned that Nate was a drunk. Despite all the praise that Archie had for Nate, I wasn't impressed. After grudgingly getting Nate's OK to do so, I sat with him once at his work console for a bit. While Nate was still good – certainly better at that part of the job than I was – it seemed to me that he made a lot of guesses. In light of his experience, it would be fair to say that his guesses were quite informed. But even so, they were still guesses.

I mentioned this to Archie, who reluctantly admitted that Nate was probably past his prime. Even he had noticed that Nate was drinking too much, which was affecting his health as well as his performance. Nate wasn't a mean drunk like some could be, but he was an unhappy one. Still, he had his supporters, so I just paid closer attention to Nate's work to ensure that it met standards. He was most likely aware of the extra scrutiny that I gave his work and he probably did not appreciate it. Although I was oblivious to any ill will that he might have toward me, Nate would eventually screw me over when drinking in the Ville.

One might think that drinking would be an enjoyable pastime on its own merits, but that would be wrong. Military personnel, just like other hardcore revelers, often drink to make the most of a bad situation or to relieve boredom. Regardless, simply going to a bar and consuming alcohol until blind drunk isn't enough – usually there has to be some fun or entertainment involved. We were no exception.

Before I arrived, the unit had actually developed official Ville jackets. Light weight and suitable from late spring through early fall – and particularly useful during monsoons – the jackets had a large Skivvy-Nine unit patch sewn on the back. On one side of the chest, the name or nickname of the owner was embroidered. On the other side was the favorite drink of the jacket owner. The idea apparently was to be able to walk into a bar and simply point at your chest in order to be served your favorite beverage, possibly to get past any perceived language barrier although I never had any problem getting what I wanted to drink.

Why all this was necessary was never made clear to me, but it seemed to be a very bad idea from the start. I mean, if one of our guys ever got into trouble in the Ville, such a patch on the back of his jacket would clearly identify the unit to which he belonged. And if someone ever caught the name on the front as well, the guy could be easily tracked down. Geezus, if you are going to act wild and crazy in the Ville, it seems to me that you would at least want to conceal your identity. Oh well, nearly everyone seemed to make it through their duty tours or deployments without getting into serious difficulties.

Now as to an entertaining way to drink, one of the augmentees had invented a novel way to consume booze. Cleverly, he called it a "bucket run." Koreans make wonderful brassware and American servicemen often buy brass goods to take home as trinkets. One particularly sought out item is the one-liter brass teapot. Holding a little more than one U.S. quart, these handled pots are used in tearooms for providing hot water at the table as well as in working-class Korean watering holes to serve homemade Korean liquor.

We had other intentions. With the lid removed and discarded as being of no use, the Korean brass pot became a bucket with a spout. A bucket run was notoriously simple – possibly simple-minded – and that was part of its appeal. Simple things are hard to screw up when imbibing large amounts of alcohol. The idea was to buy a new brass pot in the Ville – previously acquired pots always seemed to curiously disappear – and then rinse it out with beer to purify it. Once the teapot was ready, the guys ordered their drinks by pointing to the embroidery on their jacket fronts.

When the drinks were served, all were poured into the bucket, which is then swirled about until the liquids were mixed. A full measure of the concoction was then poured from the pot into each participant's glass. Often followed by the last four syllables of the chorus to "Oom Ya Ya," one of the group usually announced with great solemnity that it was time for bottoms up – glasses, that is, although on at least one occasion, one young airman misconstrued the command and mistakenly mooned everyone in the bar.

Well, at least partaking in a bucket run was better than being a charter member of the Loyal Order of the Sacred Slipper. That had been a spur of the moment and hastily developed fraternal organization formed when Cal, the other shift supervisor, and I found ourselves on a very rare day off together. Since we had seen each other just in passing for months, we both agreed that it was only proper that we celebrate being off duty at the same time. There were four or five others that joined us for this event.

Once we reached the Ville, no one wanted to take the time to go to the market area for a brass pot. Thinking of a perverted takeoff on Cinderella and speaking mostly in jest, I offered one of my shoes as a substitute. To my surprise, after a brief discussion on how alcohol kills germs, my proposal was accepted. Thus, the Loyal Order of the Sacred Slipper was formed.

This did not work out well for me on a number of levels. Foremost was the fact that I then had a very soggy shoe to wear to the next bar. By the end of the celebration, my shoe was falling apart. Sure, it was a used shoe to begin with, but it had been serving me faithfully for several months and I was a very cruel owner for having put it through such misfortunes.

I made it back to base with an artificial limp to keep the shoe from squishing too much. The next morning, I was back in the Ville looking for the shoe cobbler that always seemed to have some sort of sale for Americans. His shop was open but the Sale sign was not in evidence. The cobbler explained that he normally did not put it out until evening when his Korean customers would no longer be interested but the Americans would begin to drift into the Ville.

Having been involved in a game of Indian before coming to the Ville, I was experiencing its effects. While I am normally a bit conservative when it comes to clothing, this time I went beyond that and then some. Despite not being an Elvis Presley fan, I wound up ordering a pair of custom-made blue suede shoes to be picked up in three days.

They were ready on time and so was I. I knew that I would really be in style when I ditched my ruined pair of shoes for those new beauties. I tried them on and they were a comfortable fit, so in consideration of the price, I felt that I had made a good purchase. Feeling pleased with myself for having made a bit of lemonade out of the lemon of the ruined shoe, I headed for one of the barbershops in the Ville.

One of the old hands had informed me that the on-base barbers were overrated as well as overpriced. He had suggested I try his barber in the Ville. I went there once, never to return when the barber cut my hair as he wanted, while quietly ignoring my instructions. This time, I was going to Gark's barbershop.

Gark's place had a very prominent sign in both Korean and English. In Korean, the sign read "I Yong Gak." Now the family name of the president of South Korea at the time was Pak, but to make his name more Westernized, he Romanized it as Park. I Yong Gak was evidently quite aware of this, for his sign in English read "I Yong Gark."

Well, if Pak can become Park, then there is no damn reason that Gak can't be turned into Gark. The only problem was that this Anglicization was applied only to family names. In Asia, the family name comes first, so the family name of this guy was the "I," most often Westernized as Lee, Rhee, or Yi. Regardless of all that, anybody with a name of Gark gets my attention, so in I went and to hell with any Romanization malfunctions.

The two barbers were busy, as was the manicure girl. One of the barbers gestured in a friendly manner for me to take a seat. I was disappointed to note that there wasn't any shoeshine guy, but this was Korea and there were always the houseboys on base. I could see that it would be a few minutes before either of the barbers would be finished, so I picked up one of the Korean newspapers scattered about.

Holy mother tongue! I knew that my grasp of Korean was not as good as I once thought, but this was extremely disappointing. I couldn't read much of anything. Trying to avoid the embarrassment of quickly giving up, I continued to look through the paper, picking out the few words I knew and then trying to fill in the gaps of what I couldn't. I have no idea as to whether I ever came even close to getting the real story.

One of the barbers called me to his chair and asked how I wanted my hair cut. His English was astonishingly good. Then, after a pause, he asked if I could read Korean. "Busted!" I thought, except then I realized it was an honest question. I answered in my best Korean, saying that I could read some of the stories but that the Chinese characters used by Koreans were a difficulty. This exaggeration implied a level of fluency that I did not possess, although it would explain my lack of reading comprehension if anyone inquired that deeply. He laughed, saying I just needed to study and that he was pleased to hear an American even try to speak in his language.

About that time, the manicure girl came over. She was cute, but very young, maybe only 15 years old or thereabout. I gathered that when she asked me a question, it was to see if I wanted a manicure. At the time, the word "manicure" was not part of my vocabulary. Evidently, I guessed correctly since she went to a drawer to get the tools of her trade. I did know how to say that I wanted my nails cut short. As she was working, she occasionally glanced at me, shyly making eye contact.

I didn't know what to make of that, since surely she could not be trying to get me interested in her – she was way too young and far too innocent. After a minute or two, she asked me if I could help her with a phrase in English. This, too, was often used as a come-on by ladies of the Ville trying to engage airmen in conversations from which deals might eventually be struck.

I reluctantly agreed and was rather relieved when she explained that American men frequently approached her as though she were a business woman, despite her young age. I tried to explain that the guys might just be paying her compliments, but then I realized that, even if that were the case – and it most likely was not – making a pass at a woman on the street was something just not done in Korea.

She said that her English was very limited and asked me to write down the English words phonetically in Korean so that she could memorize the sounds to use in rebuffing crude Americans. The barber found me a stub of a pencil and a piece of paper. On it I wrote, "Ai ehm noh bis-nehs woe-mahn" using Hangul, the Korean lettering system. I had her practice the spacing of the sounds and getting the emphasis on the proper syllable to get her point across. She was a quick learner, and I could see that no English speaker would ever fail to understand her meaning.

Haircut done, I discovered much to my pleasure that service at Gark's shop included a choice of men's cologne as well as a short but well-executed shoulder massage. All of this amounted to less than the cost of an inferior base haircut. I left Gark's feeling great, and pleased that I had also done a good deed for the day.

Intending to have just a drink or two, I headed for the Stereo Club. There wasn't much business and the records being played were not to my liking. After only one drink, I moved on to the nearby Aragon Club. As I entered, I saw Nate and another guy sitting at the bar having boilermakers. It would have been rude of me to ignore them so I sat down next to Nate since I at least knew him.

He barely acknowledged my presence. In an attempt to do an attitude adjustment, I bought a round of three boilermakers. That seemed to have the desired effect, for Nate actually smiled at me as he raised his shot-glass in a gesture of thanks.

Regrettably for me, I should have realized that Nate and his buddy were professional barflies. I was always behind in finishing each round, and soon it became clear to me that I needed to take a break. I went to sit on a couch often used by the young ladies when they weren't talking with potential customers.

Before I knew what was happening, I was out. The next time I became aware of my surroundings, it was nearly three hours later and I was stretched out on the couch with the bartender gently shaking me. He explained that the club would soon be filling up and that I ought to go back to the base anyway. Nate had taken all of my money, leaving only enough change for taxi fare back to the barracks. I couldn't prove it, but the alcoholic bastard had gotten me drunk on my own dime and then rolled me in broad daylight in the Ville!

When Nate returned to the States some weeks later, I made certain that he saw me render him a farewell salute with my middle finger.

Chapter Nine: Military Adventures

It was colder than brass-monkey 'nads. The weather reports said that the winter of 1968-1969 was going to be another one of the coldest on record for Korea, and the evidence certainly supported that prediction. On this deployment, I was bunked in what would normally be considered a choice spot, at the end of the rows of bunks in the barracks wing. Being at the end meant more privacy and less noise since there would be only two, rather than three, neighboring bunk sets, one across the aisle and one to the side. However, bunking at this particular end also meant that the two walls of my small area were exterior cinderblock.

Uninsulated masonry conducts cold in a remarkably effective manner. Late one morning, I had stopped off at the squadron lounge for a soda that I had intended to drink while laying in my bunk reading. I didn't get much into the book before I started to doze off, so I decided to just go to bed and get a good rest before working another one of those extended mid shifts. None of our barracks spaces had room for nightstands or tables, just bunks and wall-lockers, so I put the partially consumed can out of the way on the floor under my rack. I crawled under the covers and was soon blissfully snoring. I awoke several hours later feeling quite refreshed, and after doing my Four Esses, I picked up the soda can to dump it out. The contents were an icy slush, and I was grateful that we had been given two blankets instead of the normal one.

One way to look at the overcrowded and disagreeable barracks conditions was that it discouraged guys from spending much time there. Now many would take this as justification to hit the Ville, and I would heartily endorse that line of reasoning on most occasions. Unfortunately, there was an ever-increasing backlog of material to contend with at work, and I was getting quite concerned about ever getting caught up. As a result, I now had two reasons for going to work instead of the Ville.

Once at work, I buckled down to plowing through the stacks of materials that surrounded my desk. Not long into my shift, one of the workers that I was supervising showed up. Ollie had been working for several days in a row and he was scheduled to be on break. He wanted to help out, and he had already been at work for a couple of hours. Ollie hadn't been here when I arrived only because he was tired of living on the snacks that each shift offered, so he had gone down to the chow hall for a decent midnight breakfast. I welcomed him as he got back to the chore of reducing the backlog. Only a couple of hours after that, the other supervisor Cal appeared, several hours ahead of his normal shift, which was to begin at the end of mine. He, too, was eager to eliminate our backlog. Ollie and I let him know that we were very pleased to see him.

Just before the end of the day shift, the three of us had been hard at work for many hours, Ollie for nearly eighteen, me for roughly fifteen, and Cal for nearly twelve hours. About that time, the ranking person on site from our home unit at Yokota, Senior Master Sergeant Bascomb, came through our area to see how things were going. A thought occurred to me, and after a brief conversation with Cal and Ollie, I called Bascomb over, saying we wanted to discuss a new work schedule.

I had already informed Bascomb about how we were tackling the backlog by working extra hours. He had been impressed. Now, I said that we wanted to implement a new plan of attack. Bascomb listened warily at first, as it was his responsibility to make sure that things got done without problems. He grinned widely, though, when I explained that our plan was to go back to the main part of the base and have a decent meal before returning to wade into the backlog yet again. Our condition – actually, more of a request in view of Bascomb's position of authority – was that we be allowed to work in our civilian clothes, rather than in a fresh uniform.

Bascomb didn't hesitant a heartbeat as he bellowed in a voice that could be heard around the corner and far down the hall, "If you crazy bastards want to come up here on your own time to work, then you can be in your damned underwear for all I care, and if anyone gives you any shit about that, you tell 'em to come see me!" Prior to this, I hadn't thought much of Bascomb because of how he had handled my complaint about an unrealistic workload a year or so ago at Yokota. His response at the time had been, "If you are looking for sympathy, you can find it in the dictionary between 'shit' and 'syphilis.'" Holy hierarchy! I thought his perspective certainly had changed, and Bascomb went up several notches in my estimation.

The three of us – Cal, Ollie, and I – went to the NCO Club for steaks before taking quick showers and changing into civvies prior to applying ourselves yet again to the backlog with renewed vigor and highly charged up states of mind. We wound up achieving what few thought was possible. After roughly thirty-six hours for Ollie, thirty-three for me, and thirty for Cal, the backlog was finally wiped out. Bascomb must have told everyone else working that evening to give us whatever we needed, for others gladly made chow runs for us to support us in our nonstop effort. By the time it was all finished, we were jittery from running on caffeine to counteract our lack of sleep. I had a hard time unwinding and turning off my brain, but when I finally got to sleep, I logged more than twelve hours of solid Zs,

Robert E. McCoy

minus a latrine break or two.

I had made an enemy during the work marathon, though. When it became clear that Cal, Ollie, and I were making an effort to wipe out the backlog, the airmen involved in other processes of our job jumped to get their work done before our efforts were concluded. They didn't want to be the only ones left with unfinished business.

One of these was a cross-trainee named Quentin. How Quentin ever made it through the selection process to get into this field was a mystery to many. He was a nice guy and normally mild-mannered, but he certainly was not the sharpest knife in the drawer. Quentin had to think before he answered almost any question, as nothing seemed to come easily for him. So for him to have made it through analyst/reporter training is noteworthy. Then for him to have successfully completed Korean language training was flat-out astounding.

As his part in the big push to get all of our work caught up, Quentin was given some raw data to be entered onto paper as an official record. When he looked about for an empty work console to accomplish his task, he discovered that the typewriter at the only open position did not have a functioning letter "M." Quentin was not about to be deterred from making his contribution. In a prefacing paragraph to his typewritten document, he wrote that his typewriter did not have the letter "M," leaving a blank space into which he subsequently penned the missing consonant by hand on the original and all the carbon copies. Instead, Quentin typed that he would use the @ symbol in its place.

I had never before noticed that, although the letter "E" is said to be the most frequently used letter in the English alphabet, "M" is employed often enough as well. The result of

- 98 -

Quentin's efforts was thirty-two pages that were completely unacceptable. I called Archie over to point this out since Archie was functioning as Quentin's on-site supervisor.

Archie started to laugh at the ridiculousness of the situation, and I chimed in by declaring, "What a dumb ass!" just as Quentin was coming through the door into our space. Archie instantly realized that some fence mending was needed and he took Quentin out to the console room to explain that his solution was not acceptable on documents that would be couriered back to our headquarters in the States.

A few hours later, a stone-faced Quentin dropped a properly typed version of his work in front of me as he proclaimed with intense earnestness, "I'm going to put your airborne ass outta business!" I just blew it off, knowing that Quentin did not have enough rank or influence to even come close to making good on such a threat. Even so, he never missed an opportunity to bad-mouth the airborne program, something for which he could never qualify. I supposed that I could have handled the mistyped document with a bit more finesse, but damn it, Quentin really was a dumb ass to try something like that when we were all busting our balls trying to get things done right the first time.

There was other fallout from the massive effort to get out from under the amassed workload. Everyone by now knew who the truly dedicated workers were, who were the "nine-to-fivers," and who totally slacked off. Those of us that had made significant contributions in finishing off the backlog were more than just pissed at the shirkers. We wanted vengeance!

I think that it was Cal who had the idea of holding a mock military award ceremony for the slackers. Out of several nominees, the first awardee chosen was Ted. Ted had more time in grade than many of us, and thus he technically outranked us.

Shorter in stature than most, he had obviously developed a Napoleon complex. Even though he was good at the job, he had discovered a way to avoid the constant six-week deployments away from his family at Yokota.

Many others from Yokota also had families and girl friends there but they never shirked their obligations at the expense of others who would have to pick up their slack. Ted was different in the sense that he didn't care that someone else had to fill in for him if he found a way to avoid having to go to Osan like the rest of us. He would develop some form of illness, usually the last workday before having to leave on a deployment. If it weren't a cough, then it would be a runny nose. Either malady would be enough to be prescribed an antihistamine, which would automatically ground him from flying. Being DNIF, a restriction to "Duty Not Including Flying," meant no deployment – and an extended stay with his family at Yokota.

Ted managed to avoid deployments for over three months until those of us at Osan were able to convince senior people back at Yokota to look into Ted's pattern of illnesses. Finally, we got word that Ted would be returning to Osan on the next deployment aircraft. We would be ready.

In preparation for his arrival and the impending "award" ceremony, someone donated a condom, which we unrolled onto a broom handle. Using military aircraft paint, we covered the exterior with a shiny aluminum color. On the tip of the condom, we placed red stamp pad ink. When the colors were dry, we removed it from its wooden form so that to the casual observer, it looked like a used silver rubber with blood on the tip. To us, however, it was one of unofficialdom's most despised medals, the Silver Shaft.

I had written a sarcastic citation to be read aloud as the

award would be presented to Ted. It went,

> In the face of overwhelming volumes of work, Staff Sergeant Theodore Bartone exhibited a rarely seen degree of selfishness in the avoidance of duty. His utter dedication to the slacker arts of *amici fornicus* and *fornicus offi* is almost unparalleled in the modern military. In consideration of his extraordinary non-achievements, he is hereby presented with the reviled medal of the Silver Shaft.

Despite my pathetic and contrived attempt to describe Ted's offenses in Latin, everyone easily grasped their meanings. Of course, Ted tried to leave the briefing area as the citation was being read, but we had anticipated that. Two burly guys stood before the closed door. Ted never spoke, and he left the room as soon as our presentation was concluded, leaving the Silver Shaft behind. I later heard that he went to the Ville that night and got drunk, but that is an unverified rumor.

In any case, not wanting to repeat ourselves, we never held another ceremony. Instead, on the wall of the small area we used to brief crews before missions, we posted the satirical citation with the stained condom, accompanied by a list of the runners up, to serve as fair warning to others. Ted never had the balls to take it down, but the Silver Shaft and its citation disappeared just before some visiting dignitary from the States arrived.

As it turned out, Ted's re-entry into the deployment cycle closely followed the culmination of our monumental effort at getting caught up at work. We were blessed with a couple of days off. The first night, we celebrated in the squadron lounge and one of the officers had contributed $20 out of his own pocket toward the event just to show his recognition of our dedication and spirit.

We even had our own confetti. Our noisy old Teletype Model 28 machines stored a formal record of messages by punching holes on long ribbons of reinforced paper, much like a reverse Braille system. In punching myriads of holes, the Teletype machine created the best confetti one could ever hope to see. The pieces of chad from those punched holes were no bigger than the size of a large pinhead, perhaps 1/16 of an inch in size. We had scads of chad, and that night we distributed it freely upon everyone that walked into the lounge.

As fine as it was, the chad was soon recognized as being horribly difficult to clean up. Broom sweeping was next to impossible since the slightest air movement was enough to swirl the chad back into the air just to land somewhere else. Only vacuuming them up came close to getting the job done, but we had to be very diligent to find all the chad. For several days after our celebration, partiers and houseboys alike were still finding it in the oddest of places. This led the Skivvy-Nine squadron commander to declare that chad could no longer be used for any purpose and that it must be discarded in appropriate containers. Our attitude was "no sweat" since we had already had our fun with it.

The next day, when many of us were still on our well-deserved and long-overdue break, several airmen held a Stink-Off. That event was a farting contest in which a winner was to be declared in each of three categories, the victors being determined by who made the loudest noise, who produced the longest sound, and who created the most malodorous output.

Getting judges for the contest proved not as difficult as anyone might have expected. Neither was getting a number of contestants, despite the infamous injunction to "Never trust a fart."

As any experienced person knows, producing flatulence is a risky endeavor, and not merely for those in the immediate vicinity. It is often not remembered until it is too late that farts are notoriously treacherous. They can be classified according to whether they are "dry" or "wet," which is to say whether they are totally gaseous or whether they contain some other state of matter, liquid or solid. It is difficult to reliably predict which result will occur when one makes a forced effort at production.

I doubt if anyone recalls who the winners were in the first two categories, loudest and longest. I certainly do not. Only Charlie, one of the augmentees from the States, was noted for having put forth the most putrid product ever noted in recent Skivvy-Nine history. Everyone, participants as well as judges, elected to depart the squadron lounge, the contest venue, with great speed. And even in the great outdoors, those downwind of Charlie knew that he was a true champion as he continued to compete.

Unfortunately, Charlie was eventually stripped of his victory when it was later discovered that he had not, in fact, produced true flatulence, but had actually generated a mixture of gaseous and solid state matter, a clear violation of the rules. Regardless, and for reasons that no one bothered to communicate, there was no rematch.

Driven out of the lounge and not interested in the game of stickball that was being hastily organized, Archie and I headed to our Operations compound just to check on things. Work seemed to be going smoothly and no new backlog was accumulating. Everything was under control for the moment. Just as Archie and I were about to leave for the barracks area, in walked one of the clumsiest people I have ever had the misfortune to meet.

Ethan was a walking example of slapstick gracelessness. Several months previously, he had been following me so closely that he stepped on the back of my flight boots, ripping the heel completely off. This time, Ethan was carrying an unopened can of soda when he tripped on the slightly raised doorsill. As he fell, he released his grip on the can, which ricocheted off a table leg before spinning to a rest under my desk.

We should have expected what happened next. Ethan retrieved the soda, but not before banging his head in the process. When he stood up, he unthinkingly opened the can. Soda spewed everywhere, even in Ethan's direction. In a daze, he turned first this way and then that way, trying to avoid the spray from the can that he himself held in his very own grip.

I could see that the mess was getting all over the clipboards of briefing notices and intelligence summaries hung along the wall. I was about to have a stroke but Archie reacted in less than a second. He grabbed Ethan's hand holding the can, forced it back into Ethan's chest, and quickly wrapped the flaps of Ethan's unzipped flight jacket around it to contain the still foaming output. Ethan just stood there dumbly. Not trusting Ethan to adequately clean up his own mess and fearful that he would rip the paper documents all to hell even if he did, I took care of things myself. Fortunately, little damage was done, thanks to the plasticized covers that identified the contents of the clipboards.

After that near disaster, I knew I had to get away for a break, so when Jack asked if I wanted to accompany him on a short trip to K-16, near Seoul, I agreed to go. Jack and I weren't really close as he was one of the old hands – and he could be a bit of a blowhard, as well. But a trip to K-16, also known to Koreans as Yoi-Do, would be a welcome diversion.

K-16 was a small airport on a major island of the Han River, which ran through Seoul. On the southeast edge of town, K-16 had a fledgling aero club there, and Jack was going because the club had light aircraft that licensed pilots could rent for an hour or two. He needed to log some flight time as a civilian single-engine pilot. I was not about to go flying with Jack – I knew him too well to trust him at the controls of a death-machine – but I thought I would hang out at the enlisted club at the military airport while he cavorted in the sky.

Jack let me off at the club and I went in to survey the scene. Off to one side were four U.S. Army infantry types at a table working on a beer drunk. Other than them, only a Korean bartender was in the joint. I ordered my drink and requested some quarters as part of my change. The jukebox had been quiet when I had entered but I wanted some cool jazz, so I fed the slot enough for at least an hour's worth of tunes.

I was enjoying the music and my drink when I became aware of a rumble of discontent emanating from the Army table. Though they had not yet worked up enough nerve to challenge me openly about my taste in sounds, their words were clearly addressed toward that "zoomie piss-ant over there drinking booze and playing that crap." Zoomie is a disparaging term applied to flyboys by flightless flunkies, and evidently, the army guys were annoyed by anyone who preferred whiskey to beer and jazz to country.

An inter-service brawl with me taking on four beefy ground-pounders was not particularly high on my list of priorities at that moment. Sometimes I am a quick thinker and, mercifully, this was one of them. I called over the bartender and instructed him to give the GIs another round of beers as quickly as possible – on my bill. He knew when trouble was brewing and he complied with my request without delay.

When the soldiers were given their new round, the grumbling stopped immediately and some sidelong glances were directed my way. After a short but whispered conversation, one of the ground-pounders got up to come over to my table, asking if he could join me for a while. I replied that he was welcome to do so. We chatted aimlessly for several minutes about nothing of importance, other than for me to say I was killing time while my buddy tried not to crash his rented plane. That seemed to amuse the Army emissary, and after a few minutes, he returned to his buddies – that was that.

I was pleased with myself for having averted a personal catastrophe as I continued to have more whiskey. When Jack collected me for the bus ride back to Osan, I was in a gloriously good mood that even Jack's blathering couldn't damage.

Break passed all too quickly, and it was time to get back to work. There were more materials waiting for us, although the quantity was manageable if we applied ourselves. However, after nearly two years of relentless six-week deployments to Osan, working 75-plus hours a week there, then one week back at Yokota, but still having to show up for 40 hours of bullshit busywork at Yokota, the deployments were getting tiresome.

Somebody back at headquarters in the States must have realized that people were getting burned out. Maybe they had finally noticed that the re-enlistment rate for Korean linguists was close to zero and that the Yokota squadron retention rate was down precipitously. Whatever the reason, a Priority message came one day late in 1969 announcing that an intermediate Korean language course was being developed and volunteers were needed for its inaugural class back in the States. Archie, Lew, Quentin, Ted, two other airmen, and I applied for the assignment the very day we learned that it was going to be in the States and that the duration of the training would take up nearly one full year.

Those of us deployed to Osan that had applied were accepted and we rejoiced mightily that night. When our official orders came, we were insufferably proud to be in the first intermediate class for Korean linguists. Whenever someone would ask us to do something distasteful or out of the ordinary, we would shout out, "FYGMO!" in a singsong voice. Being FYGMO – "Fuck you, got my orders" – confers a state of near-invincibility upon any airman, and we wasted no opportunity to take advantage of that.

Even though language courses in the military are demanding and expectations are high, most of us were going strictly for R&R – Rest and Relaxation – for school could not possibly be any worse than the work grind at Osan. We actually looked forward to the comparative life of ease at language school in the States as we said our good-byes to Osan in early 1970. No one at the time, certainly not me, expressed any misgivings about getting out of that crushing work environment.

Chapter Ten: Korean Diversions

It wasn't supposed to be a vacation, but some of us saw language school as being one anyway. Although none of us just coasted through classes, I didn't try to achieve any stellar academic marks either. Everybody was certain that, once we had finished the course, the odds were great that we would be assigned back to long hours of work in Korea. Consequently, we were going to take full advantage of being Stateside for a while.

Sure enough, just before we completed our classes, five of us were assigned back to Osan. Well, we had mostly enjoyed our year of R&R in the States, but some of us were fed up with the attitude of many American civilians – particularly women – toward the military at the time. I, without a doubt, looked forward to getting away from all that. Besides, I was anxious to put my increased language skills to work. This time, however, while I knew that my abilities were greatly improved, I also knew that I was not yet fluent. Only a lot of practice in Korea could get me to that point.

Once back at Osan in the spring of 1971, I settled into a new job, a really cushy flying position working straight days. I was now officially a Day Lady. The deskwork itself was actually rather undemanding and it soon became a bit boring. Nevertheless, I vowed to stick with it because of the non-shiftwork schedule as well as the extra income from flight pay once again.

I spent the first few weeks reacquainting myself with the base and, of course, with the Ville. Then it occurred to me that running the Ville as before wasn't going to help me in my desire to get really good in Korean. I decided to look up one of the houseboys I had known from my deployments to Osan more than a year ago.

Paek Mun-nam was a friendly guy about my age who had always been willing to answer the many questions I always seemed to have about Korea when I first began the long series of deployments more than three years ago in 1968. I had also heard that he wasn't opposed to having a beer or two now and then. After a few inquiries, I learned that he was now working at the base hospital, probably a step up for him. The next day during my lunch break, I went there and asked around. It wasn't long before I was pointed in the right direction to find him.

Mr. Paek seemed genuinely pleased to see me, and his associates looked impressed that an American would bother to find him. Evidently, many airmen saw their houseboys as nothing other than servants. In any case, Mr. Paek and I agreed to meet right after work at a tearoom just outside the main gate of the base.

I was the first to arrive so I picked a table not far from the window but somewhat out of the way of the bustling staff, mostly very young girls who were more than a bit shy about serving one of those foreign military guys. To put them at ease, I spoke in Korean, telling the young lady at the cashier station that I had an appointment to meet someone here and I would just wait at the table if that would be acceptable. I am certain that they expected my appointment to be with a business woman.

Mr. Paek soon arrived and we decided to have a beer rather than tea. As we were catching upon local events and telling each other about what we had been doing since we had last talked, we finished our beers. Mr. Paek apologized that he needed to get home this particular night, but he wanted me to meet some of his friends when they enjoyed the Ville Korean style in a couple days. I quickly took him up on his offer to accompany them as I paid the tab. He warned me, however, that while beer in the Ville clubs that catered to Americans was cheap, elsewhere off base it was generally beyond the budget for working-class Koreans. We would be drinking makkŏlli, instead.

When I informed my buddies that I was going to hit the Ville with some Koreans, the news was met with several chuckles and a few snorts of derision. The gist of the responses was that makkŏlli was indeed inexpensive, but that it was cheap for a reason – it wasn't worth drinking. Well, I thought, we'll see about that.

However, one story that I had heard shortly after my return from language school came to mind. The clerk who worked in our airborne section had his desk in the same large office as the junior officer and the senior NCO that ran the program. It seemed that the clerk had a taste – perhaps more likely, a budget – for makkŏlli that he would frequently indulge.

The others in the office were always well aware of the days following these indulgences, for makkŏlli had the undesirable after-effect of producing a great volume of a rather odiferous intestinal gas. It was quite common to hear a loud "Aw, for chrissakes, man, that is foul!" emanating from the office to be quickly followed by the other occupants striding out of the now-contaminated space with scowls on their faces. I know of one occasion when the clerk was actually dismissed from duty so that work could get done without the need for gasmasks.

No American was able to provide me with a meaningful description of makkŏlli, and thus I was looking forward to my night in the Ville with Mr. Paek and his buddies with both eagerness and trepidation. Shortly after work, I met Mr. Paek at the main gate, and he introduced me to the four work associates with him. Following a narrow and winding dirt lane that wandered through parts of the Ville I had never realized even existed, we shortly arrived at a non-descript fence with a dilapidated gate that opened onto a very small courtyard in front of a one-story house-like structure. The building had two rooms for customers on each side of a narrow hallway that led to a kitchen and a back room for employees, and to an outside toilet.

The proprietress, a middle-aged Korean lady who still possessed much of her youthful beauty, greeted us at the door. Behind her were several young kisaeng girls who all echoed her entreaty to come in and enjoy their hospitality. Kisaengs are similar in concept to the Japanese geisha, although in small villages like the one just outside Osan, they generally are not quite as accomplished in the arts of poetry or music. Regardless of skills, they are not prostitutes and, accordingly, any ill-mannered behavior will get the offending person ejected, usually by force, from a makkŏlli house.

We were shown to the first room on the left after we removed our footwear. Mr. Paek told me that rubber slippers were available if patrons ever needed to use the outhouse. The room had two low tables set end-to-end and covered with a brown paper that reminded me of the stuff used by butchers in days past. It presumably served as a disposable tablecloth. I don't recall who placed the first order, but soon we had one of those Korean brass teapots filled with makkŏlli delivered by two giggling kisaeng girls, both of whom were barely out of their teens.

They poured each of us a small cup of the brew and everyone but me took deep and noisy sips from their cups. I tentatively took a small sip – mindful that everyone's eyes were on me to gauge my reaction. I was surprised but not completely put off by the taste and consistency. I was no longer a makkŏlli virgin, but I was not yet a fan of it, either.

Makkŏlli is often defined as Korean homebrew made from rice and wheat flour, a description that is totally inadequate. It would be much more appropriate to say that makkŏlli looks and tastes like fermented milk-of-magnesia. It is a pale yellow cloudy liquid that is not homogenized, so it requires constant stirring to prevent fermentation sediment from drifting to the bottom of its container. It is also not pasteurized, but few imbibers worry about that since it has a higher alcoholic content than beer – and everyone knows that alcohol kills germs anyway, so there couldn't possibly be any problem.

After the second pot was consumed – I was now drinking my share – a third arrived with side dishes of peanuts roasted in the shell and pears cut into bite-sized pieces with toothpicks next to them. It seems that the goodies come out only for customers that spend a little money.

Into the third pot, I had a sudden moment of clarity in which I recognized that I was now speaking more Korean than I ever had before. The slight alcoholic haze had removed my self-consciousness enough to loosen my tongue and, although I knew when I made some grammatical error or groped for a word, everyone seemed most tolerant. Holy hesitations! I could get to like this way of practicing my language skills.

Somehow, I got through the evening without saying anything outrageously stupid or violating some unrecognized Korean custom. As I made my way back to the base, I wondered if the affects of the makkŏlli would hit me as badly as they did the clerk. The next day, I was not disappointed, and I felt obliged to spend as much time away from confined indoor spaces as possible. I was also very glad that I had remembered to take some Bacchus-D before going to bed.

As I mentally reviewed the various conversational topics of the previous evening, I could remember only some of the new words I had learned and none of the delicately offered corrections to my grammatical errors. To remedy that, I began to carry a small notepad whenever I went to the Ville for any reason. Even when drinking, I would often pull out my pad to make note of something, and my Korean companions soon got used to that.

There were a lot of things I needed to keep in mind when out on the town with Koreans, one of which being who pays for the evening's festivities. Most of the time when airmen are in the Ville, each person pays for his own poison. I learned just how this is different in Korea as the result of a prank that Mr. Paek and his buddies played on me one evening.

As we approached the entrance to the makkŏlli house we had visited a few times before, I was pushed to the front of the group. Normally, out of respect, I would hang back to be close to last entering any Korean establishment. This time, I was forced to be first. The proprietress and her kisaeng girls greeted me as though I were the leader of the pack. Something began to feel odd, so I turned to Mr. Paek and asked him what was going on. He just grinned and said that I would have to wait and see.

As we began our evening, I noticed that larger plates of peanuts and fruit were appearing, and they were appearing more frequently as well. Mr. Paek and the others seemed to be having more fun than normal. Finally, when it came time to call it a night, the bill was presented to me!

It seems that he who enters the drinking establishment first is announcing to everyone that it is his party, that he is the one buying for the night. After a moment, I realized that was only fair, since I had never been asked to help pay for our previous excursions and my offers to do so had been declined. In fact, as several thoughts flashed through my mind, I was able to recall that all of the Koreans had paid one by one. It was indeed now my turn.

Everyone probably knew that I was unaware of this custom, and they all offered to chip in if I did not have enough cash. I could not accept their kind gestures as I felt that it would have been a loss of face for me to admit that I was not prepared. Holding my breath, I looked at the bill. Including a generous tip, it was still under $20 for the five of us – and the peanuts and fruit were not free as I once thought. Holy hangover! The five of us having a good time for that amount of money? Drinking with the guys could be just as expensive as that and not as rewarding.

Even though I paid the bill without any financial concern – and in good humor for the rather subtle reminder that it was my turn to buy – I told myself to pay closer attention in the future to things like this. I did not want to be seen as a cheapskate or slacker that had to be reminded to step up when it was his time to do anything.

But despite the slight embarrassment, there was a silver lining in this experience. By having paid my dues, so to speak, I felt that I had become a full-fledged and accepted member of the group. So, instead of addressing my friend as Mister Paek, I referred to him by his given name of Mun-nam, just like his Korean buddies. At first, he objected strenuously, saying that he was *several months* older than me and thus deserved far more respect.

I knew from his demeanor that he was only toying with me, but I did surprise him by agreeing to address him as Elder

Brother, but I did so in a tone of voice and with a slight bowing of my head to imply that he was years older than he actually was. He grimaced in mock annoyance and then relented with a wide grin, saying, "You are right, we are equal, truly, you son of a dog!" He then said that I needed a Korean nickname, and that mine would be Dragonfly. It was fitting, he claimed, because I was a flyboy. From that point on, nearly all Koreans addressed me as Dragonfly.

The next time we met, Mun-nam said that we ought to try a different place, one close to where he lived that had just opened up. No one objected, so off we went with more than a bit of curiosity to visit the new makkŏlli house. A big sign over the door announced that it was called the Jinwi Jip. I knew that jip meant house, but I did not know the meaning of Jinwi. Since I was aware that names often have significance, I decided to look it up in my dictionary back at the barracks.

I had to laugh out loud when I looked up the definition in my Minjungsugwan Korean-to-English dictionary. Somebody must have had a sense of humor to label a working-class drinking establishment as "The House of Truth." On second thought, however, it made perfect sense, for it has long been said, beginning with the ancient Greeks and Romans, that in wine there is truth. Well, fancy that, I thought, Korea is not so different from the West after all.

Mun-nam and his friends and I did not hit the makkŏlli houses all that often, perhaps only once a week or so. But I found that I preferred going to that type of drinking establishment rather than the clubs that catered strictly to Americans. First of all, the club music was far too loud, the airmen were always somewhat rowdier than I prefer, and the whole atmosphere was losing its appeal for me. Besides, I could speak Korean in makkŏlli houses where English was generally not used.

I also found a perfect place when not hanging out with Munnam and his friends. Along the path to one of the clubs frequented by the military was the Tong Paek Jip. I was confident that I knew the meaning of this name – Eastern White House, one more example of Korean humor – and I continued in that belief until one of the old hands in Korea pointed out that it could just as easily mean Camellia House. The camellia is a type of flower often used in making tea. The only way to be sure would be to see how the name was written using Chinese characters, rather than in Korean letters, but the sign over the door was written only in Korean. However, based on the open layout of the place and the fact that it had normal tables and chairs, it is quite likely that it had indeed been a tearoom in its beginnings. Thus, I disappointedly admitted to myself that it was quite probably the Camellia House.

These days, though, the Camellia House served beer, makkŏlli, and various Korean hard liquors. It was a true bar, and it consequently had no kisaeng girls. The middle-aged woman running it was simply referred to as Mom by everyone who patronized the place. I went there often enough that occasionally a group of Korean men would invite me to sit with them at their table. Perhaps it was only a case of getting the richer American to spring for a round of drinks – which I would gladly do – or maybe it was simple curiosity as to why an American would come to this type of place to get his buzz on.

Koreans have their own term for getting a buzz on. They call it "getting the engine started," meaning that they are starting to feel the effects of drinking. Getting the engine started is quite apt since Koreans tend to be a voluble people, and they can get emotionally charged up when imbibing. Discussions can become intense and tempers can briefly flare up during particularly contentious arguments. Even so, actual fights are extremely rare, since everyone soon calms down and things quickly return to normal. Holding a grudge is almost unknown.

If the Koreans inviting me to their table didn't have their engines running too much and they seemed to be in an affable frame of mind, I would accept. After invariably having to explain my reasons for being there, I would frequently be asked questions about the States or to provide my take on some current event that had captured their attention. I found that I was sometimes hard-pressed to come up with answers to their questions. The vocabulary was certainly a challenge at all times, but what most often gave me pause was responding to a point of view that came from a different perspective, another culture. I learned a lot about working-class Korea from some of those late evening less-than-sober exchanges, and I considered those experiences invaluable.

Chapter Eleven: The Ugly, the Bad, and the Good

Not everything about hanging out with Koreans involved makkŏlli. After all, no one can go about just drinking the cheap shit and having a good time. On rare occasions, the group of us would go to the Venus Club, a nightclub of sorts but with a decidedly Korean twist, to drink beer. At first, I thought the name of the club was "The Penis Club," for that is exactly how the neon sign had it. I was confused enough to ask Mun-nam why we were going to a club named after the male organ. After a several seconds of laughter by all of the Koreans, I was reminded that the Korean alphabet had no "V" sound. By convention, a "P" was used instead. Being reassured that it really was named after the goddess of love, I had to smile at my failure to recognize the name for what it really was.

The Venus Club was located on the second floor of a building that used to house a club that catered to Americans. For an unknown reason during my year back in the States, the American club had moved to another location, leaving a perfectly good barroom open for a Korean enterprise. The room itself was a rectangle with a disco mirror ball hanging from the center of its high ceiling. Around the perimeter on three sides were large curtained booths that could hold up to eight people in four wide upholstered chairs set around a table. The entrance with a manager's station and a service bar were on the fourth wall, all of this surrounding a modest dance floor.

Bar girls populated the club to serve not only as waitresses, but also as dance partners and coquettish booth companions – for a price by the hour. I never understood why men would want to hang out with bawdy ladies, only to be told, "Sorry, fella, time for you to go home – alone" at the end of the evening.

However, Mun-nam and the others always wanted to go there when they were flush with money. Perhaps they were able to arrange something on the side with the bar girls, but I never saw anything to indicate that.

Anyway, after a couple of visits to the Venus Club, I knew that it was time for me to foot the bill. I expected the cost to be quite high, perhaps as much as $40, so I cashed a check at the NCO Club to have enough Korean won. In the taxi on the way to the Ville, I discovered that in my haste I had left the won at the cashier's cage of the NCO Club.

I was confident for a number of reasons that I would be able to claim it the next day, so I explained my options to my Korean friends. Everyone could wait while I went back to get the won or I could ask the manager at the Venus Club to allow us to drink on credit until the next day. They all thought that it wouldn't hurt to ask, so we continued on to the Venus Club.

I led the group into the club, pausing at the manager's station to inquire about credit. We were known, I was confident, because this was the group that always had an American with them. The manager's response was a hearty "Of course!" I wouldn't have to return to the base to retrieve my money after all, so we picked a booth and began to enjoy the evening, including a few of the bar girls.

I usually declined to have a booth companion for myself for a number of reasons. I don't like being led on, and I was aware that being seen with an American on the dance floor could be detrimental to a bar girl's desirability. After all, "good" Korean girls do not as a rule associate with skivvy honcho Americans. I also did not enjoy spending the money for empty promises.

At the end of the evening, the bill was presented to me and I inquired as to how I would sign the IOU for credit. Following a moment of stunned silence, all hell broke loose. The bar girls scattered like leaves in the wind as the manager came over to loudly berate me for being a deadbeat. I felt insulted, for I had taken the manager at his word that the club would extend me credit. He contemptuously retorted that he thought I was joking and he had answered in a like manner. There was no credit at the Venus Club.

My character was under attack. Being somewhat fortified by liquid courage, I told my Korean friends to leave and that I would handle this on my own. Mun-nam reluctantly followed the others down the stairs and out the door. A bouncer was about to roughly escort me out when I got him to stop directly in front of the manager to indignantly declare in Korean, "I pay my debts. You did not tell me the truth. I will sleep here on this floor until you allow me the credit I thought was offered in good faith. I pay my debts." With that, I broke free of the bouncer's grip to lie down in the middle of the dance floor and close my eyes. I thought that everyone was being extremely shortsighted, since it would be better to receive payment a little late rather than have to write the bill off as being run up by a stupid American.

Within minutes, a rough-looking older Korean man in a wheelchair prodded me with a wooden rod. He identified himself as the owner and demanded in an angry tone that I explain myself, insisting that I use English. I restated my case and added that our group had been patronizing his club on and off for some time. I also added that in my hurry to not delay the group in starting the evening, I had forgotten my money at the NCO Club. I thought that we would be recognized as good customers and that was why I had requested approval to run a tab.

After consulting off to one side with the manager, the owner returned with the list of charges for me to sign, stating gruffly that I had until the next military payday to wipe the debt clean. "Yeah, now he realizes that I intend to pay," I thought. I told him that it would be paid well before that, most likely by the end of the day tomorrow. He bade me a brusque goodnight as I left.

Right after work the next day, I hustled to the cashier's cage at the NCO Club. As I expected, my money had been set aside for me. Mun-nam and the head cashier were close acquaintances and as a result, I always received preferential services from the cashier and his subordinates. I also made it a point to tip those Korean workers there, knowing that doing so would always be to my advantage.

After a relaxing dinner at the NCO Club and with a wad of won safely stashed in my pocket, I headed to the Ville and the Venus Club. When I entered the club, the manager showed surprise as I presented myself to ask for the owner. He curtly told me to take a seat in one of the booths but to leave the curtains open. I did so and soon an extremely attractive woman probably in her late 30s slid into the chair opposite me. Although this woman was perhaps a decade older than me, under different circumstances I would have made my appreciation known in a heartbeat.

Such thoughts fled my mind as she explained that she was the wife of the owner. He was not feeling well and she would be handling this affair on his behalf. She spoke nearly perfect English in a soft voice saying, "My husband is well-known in some areas and he has unusual business partners that you would not want to meet. It is good that you are here to pay off your obligation so soon. It shows that you have honor."

I was quite taken aback to suddenly realize that I had unwittingly gotten myself into a part of Korean culture that I had only heard about and never wanted to experience – the Korean underworld. After only a brief hesitation as I digested the import of what the lady had said, I asked for the bill that I had signed. She readily produced it for me to see, not letting it out of her hand until I handed over the won in exchange.

As I excused myself to leave, she admitted that she did not think an American would have had the courage to do what I had done last night, let alone show the integrity to follow up on the obligation today. She got up to accompany me to the exit. Her last words to me were, "You now have credit here, but do not abuse it. Do you understand?"

Holy hoodlums! All I could think was that the situation could have turned out really ugly. If I had not insisted on paying, I might have been jumped in some alley by some of those "unusual business partners." When I relayed my experience to Mun-nam and the others the next time we met, they were absolutely amazed that I had pulled it off, saying that I must be the luckiest dumb ass in the world. I just laughed – and did not tell them that I agreed with their evaluation of my mental capacities.

On the way back to the base after resolving my credit predicament at the Venus Club, I stopped off at the Camellia House to see if any of the regulars were there for me to sit and drink with. Once inside, I was disappointed to see that the only people besides Mom were two old men at a table in one corner arguing and a Korean woman sitting by herself along the back wall.

Since Mom had seen me, I was obligated to stay and have something to drink. Before I could sit, however, Mom came scurrying over to me to quietly suggest that I sit with the woman who was alone. Mom actually gave me a push

whispering in English, "You and she talk, go now!"

What the hell, I thought, the worst that can happen is that the woman tells me to take a hike. I can't get blamed for any ruckus because Mom would be the one who started all this. I took a better look at the woman and was surprised to note two things. First, she was not dressed as a business woman but was outfitted in conservative but casual Western clothes. Second, she was a very presentable woman roughly my own age.

I could not think of a good line as I approached her table, so I just blurted out the truth. I said that I often came to the Camellia House to practice my Korean with some of the other customers who were willing to talk with an American. I continued that it was Mom that suggested that I ask if I could sit with her.

She politely gestured to the chair opposite her without a sound. As I sat down, I told her my Korean nickname of Dragonfly and asked for hers. In lightly accented English, she replied that her name was Son-hŭi but that everyone called her Sony. I took a chance and said, "If I were a Korean lady, I would not want to be named after a Japanese radio." She paused and then gave a short laugh, looking at me with interest for the first time.

Reasoning that I was on a roll here, I continued by declaring that, as pretty as she was, she should be called Myŏng-ja for her brilliant smile. Her face lost its warmth as she quietly but intensely announced, "Do not bullshit me. I don't need any bullshit tonight." I quickly apologized and asked if she would be willing to speak Korean with me.

She agreed and then hesitatingly inquired, "Do you really think that I have a nice smile?" I grinned in return, responding, "No," and hesitated just a bit to toy with her before continuing, "Your smile is nice, truly, but it is your eyes that I find lovely."

Sony laughed without reservation and, for the first time since I had approached, I could see her begin to relax.

Sony had an empty glass in front of her but since she did not seem intoxicated, I suggested that perhaps we could have some conversation over another round. She accepted, and Mom, who had evidently been observing our interaction, quickly came over with two O.B.s and fresh glasses. As she left the table, Mom looked at me over her shoulder and winked as she grinned.

Sony and I talked at the Camellia House for more than an hour. Although we consumed only the two beers, Mom did not pester us to buy more. Long before midnight, I said that I had enjoyed our conversation very much but that it was time for me to get back to the barracks. Without making eye contact as she touched my hand briefly, Sony murmured that we could continue to talk where she lived. Of course I thought that was a splendid idea.

It was a short distance that we easily covered in silence. As I followed Sony into her place, I was surprised to see that it was not one room in a house but a nice apartment with a curtained archway between the front and back rooms. In addition to a small Western-style couch and a table with two chairs, the first room had a modern refrigerator, a hot plate, and a small TV. The room in the rear was obviously the bedroom. I was impressed. I knew from her speech and behavior that she was no business woman, so I concluded that she was a very successful shop owner.

Now that we were together and out of the public eye, I wondered at her sudden quietness. Since I didn't think she had changed her mind about me, I guessed that it was likely that she was waiting for me to make the next move. I felt a bit awkward, for there had been no flirting or other courtship behavior back at the Camellia House, other than the invitation to her home. Fortunately, the processed beer chose that moment to make itself known. She excused herself to the back room to use the chamber pot and then asked me if I knew how to use it.

That appeared to break the ice a bit, for she then looked at me to say with a bit of defiance that she needed someone to talk with her tonight. Given her earlier comment about not wanting any bullshit, I realized that something must have upset her before I arrived at the Camellia House. It seemed that somehow I had been chosen to comfort her. Not quite sure how to go about that, I slowly approached her and gently gathered her into my arms just to hold her.

Speaking so quietly that I had to listen closely, Sony asked me to tell her again that I found her attractive. I did so with honesty and restrained ardor. Sony was looking for reassurance, as it seemed that whatever had happened was causing her to question whether she was appealing. That night, I did my best to convince her that she was the most desirable woman in the world. Sony was a willing and very active recipient of my efforts, rousing me two more times to finally conquer her insecurities on that point. When we finally slept, I was exhausted.

In the morning, Sony was again quiet and I felt it best to leave. She said that she would walk with me to the base. That was fine with me, but I mentioned that I wanted to stop at a drug store for some Bacchus-D.

After experiencing its recuperative powers before, I had since taken the time to read the ingredients on the back label. Bacchus-D contained Vitamins A, B, C, D, E, and K. It also had significant amounts of nicotine and caffeine. My depleted body demanded caffeine. I got a bottle for Sony as well and we both quaffed them with relish.

Once at the main gate, I thought that we would say our good-byes, but Sony proceeded through the checkpoint right with me, flashing a military spouse ID card. I was shocked to realize that Sony was the wife of some military guy. As soon as we were out of earshot of the gate guards, I straight-out asked her if she was married. She looked away for the briefest of moments before turning to face me with an unrepentant look as she said, "I am married, yes, but that no longer matters. Does this bother you?"

I was indeed bothered, but not for any religious reason. I was trying to formulate a delicate reply when Sony, seeing my hesitation, interjected that she understood if I was concerned about having broken one of the Ten Commandments, she herself being Catholic. I was about to deny any concern for Christian taboos when it struck me that Sony had unwittingly provided me with the only non-judgmental explanation for any worries I might have.

I falsely confessed that I needed time to think about what we had done, that while I enjoyed our time together and wished we could see each other again, that was probably not a good idea. Sony seemed to accept that. We gave each other a brief friend-like hug and she walked off toward one part of the base while I continued on to the Skivvy-Nine barracks.

The real reason I was uncomfortable was that I did not want to get in the middle of some domestic difficulty. I had heard of too many American-Korean relationships in which a minor spat became a very major problem when one or the other was found to be cheating during what could have been just a temporary breakup. I also knew that one of the most dangerous places for a guy to be is in a bedroom that is not his own.

I never saw Sony again, and I never told Mom of the Camellia

House or anyone else about what had transpired, but no man could ever forget a night like the one I had spent with a woman like Sony.

After my escapade at the Venus Club, I told Mun-nam and the others that I wanted to avoid the place for a while. They all understood and decided that we would revert to the House of Truth and drink makkŏlli even though they all liked beer and I preferred whiskey.

There were a couple of differences between the makkŏlli house where Mun-nam and the rest of us normally gathered and the House of Truth. The first is that the House of Truth was in much better repair due to its newer construction. Everything just looked better, neater, cleaner, brighter.

Another difference was that the kisaeng girls at the House of Truth were even less skilled in reciting poetry or singing. That really wasn't a problem since the only truly talented songstress at the other place had been the proprietress. Unfortunately, one could not request only her to perform for that would have been an insult to the less-gifted girls. Consequently, the relatively unskilled girls at the House of Truth weren't an issue.

Perhaps in compensation though, the House of Truth girls were willing to try out new ways to entertain their customers. I had the idea to introduce everyone to the game of Thumper. As we traditionally sat on the floor with legs folded under a low table, establishing a rhythm by slapping our thighs or stomping our feet was not practical. Instead, we used chopsticks to beat out a cadence on the table. Instead of using names, though, everyone just picked a number.

Another difference was that the House of Truth did not mind if its kisaengs got a little tipsy as they entertained. The girls were quite willing to play Thumper since it became as much fun for them as it was for us guys, and the management sure as hell didn't seem to mind. More people drinking more makkŏlli had the benefit of causing us to buy more, and that was good for business.

However, the most significant difference was that the Truth kisaengs were more pragmatic in their relationships with the customers. That is not to say that the women were for hire, but they occasionally were coaxed into becoming mistresses of customers they favored. Before that could happen, though, the ladies expected some sort of relationship involving friendship and respect to develop.

There was one woman there, a Miss Yang – somewhat older than the rest and with a slightly crooked tooth – who interested me. More than anything, it was her spunky personality and her outgoing demeanor that caught my attention. She also seemed more curious than the others about the American who was making an effort to understand whatever he could about Korea and its culture.

After I had cautiously and mildly flirted with her a few times during our patronage of the House of Truth, Mun-nam uncharacteristically brought things out in the open. He and the others evidently had noted the verbal back-and-forth between the two of us. He teasingly questioned, "Why don't you and Miss Yang go talk in the corner over there?" I was embarrassed – but not nearly as much as Miss Yang who dropped her gaze and covered her face with her hands. She would not even look at anyone. The other kisaengs giggled like schoolgirls, while the guys just grinned. Shit, I had to do something.

I summoned my dignity as best I could to declare, "I came here to consume makkŏlli with my friends and that is all I will do." Realizing that Miss Yang could take my words as a rejection, which would be the very last thing that I wanted, I hastened to add, "I do not say that Miss Yang is not appealing. She is that indeed! However, I mean to say that if Miss Yang desires my attention, it will be as she wishes." With that, I looked directly at Miss Yang, who had dropped her hands from her face to stare at me during my proclamation.

After I finished my short sermon, I drained the remains of my makkŏlli cup in one swig to set it down emphatically. In an attempt to break up the seriousness with a bit of humor, I assumed a pompous tone of voice to query, "Well, who will fill my cup?" Mun-nam reached for the makkŏlli but Miss Yang stretched out to take the pot from him. As she poured, she gave me a look to make sure that I was watching her serve me. I was flabbergasted – and then delighted – as the meaning of her action washed over me.

Later, as we left the House of Truth, Miss Yang drew close to me and daringly admitted that she would not be offended if I showed her attention. I asked her when she was free and we agreed to have lunch at a nearby tearoom in two days when I was off duty during the day. This exchange did not escape the attention of my drinking buddies who razzed me mercilessly for a while. I did not care one bit as I just grinned.

Miss Yang and I settled into a comfortable and caring intimate relationship that lasted for months. When the end of my assignment in Korea approached, she presented me with a gift, a hand-crocheted under garment. I was very moved by her offering, knowing that I would always remember our relationship with deep affection.

Chapter Twelve: Going Golfing

Some of the guys with whom I worked were beginning to comment that I spent a lot of time with Koreans. At first, I thought nothing of it, knowing that they could choose to improve their own knowledge of things Korean and reap the benefits that I enjoyed, if only they wanted to do so.

Then I began to sense some animosity about my not hanging out with them after work. I hadn't realized that everyone missed me so much. Actually, I really didn't think that was it; it might have been that they felt I was being standoffish. Whether they missed me or thought I was being aloof, the cause really didn't matter, but the result did. Perhaps I needed to spend more time hanging out with my coworkers.

When I heard that Lew and Zeke were getting a foursome together for golf the upcoming weekend, I asked if I could tag along even though I was not much of a golfer. That was fine as they both said that they were just amateurs themselves and that it was a good excuse to get out in the fresh air and smack some balls around.

Lew was still the same as he was before the intermediate language class – usually arrogant, occasionally offensive, and always entertaining. Zeke was Lew's groupie and everything that Lew did, Zeke copied. Not the brightest bulb to ever glow, misfortune seemed to follow Zeke wherever he went. After being bitten by a stray dog at a lakeside party near the Paradise Club in the spring, Zeke had to undergo a series of rabies shots because the dog could not be captured for testing. Another time, he had gone wading in the golf course water hazards to retrieve golf balls for free, only to come out with his lower torso and legs covered with leeches. I shuddered as I realized what would have been the result if Zeke had not kept his briefs on.

Archie joined us that Saturday to complete the foursome and I was pleased that he did. A couple of years older than the rest of us, he was probably the most reasonable and sane person in our group. To save money, we all declined to have caddies. We intended to do only the nine holes walking and carrying our own gear.

I am absolutely horrible in teeing off due to my fear of grounding the club. As a result, I almost always top the ball, causing my shots to fly off only a few feet above the fairway until gravity pulls them down and they eventually dribble to a stop not more than a hundred yards or so out. Even using a brassie or a spoon instead of a driver doesn't help. I just don't do well with woods. I do better with approach shots requiring an iron and I am not at all a bad putter.

In the aggregate, though, my skill set put me at the low end of the scale as a golfer and my scores reflected that. Nonetheless, I do have fun when out on the course with the guys. The nine-hole course at Osan added a few challenges of its own, however, causing a great deal of consternation for me as well as providing a lot of amusement for the others.

Holes One and Two at Osan are routine Par Fours, first a dogleg to the right and next one to the left. I managed to get through these two holes in only 10 strokes while Lew had 8 for the best score. I dreaded what was coming next.

Right in front of the tee on Number Three was a significant water hazard. In my mind, water hazard was an understatement since it was actually more like a large pond, roughly 50 yards across. I was absolutely convinced that I was going to lose balls here. Sure enough, my first two drives went directly into the water, one immediately going in like a bullet and the next skimming like a flat stone only to sink in the middle of the pond. Lew and Zeke were howling like I was putting on a comedy show. Even Archie was chuckling.

Archie eventually came over to suggest that I use a 2-iron, and not to worry about the excess altitude I would get but to think instead about the distance through the air that would be enough to carry the ball over the water. I didn't merely tee off; I smacked the ball with all of my frustration behind my swing and was pleasantly surprised to see that Archie's advice had worked. Holy hotshot! Not only did I clear the water, I got more distance than any of my drives using woods ever had. I was an "iron man" from that point on.

Not counting the two balls dropped into the water, I was approaching the green on Hole Three in just two shots, which would have been good for par. The far edge of the green of this hole bordered right on the base perimeter fence. As I prepared to chip onto the green, all of us failed to note the little Korean kid watching intently from just on the other side of that fence.

I made my chip shot and was happy to see that it rolled to a stop not much more than a club length from the hole. What I was not happy to see was that the kid had snuck through a loose flap of the chain-link fence and was now streaking for my ball. I knew what was going to happen before it did. The little urchin snatched up my ball and sped back through the fence in retreat to the other side.

My ball was now hostage to this enterprising little bastard who had no mercy. "You gimme fibu dollah, GI!" he shouted in his best English as he brandished my ball above his head in triumph. I was not amused by his failure to pronounce the word "five" properly. All I knew is that he had ruined what was likely one of the best shots I would have that day – and after the water hazard, I was out of spare balls. I needed that one back.

I strode across the green toward the fence with the intent of climbing through it to run him down until his little lungs burst. Archie pointed out that the hole in the fence was not big enough for me and that the little urchin could probably outrun my sorry out-of-shape ass in the first place. Lew was about to let loose with one of his profanity-laced outbursts for which he was well known. Archie stopped him, explaining that doing so would only drive up the cost for me to get my ball back.

Instead Archie took out his spare pack of Juicy Fruit gum that he was using as a crutch during his effort to stay off cigarettes. Waving the gum in his hand, he slowly approached the hole in the fence while telling the boy that he could get more for the pack of gum in the Ville than "fibu dollah." The kid knew better. "Choon gum one dollah," the little bastard scoffed in contempt.

I had an idea. Kids everywhere love balloons, so I pulled out a three-pack of condoms and showed the kid how to unroll his own personal balloon. His eyes widened and a big grin spread across his thin face. "I give you these three balloons, you give me my ball," I offered. We had a deal!

With two packaged condoms in one hand and the unrolled one flapping in the other, the kid ran off to show everyone what he had. I had to laugh as I thought about how his mother or father would react to a young boy coming home with a pack of condoms that he had gotten in trade from some pervert American.

Focusing once again on our game, we teed off on Four, the relatively short and straight fairway of which was like a valley – down from the tee and up again to the green. Everyone made par on the hole and we moved on to Hole Five.

Five was probably the most unusual hole on the course, if not in the world. The tee was on top of a command bunker that had been built and then covered with several feet of earth to camouflage it from aerial view and protect it from enemy fire. That wasn't the challenge, for in fact the twenty or so feet of additional height was actually a benefit for those wanting more distance off the tee.

The challenge was all those communications antenna guy-wires that crisscrossed the fairway. It was not uncommon to hear a reverberating twang when one of the wires was struck by a tee-shot. Often enough, this occurrence would shortly be followed by a robust litany of military expressions best left undescribed.

Occasionally, though, a shot would get through or would ricochet advantageously off the wires. Regardless, I chose to aim at the wires for two reasons. The first is that I am a bad enough golfer that by aiming at them, I would likely be assured of not hitting the wires. The second reason is that, if I did hit them, then perhaps I could do enough damage so that the guy-wires would eventually fail. It seems that many of the golfers shared my enthusiasm for destruction. We all ignored the consequences of having a guy-wire fail, causing a tall radio mast to collapse. Besides, all the damage seemed to be only to the golf balls anyway.

I performed adequately, for me, on all the remaining holes now that I was driving with a 2-iron rather than a wood – until we reached the ninth hole. Nine was the longest hole of the course and I did not want to have to do two approach shots from the fairway. I decided to try my wood driver once more. The other three failed to draw my attention to the gaping trench about 50 feet in front of the tee. There was a long section of 30-

inch cast-iron pipe lying on the ground next to it. Both the trench and the pipe crossed the fairway at right angles to present a formidable obstacle for a duffer like me.

Everyone else had teed off ahead of me while I was psyching myself up to get some altitude and distance with the wood. I wound up my backswing and let go with all that I could muster, and I was gratified to hear the sound that comes only from having hit the ball squarely. What I didn't expect, however, was for my ball to hit the pipe. It did exactly that with a frighteningly loud clang that startled all of us as my ball promptly disappeared from view.

It seemed like several seconds went by as we looked up and down the fairway, to the right and to the left, trying to spot where my ball was. Then we heard a soft plop on the ground a few feet behind us. There it was, my ball. With the energy of probably my most powerful tee-shot ever propelling it, the ball must have hit the rounded side of the pipe at the precise angle necessary for it to ricochet in a tall vertical arc that would curve it back behind where we all had been standing.

At first, we thought that this was hilarious, and even I could see the irony in having my mightiest drive go for negative yards. It was a few minutes before we realized that, had the ball rebounded straight back at us at with the velocity it must have possessed, someone would have been seriously injured. It was very strongly suggested that I go back to using a 2-iron to play out the last hole.

I made a stop at the pro-shop specifically to complain about that pipe but the guy behind the counter showed no concern whatsoever as he replied, "Osan is sort of a combat zone and Nine is under construction right now, whaddya fuckin' expect?"

It was clear to me that my swing needed help, so I decided to use the practice range with a bucket of balls. No matter how I tried, I just couldn't get enough altitude with a wood. Even though I was moderately successful in using a 2-iron in place of a driver, I felt that I was sacrificing distance needlessly. I needed to master the woods.

After several balls flying off the tee just inches above the ground and rolling no further than a hundred yards at best, I conceded that I required professional help. I sought out the resident pro who told me that he was absolutely, positively certain he could help me – for a steep price. I declined to invest that much in a game that I knew I wouldn't ever play that often.

Giving up in disgust, I retreated to the NCO Club for an early dinner and some help to soothe my soul in the form of some spirits. My medicine worked its wonders, for by dusk I had not a single care in the world. By then, I had even forgiven the little bastard who had held my ball hostage. After all, I at last reasoned, he might have only been trying to earn some money for his family. Hell, the poor little guy had been thrilled to get some military-issue condoms to play with. How sad is that, I wondered, thinking that I should have given him the five.

Ruthie, the waitress supervisor, came over to tell me that I ought to eat something if I was going to continue to drink. When she brought me a hamburger, I told her the whole story about how the sad little urchin had captured my ball and how I got it back. She snorted as if in disgust and then looked at me for a bit before saying, "You should go to bed before you get really drunk and decide to give away all your money."

Chapter Thirteen: Difficulties

Mid afternoon one Sunday, I was looking for Kent, one of my other coworkers. Several of the guys in our unit had been talking about his latest escapade as he was returning to base from the Ville and I wanted to hear about it from the man himself. I found Kent just coming out of the shower after a workout at his martial arts gym down in the Ville. Often recognized around the base from his numerous on-base bouts and exhibitions, he was working on becoming a Fourth Degree Black Belt in taekwondo.

Kent had gotten into taekwondo to overcome a tendency to gain weight. In finding the solution to that problem, he also found a new way of life that included eating properly, drinking very little, and generally behaving himself. However, that is not to say that Kent was against having a little fun now and then. He could be a Ville rat like the rest of us when the occasion warranted.

Once Kent was dressed, we went to the NCO Club so that he could eat. He ordered two deluxe cheeseburgers, one with onion rings and one with fries, along with a large iced tea. Kent had really wanted a vanilla milk shake but he said that he was cutting back on his calories. Over lunch, he told me about his recent experience. It had not taken place in the Ville as I had originally thought, but at the parking lot just inside the main gate of the base.

Then he asked me if I knew much about the latest incident with the Drunk Bus. I said no, only that I would rather walk than ride it. He agreed that the risk of falling into one of Osan's deep benjo ditches was preferable to riding that particular bus.

Benjo ditches were really not open sewers like their

Japanese label implies. It is just a name that came about so distant in the past that no one recalls its origin. Perhaps the Japanese built them during their occupation of Korea up to the end of World War II. Regardless, the ditches were deep to handle all of the run-off that occurs during the monsoon season and they were lined with large cemented-in stones to prevent erosion from the force of the rushing waters.

To the unwary, they can be very dangerous, as one airman new to the area learned. He had gotten off a crew bus one rainy night and walked directly into a benjo ditch that was about six feet across at the top and five feet deep. He smacked his forehead severely enough that he was grounded for a few days until the flight surgeon was confident that he had not suffered a concussion.

Well, by now most base residents knew about benjo ditches and the need to be careful when walking about the base after dark where there are no streetlights. Consequently, when not completely sober, it can be quite a temptation to take the Drunk Bus to avoid a long and potentially dangerous walk from the main gate of the base to the barracks area.

As Kent began his tale, it soon became clear to me that I would have to be crazier than I already was to ever take the Drunk Bus again for any reason. Kent had been returning from a late martial arts workout in the Ville a few days ago. He was aware that he was cutting it close and he did not want to get to the base after the South Korean curfew, which went into effect at midnight and the base gate would then close to all but duty-related traffic.

Kent made it back to the base just in time, but he had missed the next to the last bus that traveled from the gate parking lot all over the base, quickly and safely delivering revelers to their respective barracks area. There was still that last bus, though. The last bus, most aptly labeled the Drunk Bus, was always filled with the drunkest and rowdiest of airmen. Even under the best of conditions, riding that bus was not a pleasant experience. Fights were not unknown and various alcohol-induced maladies were routine. The wary airman did not ride that vehicle.

Kent knew that walking was preferable to the Drunk Bus so he headed out on the now unused steep and narrow lane that went over a hill to the barracks area. This lane was challenging to navigate since it had no streetlights – but it also had no benjo ditches and it certainly had no Drunk Buses. The lane eventually reconnected with the less direct route used by the Drunk Bus, just after the point where the main road bent sharply to the right.

As Kent started up the hill into the gloom, he looked back to see that the recent fad of foolhardiness on the Drunk Bus had already begun. Drunken riders seemed to think that it was amusing to see how much they could rock the Drunk Bus from side-to-side by swaying their bodies as they hung onto the overhead grip rails running down the aisle of the bus. Usually, this did not go precariously far and it nearly always stopped once the bus was in motion. This night, however, neither limit was observed.

As the bus started out of the parking lot onto the main road, Kent saw that it continued its sidewise rocking. He thought that it would stop by the time the bus got to that acute right hand turn where Kent's small lane would meet up with the bus route. As Kent crested his hill and looked ahead, he could see by the streetlights of the main road that the bus was on its side with guys crawling out its back door. The bus had overbalanced due to the side-to-side rocking while the bus had been at the apex of its sharp turn. It had slid on its left side across the road and had come to rest with the nose of the bus dangling over one of those deep benjo ditches.

I later learned from my Korean buddy Mun-nam that the hospital ER had treated some riders with broken arms and wrists along with several other lesser injuries that did not affect duty status. Kent had little sympathy for the injured – I had little myself – in light of the incident. Then I told Kent that what I really wanted to hear about was another incident in which he was directly involved. With a smirk, Kent began his story.

A few days prior to the Drunk Bus incident, he had come back from the Ville looking forward to getting a couple of chili dogs from the Roach Coach that was always at the main gate, serving hungry partiers returning to base in the late evening hours. After waiting in the long line for several minutes, Kent placed his order and was patiently standing nearby for his goodies. He did not see the two bigger guys come up to stand a little off to one side near the food delivery window of the Roach Coach.

Kent's order number was called and he moved toward the window to pick up his two tantalizing chili dogs. Before he could claim his food, one of the two guys that had been standing off to the side grabbed the plate of chili dogs and started to walk away while the other stepped in front of Kent and told him to give up or face the consequences.

At that point, another guy further back in the line shouted out to the two would-be food-nappers that they didn't know who they were messing with. The third guy pointed out that he had seen Kent demolish all of his opponents in several taekwondo matches over the last few months. The guy informed Tweedledee and Tweedledum that they were about to become unwilling participants in another awesome smack down.

There wasn't much time for contemplation since Kent had put his watch in his pocket as he strode over to the guy holding his chili dogs. He announced, "You have a choice: I get my food or I beat the shit outta your punk ass – *now!*" With very little hesitation, the chili dogs were handed over accompanied by a hastily mumbled apology for not knowing who Kent was. Kent replied that he would kick both their asses if he ever saw them try that again, no matter who the intended victim was. The two guys scurried off into the night with no further ado. Kent turned to the friend that had warned them to say, "Your friends ought to thank you. I was starting to look forward to another workout."

As expected, it had been an interesting story, but there was another reason I wanted to talk with Kent. It was about a problem that Frank, one of our coworkers, was having due to one of his odd habits. Frank had taken to wearing an Australian bush hat and he assumed an Aussie accent at times as well. Most guys simply thought that Frank was weird, but one of the guys we worked with seemed more than merely put off by these oddities.

The one coworker, Vince, seemed to have it in for Frank and was continually taunting him. Even on his best days, Vince always had a scowl on his face with little good to say about anything to anyone. At work, he was sullen enough that the rest of us didn't want to associate with him any more than duty required. More than once Vince told Frank that he didn't like his hat and one day he was going to do something about it.

There was a party in the Ville coming up that all the guys in our flying section would be attending. It was a significant milestone for the airborne contingent of Skivvy-Nine and everyone would likely want to make the most of it. Vince evidently intended to do so, too. He let it be known that he would slice and dice Frank if he showed up at the party wearing his Aussie hat.

Archie had joined Kent and me at our table and the three of us reflected on how this was going to play out. Everyone knew that Vince carried a knife, and some of his friends said that he wasn't afraid of using it. I think that it was Archie that came up with the idea that Vince would have second thoughts about using a blade if the three of us accompanied Frank to the party – all of us wearing Aussie bush hats.

We three headed down to the Ville for a clothing store that catered to military tastes where we had seen knock-offs of Australian bush hats on sale for only a couple of bucks. On the way, Kent told Archie and me that he had rented a small place off base as his off base hideaway, so to speak. At Kent's urging, we stopped off to have a look at it.

It was a one-room affair in a larger traditional Korean house. Traditional Korean houses are built in the shape of an L or a U and usually have at least four or five rooms. Kent's room was about 8 by 12 feet and situated on the end of the house that was furthest from a rather primitive kitchen but closest to the outhouse. That meant he would get the least amount of heat from the under-floor heating system. However, he would be closer to the comfort station, as it is called in Korean. It was through his association with the off base taekwondo gym that he was offered the room.

It was starkly furnished by American standards, containing only a Korean bed, two small cabinets, a low table, a Korean charcoal heating stove on the outside wall, and some of Kent's clothes on wall pegs. I wasn't terribly impressed until Kent pointed out that on a number of occasions, he was able to persuade business women to come to his humble abode for dalliances when the ladies weren't busy working. It was then that it occurred to me that I should look into this type of arrangement for myself.

After Kent secured his sliding door with a newly installed hasp and Master Lock, we went on to the Lucky Clothing Store. There we purchased our knockoff Australian bush hats to wear at the upcoming party. To keep everything under cover, we made certain that the shopkeeper would be open for business on the day of the party so that we could leave the hats there and pick them up on our way to the festivities.

The big day arrived and the four of us – Frank, Archie, Kent, and I – stopped off at the hat store to pick up the hats. Frank was amused that we were going to accompany him to the fest while wearing our headgear. His amusement did not last long once we entered the rented club.

Inside, Frank continued to wear his hat while the other three of us removed ours out of habit. As we allowed our eyes to adjust to the relative dimness of the club after being out in the full sun, Kent saw Vince start to move toward us. As he approached Frank, Archie suggested that we put our hats back on.

Vince faced Frank and said in a flat tone, "I warned you I was gonna cut you if you came in here with that hat. Now here you are with that piece o' shit hat. Guess I gotta do something 'bout that." He put his hand into his right pocket for the knife we all knew was there. Vince hadn't noticed that all four of us were now wearing Australian bush hats.

Kent had stepped up to move Frank slightly to one side so that Vince was then facing Kent as well as Frank. Kent reached out to lightly touch Vince's arm before his hand left his pocket, saying, "When your hand comes out, it had better be empty. If it isn't, I'll take your knife and cut you FWD." I had never heard of FWD before but I later learned that it meant "fast, wide, and deep" – a term used primarily in reference to knife fights.

Vince hesitated for a second or two as he slowly realized two things. First, that all four of us were wearing Australian bush hats and that Archie and I were now standing behind him. Second, and probably most important, Kent had his game face on and his glare of determination was truly intense. At last, Vince slowly removed his hand to show that he had nothing in it, before mumbling that he had only been joking.

"Fuck you and the horse you rode in on, you dick-headed dingleberry!" was Kent's response. As Vince walked to the far end of the club's bar, tension began to ebb a bit. No more was ever said about Frank or his Australian bush hat, and most of us proceeded to get cheerfully drunk.

Later, on the way back to the base from the party, Archie pointed out a sign in English on the side facing the base and in Korean on the side facing the Ville. The English side read "We Koreans are grateful to you American servicemen for helping to protect us." The Korean side read, "We should extend the American Forces personnel every convenience."

Isaac, one of the guys walking with us back to the base gate, snorted in scorn before declaring, "If they really meant that, we'd be getting drunk and laid for free." I mentioned that drinking in the Ville was cheap enough, and it was kind of neat to hear the latest American Top 40 songs – usually before the Armed Forces Radio and Television Service playlists were updated by the lame-ass civilians back in the States. As for getting laid, Archie said that all Isaac needed to do was work on his language abilities and his social skills, either of which would go along way toward remedying any lack of poon on his part.

Most of us recognized that business women really appreciated a kind word, and if a guy developed a sincere friendship with one of the ladies, well .... Let's just say that the benefits of doing so far outweighed the effort involved. A little language goes a long way. Some guys, though, just don't get that, and Isaac was one of those unfortunates.

I had met Isaac when back in the States for my intermediate language course. I had agreed to play handball with him one time and I came away from that experience thinking that I would rather play with a venomous snake. Isaac had a malicious temper at the end of a very short fuse. He was somewhat like Lew, only worse, and he did not have any of Lew's entertaining ways. In short, he was just about a full-time dick-head dumb ass.

I could not understand why Isaac complained about getting laid since he had somehow managed to convince a business woman to marry him. Archie as well as several others also wondered about that. Not long after the party involving the Australian hats, we learned just how great Isaac's marriage was.

Isaac was late for work one day. In our line of work, that was a big no-no. Just about the time that Archie had to decide whether to inform the authorities that an airmen with access to classified information was missing, Isaac limped in with two black eyes, a stitched-up jagged cut across the bridge of his nose that continued over his right forehead, and various other abrasions about his hands, face, and forearms. As he began to justify why he was tardy, we noticed that he was speaking in a garbled voice. He explained that he had severely bitten his tongue, which was still quite swollen.

Piece by piece, we learned that Isaac and his wife were not

on the best of terms. "What a shock," I thought sarcastically to myself. I did not want to interrupt the story and have Isaac direct any anger toward me, so I kept my observations to myself. The only questions from any of us were in the form of, "So what happened next."

It seems that the previous evening, Isaac had returned home late to find a note from his wife stating that she was fed up with his caustic temper and disrespectful behavior, and that she was leaving him and his pathetic johnson for good. Holy shortcomings! "Geez, that explains a lot of his behavior," I thought. Isaac was beside himself with rage. Despite most martial arts students being taught to master their emotions, Isaac had an anger management issue that did not improve his innate selfishness and acidic arrogance.

He eventually realized that he could probably track down his wife by going to the old Korean woman who had been his wife's auntie before marriage. From her, Isaac had been able to tease out that his wife was likely in the company of a certain Korean man, probably at some Korean drinking establishment in the vicinity.

Isaac became even angrier at the thought of his wife being with a Korean as he went searching for the pair. Shortly before curfew, he found his wife in a hole-in-the-wall makkŏlli joint nobody had ever heard of. She wasn't with one Korean man but four, and they all seemed to be having a good time. According to Isaac, his wife declared her intent to service all four of the men, saying that they would probably satisfy her better than he ever did. I was extremely surprised to hear Isaac relate this last part since it was directed at the one activity that most red-blooded males pride themselves in.

Isaac could not contain himself. Since he had been studying

taekwondo, he was certain that he could take four Koreans in their 30s, several years older than he was. However, Isaac failed to consider a great many factors, each of which had contributed to his painful condition.

It did not occur to him that Korean life is a tougher, more demanding one than that of a privileged American. Consequently, those Korean men were probably in far better condition than Isaac, despite his efforts at taekwondo. It also did not occur to him that these Korean men themselves might be practitioners of taekwondo or have some similar skill. And he ignored the fact that there were four of them.

The confrontation lasted for only a very few minutes before Isaac was lying on the dirt floor of the shack, moaning in a semi-conscious state. The four had quickly and undeniably given Isaac a timely world-class lesson in the martial arts. The group then fled, Isaac's wife willingly going with them as they departed the scene. The proprietor summoned the Korean police, but then declared that he had never seen the four Korean men before and that he most certainly did not know their names.

The Korean police attempted to question Isaac but he was quite uncooperative, demanding to be released to the military authorities in accordance with the Status of Forces Agreement (SOFA) between the U.S. and the South Korean government.

Actually, Isaac had his information all wrong. The first true SOFA agreement between the U.S. and South Korea had been signed into effect in 1967. At long last, it did away with the concept of "extraterritoriality" enjoyed by U.S. military personnel in South Korea. Extraterritoriality is the state of being exempt from local laws, meaning that Koreans could not charge American servicemen for crimes committed off base. All incidents involving U.S. military personnel had to be referred to the military for investigation and prosecution as determined by the U.S. In the past, most U.S. servicemen were simply reassigned out of country as rapidly as possible, rather than face charges for something they did off base.

Now, however, under the SOFA agreement, American service personnel were subject to Korean law when off base. All that was required of local authorities was that they had to immediately notify the nearest U.S. military authorities that airman so-and-so had been arrested for such-and-such a crime. Under SOFA, South Koreans afforded airmen under detention better treatment than locals usually received, but that really did not apply to Isaac's case. He had gotten into a fight with some Koreans who were no longer around to make a case and the makkŏlli house owner would be interested only in asking for reimbursement for the unpaid bill – but only if his drinking establishment was registered with the authorities.

The proprietor volunteered that, although Isaac had started the fight, he clearly got the worst of it, as could be seen by Isaac's condition, and that all he wanted was for the commotion to go away so that he could close up shop and go home. After a few minutes of listening to Isaac's gutter-mouth ranting, the Korean police were more than willing to dump the obviously uncivilized and offensive foreigner off on the Osan military police who took him to the base hospital for treatment.

I never learned how – or even if – Isaac and his wife resolved their difficulties. I felt that she would be well rid of him, despite losing a chance for U.S. citizenship through marriage to him – if that had been her ultimate goal. Even so, she had likely decided that escape from the life of a business woman was not worth the discord and strife that living with Isaac would bring.

Chapter Fourteen: Korean Outings

I felt that I was spending too much time with Americans and being on base instead of hanging out more with my Korean buddy Mun-nam and learning more about Korean culture. Consequently, when Mun-nam asked me if I knew anything about the Mt. Song-ni National Park in the central area of South Korea, I was quite curious.

Mun-nam described it as very scenic with a very old Buddhist temple in completely natural settings reached by walking paths, a number of communal hostels or small bungalows for rent, and a pavilion that could be hired for special occasions. Low hills and little vales were scattered throughout to make for an unending source of different vistas for those willing to do a bit of exploring. All in all, it sounded like a great place to escape the routine of life on base.

What Mun-nam said next was a real eye-opener. It seems that the Korean workers had negotiated a spectacularly sweet deal with a former base hospital commander, an agreement that had continued unbroken for some years. In late summer or very early fall, after the rainy season had ended and while the weather was still pleasantly warm during the day, the few Korean hospital workers that could be spared to be away from work were permitted to use an Air Force bus and gas ration card for a short vacation, this year to Mt. Song-ni.

That an Air Force vehicle and military gas rations could be used for such a purpose was absolutely astonishing. What Mun-nam told me next, though, was equally amazing. Typically, an Air Force bus had seating for 35 passengers and, setting aside the issue of U.S. government property being used in a normally unauthorized manner, it would be far too large and therefore unjustified, if the riders consisted of only a dozen or so Korean workers going on holiday. Well, it seemed that the mistresses of those Korean workers would occupy the extra seats. The only requirement, though, was that was the driver of the bus had to be an American. That had already been worked out since one of the airmen who worked closely with the Koreans at the hospital would fulfill that role, and his Korean girlfriend would accompany him. Mun-nam asked me if I would like to come along since there was room.

I felt quite flattered to be asked and I accepted immediately. Mun-nam said that the cost was just about $15 per person and that meant each Korean paid roughly $30 for his mistress and himself. Mun-nam suggested that I would need someone to keep me warm during the cool nights in the mountains. When I pointed out that I did not have a close relationship with anyone at that time, he offered to set me up with a blind date for the trip.

He saw my hesitation and responded that he knew the type of women that appealed to me from my interactions with the various kisaengs at makkŏlli houses and that he would not disappoint me. Besides, he said, it would be good for me to see one more aspect of Korean culture. I reluctantly agreed, thinking that if the lady and I were incompatible for whatever reason, we could both just have to share a bed without obligation on anyone's part.

I still had one reservation, however. "What about the other Korean men and their ladies?" I inquired, stating that I knew that many Korean men objected to seeing Korean women in the company of foreigners, and Korean women were particularly disapproving of that as well. Mun-nam assured me that I already knew many of his co-workers going on the excursion through our makkŏlli house nights and that they had vouched for me being no typical uncouth American. As for their mistresses, they were hardly in any position to take a superior attitude. Well, OK, I thought, this is going to be a great adventure.

Mun-nam did ask a favor, "Could you buy as much beer as your ration card allows? It is much better than O.B., as you know, and cheaper on base, too." Each military member was allowed eight cases of beer per month, but I never used my ration for myself, instead buying as asked on behalf of airmen who had expended their rations. It wasn't that those guys drank that much, they probably sold the beer on the black market in the Ville to fund their own activities. This time, however, I would keep my rations for the month to myself and donate eight cases of U.S. beer to the cause. Mun-nam was very appreciative, and he informed the others of my generosity. It really wasn't that grand a gesture, though. Beer sold for ten cents a can when bought by the unrefrigerated case at the NCO Club. My total contribution would be less than $20 – and would more than likely exempt me from any other incidental expenses during the trip. The biggest problem would be to haul that much beer from the NCO Club to my barracks room and then to the bus, a task I realized that could easily manage by taxi.

I got approval for my leave of absence and on the day of the trip presented myself at the hospital parking lot very early in the morning with the beer. Everyone's luggage was packed in the last two rows of the bus, and a clean-looking 32-gallon galvanized steel trashcan half-filled with ice occupied the aisle between those rows. That blocked the rear emergency exit, but I doubt if anyone gave much of a rat's ass about violating safety regulations. I was introduced to the other airman who had also brought his eight cases of beer. One of the Korean guys was already pulling out two of the 16 cases to be iced down for the trip of roughly 100 miles that would take about three hours due to the roads and terrain.

Mun-nam mentioned that we would be making one very quick stop in the Ville, once we were out of sight of the base, to pick up the ladies. I was more than curious about Mun-nam's expertise in choosing my holiday companion. At the designated spot, I paid close attention as the ladies boarded the bus. I was a bit nervous, like I was going on my first date. I hadn't realized that Mun-nam had gone to the front of the bus and was now walking back down the aisle towards me closely followed by two women.

He gestured for one of them to sit in the row ahead of me and, as I stood up to meet my arranged date, he introduced me to Ok-ja, the taller one. I was relieved to note that, while she was my age or perhaps very slightly older, she was pleasant looking and that she, too, was wearing a self-conscious smile. I gave her my name in Korean – actually my Korean nickname Dragonfly – and invited her to sit down in my row. I was gratified to see that Mun-nam and his lady were in the row directly in front of us and that his lady and my date seemed to be on very good terms already, perhaps old friends.

After a few moments, Ok-ja turned to me and said that she wanted to speak in English because she did not get the opportunity often enough these days. Her English was not perfect – but it was quite acceptable, certainly better than my Korean – and we could understand each other without any effort.

I began to relax as I recognized that Mun-nam had done quite well by me. Now, all I had to do was to live up to whatever expectations everyone had of me. Ok-ja and I began an easy give and take conversation in which she inquired as to what I thought of Korea and how I came to be involved in things far beyond what most American servicemen care about. I learned that she had worked in the office of some international manufacturing company and that was where she had been able to refine her high school English. Soon I sensed that at least some of her anxiety about being with some unknown American was slowly melting away.

I gathered that she had been married for a while, but she did not specify how or why that had ended. I was quite intrigued since a divorced Korean woman is a bit of an outcast in Korean society. I thought that it was odd that Korean men tended to prefer inexperienced ladies in marriage – but it would have been a breach of Korean etiquette to ask for clarification. Nonetheless, I also got the impression that she wasn't really interested in being constrained by such a relationship again because she was now satisfactorily established in her own life. Regardless, her chances of remarriage – at least to a Korean man – were not at all good. Perhaps her situation was a factor in her agreeing to go on the trip with some American, particularly if trusted Koreans had vouched for his character.

Since we were finally out of town and on the highway going south, the beer was broken out. I was mildly surprised at first to see that Korean women had no problem in letting their hair down and having a good time when the opportunity presented itself. Then I remembered the stories I had heard about Korean ladies playing the Korean card game called Flower Battle and how the games were often helped along with generous amounts of soju, the rather fierce Korean liquor, or beer.

Koreans love to gamble and they get very excited and sometimes quite emotional when their engines are started. I know this to be especially true of women when they are engaged in a game of Flower Battle. The deck itself consists of 52 cards, not much bigger than one inch by two inches in size, but of a thick construction intended to withstand the custom of being theatrically thrown down. It doesn't matter whether it is in triumph or disgust – it is the drama that counts. The suits are of different colorful flowers, each suit having four variations of its particular flower, one for each season perhaps. The games can be complex and although I often tried, even the youngest opponent always beat me, usually quite severely. I am above average at pinochle or poker, but certainly not at the Korean game of Flower Battle.

The women on the bus were drinking as much as the men, and since the drive would be another three hours, it was decided to ice down another case of beer just to be safe. I smiled, realizing that everyone was going to have a fine time.

About half way to our destination, one of the women called out for a potty break, using a rather common term that brought laughter from some of the men. A couple of the ladies responded to the laughs of disdain that it wasn't fair since men can relieve themselves almost anywhere, and that they usually did so without regard for propriety, unlike women who usually exercised some discretion.

I noticed a smile playing about the lips of Ok-ja as she listened to the slightly risqué discussion about men and their tendencies, particularly when one of the ladies said that, as for herself, she was grateful that men are different from ladies, an unmistakable reference to anatomy, rather than toilet habits. Then everyone recognized that we would have to abandon that line of conversation, for to continue would have meant going beyond publicly acceptable limits. Fortunately, it was only a minute or so more until the driver pulled over next to a sizable clump of trees. The ladies disappeared into the woods while the men went to the other side of the road into the weeds.

We arrived at the park in mid afternoon with a few of hours of warm sunshine remaining in the day. Mun-nam explained that he had arranged for the four of us to be together in a small bungalow that had two small sleeping alcoves off a central gathering space. Since the alcoves were on adjacent walls, there was a bit of privacy due to the right angle between them. He continued that meals were taken communally with the men eating at tables separate from the women. I shot a quick look at Ok-ja to see her smile timidly back at me.

Supper was typical Korean fare, nothing fancy, but it was tasty and plentiful. I made a point of asking for more kimchee and I tried to slurp my soup as loudly as any Korean. I stayed away from the potent liquor that was available for those that wanted it. I had consumed a couple of beers on the bus and I judged that to be enough for me in the alcohol department for the day. Besides, even though I had no idea about what – if anything – would transpire that evening, I did not want to have a buzzing head when bedtime arrived.

After dinner and a short walk, we four retired to our bungalow to play cards and talk for a short while until it was time to retire. Morning would come early if we expected to eat at the communal dining hall. In deference to the ladies' modesty, Mun-nam and I went outside for a few moments while they prepared for bed. When I approached our small alcove, I saw Ok-ja covered up in bed but on her side facing where I would be. The light bedding could not conceal that she had been blessed with a wonderful amount of womanly curves. With a timorous grin on her lips, she softly wondered aloud whether I was bashful.

Surprisingly, I was for some reason, and besides there was Mun-nam and his lady just around the corner, so I sat on the low bed with my back to her and the other alcove while I undressed. As I turned to recline on my back, I saw that she was holding the covers open for me but in a way that kept most of her body tantalizingly covered. I reached for her but she hesitated before coming into my arms. She was concerned that I would think her a woman of low character if she gave in to me so readily. I thought, but did not say, that it would be stupidly hypocritical of me to think ill of any woman who was willing to go on such an excursion with me. I did say that I saw her as proper woman and that I could tell from her behavior and mannerisms that she had come from a family of good standing.

I continued by saying whatever we did, just sleep or talk or whatever, it had to be in full harmony with what she thought was best for her. I explained that otherwise, it would be a loss of face for me, and I would feel badly for both our sakes. My statement was no pretense, and I was just about to cease any more whispered attempts to dispel any concerns she might have about her reputation in my eyes when she hushed me with fingers over my lips. Ok-ja solemnly replied that it would be a loss of face for her to not make certain that I was happy.

Holy stalemate! The conversation was getting too serious for me, so I tried a little humor by saying, "Well, I like my face and I like your face, so let's do our best to keep both our faces on." For once, I was glad that we were speaking in English, for I knew damned well that I could not have pulled that off in Korean. Ok-ja poked me in the ribs before she whispered that she just wanted to make sure I understood, even though she was certainly no virgin, that she also was no woman of the night, either. I told her that I had sensed that from the moment we first spoke – as she pulled herself over to be on top.

I don't know whether we disturbed the others, for all I remember is that Ok-ja joyously got as much out of our being together as I did. The next morning, when we went walking around the grounds after breakfast, it seemed completely natural for us to be holding hands. Mun-nam enjoyed teasing me about that for a while until Ok-ja gently chided him for trying to embarrass me. I realized that this was a woman that I could really get to like.

The two of us decided to leave the group and go exploring the park on our own. Ok-ja said that she had read up on the park and thought that there was supposed to be a small stream in a nearby meadow that she would like to see. It turned out to be a splendid sight and we dallied there like children, splashing in the shallow waters trying to catch minnows. On the way back, I saw a rocky promontory that called out to be scaled. We found a safe route up and we were rewarded with a grand view of the area in which we were staying.

We returned to the bungalow in late afternoon, starving although we knew that it would be more than an hour before the communal hall would serve dinner. I remembered that I had packed a box of Forever Yours candy bars, my favorite, and I also knew that Koreans loved American sweets. Ok-ja and I each had a one to tide us over until supper.

I had mixed feelings when I learned that the men would be gathering in the communal hall that evening to drink and entertain each other with songs or poems while the ladies would be off doing whatever appealed to them. While my original intent in coming on the trip with Mun-nam was to learn more about Korean culture, I now wanted to be with Ok-ja. With a laugh, she pushed me out of the bungalow with Mun-nam as she assured me that she would be waiting and asking me to not get stinky drunk.

I heard a few new Korean songs that night – and learned another Korean custom. One member after another of the group had to entertain the rest with a song or a story, but I was quite unprepared and totally embarrassed. I knew no classical song or epic saga in Korean – what the hell was I going to do? The only thing I could remember from language school was a tale about a young girl who lost her rain boots at school and another about a dying man who passed on when the last leaf on his beloved tree fell as the first snows arrived. Although I could muster the Korean vocabulary to narrate them, neither of those sad stories would do. Mun-nam provided the solution: just be yourself.

Long before the progression around the table reached me, one of Mun-nam's co-workers hollered out, "Let's hear the American now!" After a brief protest that I knew was to no avail, I slowly arose to announce in Korean that I had been ambushed, that if I had known of this custom, I would have made some sort of preparation. Even knowing about this tradition, I would probably only duplicate the effort of another. Therefore, I would give them something only an American could give them – Jabberwocky by Lewis Carroll.

I explained that long, long ago Lewis Carroll wrote poems for children using nonsense words – I said "sounds without meaning" – just because of how they suited the ear. Without further ado and hoping to forestall any criticism, in English I launched into the three verses of Jabberwocky that I could confidently recall, accompanied by greatly exaggerated gestures and facial expressions.

Jabberwocky
by Lewis Carroll as recalled by Dragonfly

'Twas brillig, and the slithy toves
Did gyre and gimble in the wabe;
All mimsy were the borogoves,
And the mome raths outgrabe.

And as in uffish thought he stood,
The Jabberwock, with eyes of flame,
Came whiffling through the tulgey wood,
And burbled as it came!

One, two! One, two! And through and through
The vorpal blade went snicker-snack!
He left it dead, and with its head
He went galumphing back.

By the time I was finished, my theatrical performance had made me quite self-conscious and I was more than ready to relinquish the floor. Perhaps it was just my overly dramatic rendering of the poem, or maybe it was the cadence of the foreign sounds that rhymed in a pleasing fashion, but more likely it was the fiery Korean liquor that caused the outburst of applause and cheers of approval. I sat down in relief as Mun-nam slapped me on the back as he repeatedly said, "I told you! I told you!" I got a little drunk, but not stinky drunk.

The next two days at Mt. Song-ni were much like the first, passing all too quickly. On the road back to the Ville, I reflected on what had been a very delightful experience for me. I had sensed that Ok-ja had found everything to her liking as well, and as a result, I was totally unprepared for what she told me as she gathered up her things in preparation to leave the bus as it was approaching the Ville.

She matter-of-factly declared in a low voice that, even

though she thought that I was a very interesting man and that our time together had been particularly enjoyable, she would not see me again. Reading the stunned look on my face, she quietly explained that there were things about her and about Korea that I did not yet understand. Anything that might have started between us had to end now. I knew better than to protest, but I rode the rest of the way back to the hospital parking lot in silence, not looking at anyone as I nursed a hurt that was as stinging as it was surprising. A rare woman had broken up with me, and I did not like how it made me feel. Mun-nam absolutely refused to offer any explanation or comment, other than to say that women are unknowable at times.

The incident made me think back to another outing some weeks earlier with Mun-nam and the others when the shoe was on the other foot, when I had done the dumping without any regard for the feelings of someone else. Mun-nam had asked me to go fishing with the gang at the river north of the base. When I pointed out that I had no fishing gear, he laughed as he replied that fishing is done differently in Korea and that I should just bring swimming trunks and a towel.

We took a Korean public bus for a few miles to the north of the base before getting out to walk the rest of the way. I made sure to take my turn carrying one of the bags of supplies for our adventure. It wasn't long before we got to the bank of a wide but very shallow river than ran clear over a generally smooth pebbled bottom. The river had several dozen people wading about in the vicinity and I began to wonder how we could catch anything with all that commotion scaring the fish.

Away from the bank and in a clump of low tress but still in plain view of anyone who cared to look, the guys began to change into their swimwear. Thinking, "To hell with Western modesty," I did the same and discovered that no one was watching. People around us must have been aware that we had arrived and would be changing clothes, so gazes were politely averted from our direction for the time being. Geezus, in the States more than a few people would have been gawking and somebody would have complained about all those men exposing themselves. I could easily imagine some old biddy back in the States exclaiming, "And, Officer, I even saw his pee-pee!"

Our packs were opened in preparation for the picnic. Out of one came four bottles of Korean orange soda and two of Jin-ro soju, the distilled drink of choice for working-class people. In my mind, its taste was similar to vodka but it also had a smell reminiscent of musty earth. I could drink it although it was certainly not my beverage of choice. Into one of the Korean brass teapots went two orange sodas and one soju. A supply of small paper cups, probably appropriated from a hospital water fountain, served as our drinking mugs.

I was dispatched to fill another pot with water as clear of any floating debris as I could find. Boiling the water would take care of any bacteria and such. Mun-nam and two others started unrolling a seine and I then understood how the fishing was done, but I was not certain that they would capture anything with all the people splashing around. Holy mackerel! I was quite wrong, for within just minutes, the seine had snared several dozen flopping green-gray minnows that were quickly field-cleaned and tossed into the pot of now boiling water.

Balls of cooked rice were cut open and the boiled fish inserted along with a small amount of Korean red pepper paste to add some kick to the otherwise bland food. It wasn't great but it wasn't bad, either, and I was getting hungry in any event. The soju helped me in getting my fill of the rice and fish.

After eating, we went into the water. As shallow as the river was, there was no danger of drowning from cramps, although swimming was possible for short distances in various parts of the main channel. One of the guys noticed a cluster of bikini-clad ladies in their early to mid 20s just upstream from us. They were cavorting in the water and making a lot of noise, totally oblivious to us.

Mun-nam suggested that we go sightseeing in that direction. Spreading out like a school of sharks, we swam or used our hands to pull ourselves against the flow of water until we were only a few feet from the nearest young lady. When she saw us, she let out a shriek and hastily moved toward the others who then gathered together for mutual reassurance.

We were easily able to dispel any fears they might have had about us, particularly since we were in broad daylight with dozens of others within hailing distance to come to the rescue should any of us be foolish enough to try anything. One of the guys invited them back to our spot in the shade for some rice and fish and all of the ladies took advantage of the offer.

I wasn't about to make a play for any girl out in public since I knew all too well how badly that looked in the Ville to see airmen call out to every sweet young thing they happened to come upon. Hence, I was a bit taken aback when one of the ladies turned to me to ask in English how I came to be with a bunch of Korean guys. Her question was posed in a way that I thought implied her availability – if I were up to the challenge, but maybe that was just her way of speaking in a language that was not her native tongue.

After polishing off all the leftovers, three of the women stuck around – because we still had soju – one of which was the lady who had wondered why I was there. I had explained my interest in not being the typical American serviceman and wanting to see as much of the real Korea as I could. Taking a swig of soju, she continued her interrogation to ask if my interest in Korea meant that I didn't go to the American clubs in the Ville. I laughed my way out of being put on the spot and replied that, of course I went to the clubs. After all, I was a typical male, American or otherwise, wasn't I?

She understood what I meant and she then coquettishly suggested that it would be worth my while if I came to see her when she was working at the Arirang Club. I was put off by this rather blatant solicitation and I declined her offer in a needlessly abrupt fashion. I saw a flash of hurt on her face before she collected herself to huffily say in English, "Do not misunderstand what I meant. I was only trying to get customers for the club."

As I saw her expression change, I realized that I had hurt her feelings for no good reason. Once again, I had been reminded that business women are people with sentiments just like the rest of us, but I didn't know how to correct my poor manners.

The ladies stayed around to help finish off the soju as we packed up our gear to leave, and it seemed that we would be walking back to the highway together. Mun-nam pulled me aside to remind me of the one lady that had expressed some curiosity about me, and that I ought to walk with her just to return the courtesy. I think he was expecting me to make up for having shot myself in the foot during our conversation earlier.

As we started off, the ladies were in a group ahead of us guys but we all were close enough to talk if we raised our voices a bit. It was clear that there was a cluster of now modestly clad young ladies being closely followed by a crowd of slightly older men. After a few moments, I lengthened my stride to fall into step with the young lady that I had offended. I asked her if we could talk while we hiked back to the main road, and although she agreed, it was not before giving me a suspicious glance.

It was nothing but idle chatter, like the air smelling good in the country and the quiet being so nice with no vehicles around. We parted on sociable terms when we reached the road, but we both knew that I had not overcome the blunder I had made earlier in callously rejecting her invitation to the Arirang Club. First impressions can be lasting ones, and I sure as hell had not made a good one with her.

Chapter Fifteen: More with Mun-nam

Hanging out with Mun-nam and the other Korean guys was interesting, educational, and – best of all – always entertaining. All of my Korean friends knew that I had a deep interest in their country and culture, and many of them found ways to include me in their various activities.

One day, Mun-nam asked me if I had ever seen what a Korean farm looks like. My response was that, except for a short vacation to the Onyang Hot Springs Tourist Hotel years ago and our joint trip to Mt. Song-ni National Park, I had never ventured much beyond the area around the base and the Ville. I knew that he didn't mean Seoul, since everybody sooner or later goes to the "big city" for one reason or another.

Mun-nam invited me to go with him to visit his "war house," a trip that would take all day to go and come back. When I looked a bit confused, he informed me that Koreans often referred to the home of their in-laws as the war house. He went on that, although he got along well with his wife's family, there was often discord between the relatives of the wife and those of the husband if things were not going well.

From my perspective, Mun-nam and his wife were happy together. Mun-nam was a hard worker who brought home very good money from his job at the base hospital. His wife had her own beauty parlor, so I concluded that, between the two incomes, they must have been doing well enough. More importantly, each seemed to appreciate the other.

The only possible source of friction, as far as I could tell, might be the presence of Mun-nam's aging mother living with them. His father had been killed during the Korean War and, as the only son, Mun-nam was obligated to care for her in her declining years. It was rather common for Korean wives to be faced with this arrangement, and most just took it in stride as being a fact of life, part of the culture in Korea. Eventually, the daughter-in-law would become a mother-in-law in her own right, and the cycle would continue.

When I learned how Mun-nam's father had died, I was appalled. During the Korean War when Mun-nam was less than ten years old, his father had been killed by a bomb dropped from an American aircraft on a close-in ground support mission near where the family lived. I never inquired as to the specifics of that tragedy for, if he had wanted me to know anything more, Mun-nam would have told me outright.

Mun-nam said that he experienced no anger at the time – and that he bore no grudge now – that he had felt only the grief of losing his father, simply because it was wartime during which a great number of Korean civilians became casualties as battles raged and raged all around them. It was something that just happened in the course of war, he had said as a final explanation of that event. I was stunned into silence, feeling that I should say something, but I had no words. I finally said, in English, "I don't know what to say." Mun-nam gave a wry grin and replied, also in English, "There is nothing for you to say, truly, my friend."

I was also shocked that, having lost his father to an American bomb, Mun-nam as an adult had sought out employment from the Americans on base. Perhaps, with life being so tough in Korea, such heartbreaks are more readily accepted, or perhaps it was the practicality of a better job with unequaled wages on base. Maybe it was just fatalism from having experienced the dangers and devastating losses of the Korean War. Most likely it was a uniquely Korean mixture of all of that. I also knew that Mun-nam was smart enough to seize any opportunity that came before him.

For several long minutes, in light of Mun-nam's sobering revelation, I felt quite out of place, despite the fact that he and I were now becoming very close friends. My thoughts must have been reflected by the look on my face, for Mun-nam punched me lightly on my bicep as he told me to put it in the past, just as he had.

All this was in my mind as I asked if there was anything that I, as a non-family member and a foreign guest, could bring on our trip to his "war house." His one word response got a quick laugh out of me: batteries. It seems that on the farm where his in-laws lived, there was no electricity, no newspapers, and no telephone. The only connections with the rest of the world were by walking or taking an ox-drawn cart to the nearest town about an hour away, by mail that was picked up only when a delivery was made, or through listening to the news broadcasts tuned in on a transistor radio – hence, the batteries.

Mun-nam suggested that I buy American batteries on base because they would be of higher quality and last longer than the ones available in the Ville and they would probably be priced about the same, anyway. I went to the BX and got a box of yellow Ray-O-Vac nine-volt rectangular batteries along with some red tissue paper in which to wrap them. The package was small enough to be easily concealed in my jacket when I passed through the base gate to the Ville.

On Saturday, we set out just after nine in the morning on a Korean bus for Suwŏn, the larger city just a few miles north of the Ville. The old vehicle was in a rather dilapidated condition – bouncy and noisy and slow – but it was cheaper than a taxi and it definitely was better than walking. The bus stopped at the side of the road near the middle of Suwŏn to let us out by an area often used as a taxi stand. While Mun-nam started looking about for a taxi to take us the next part of the way, I was thinking that for a town claimed to be more cosmopolitan, it certainly was unimpressive, just a bigger version of the Ville. The taxi took us a few minutes north of Suwŏn and then turned right at Mun-nam's direction onto a dirt lane to go for perhaps two more miles before the driver said that he would go no further. Despite the lane being visible for at least another one hundred yards or so, it became considerably narrower and that would present problems for turning the taxi around. On foot, we had less than two miles left – about three kilometers, according to Mun-nam – but it was up one hill and down another before doing it all over again, hill after hill after hill.

When I saw the buildings that were the hub of the farm, I was relieved to know that our trek was over. I could see only two structures, both with thatched roofs, but they were arranged together to form the shape of the letter "U." The house itself was in the shape of the letter "L" and the other building was some sort of large storage shed. It faced the longer portion of the "L" of the house and it was far enough back from the short leg of the "L" that a low bamboo fence with a gate was used to close off the distance between the two buildings. That created a large south-facing courtyard containing a well that was off to one side. Mun-nam later informed me that the "comfort station" was just behind that bamboo gate.

Mun-nam introduced me to the rather large extended family consisting of nearly a dozen people of all ages, explaining that I was a very good friend who, unlike most American servicemen, had a deep interest in all things Korean. When he paused, I took the opportunity to slowly say in Korean that I greatly appreciated their hospitality and that I had an offering for the house. With both hands I offered the red tissue package of batteries to the oldest man who, in light of his long wispy chin whiskers, appeared to be in his 60s or older, bowing as I did so.

Even though I could barely understand his dialect, I caught just enough to conclude that he was thanking me for the gift, since he was smiling a bit as he spoke. He also said something that I thought was he had never heard an American speak Korean before and that my Seoul accent was not commonly heard in that area. He handed the batteries to a middle-aged woman who took them to one of the rooms inside.

As it was a warm early fall day, we continued to sit on the outdoor veranda floor that had been worn smooth to a faint sheen by years of use. Mun-nam hastened to put everyone at ease about what to serve me at the midday meal since I ate Korean food, even kimchee. He did make a small joke at my expense, however, playfully scornful of my distaste for bŏndegi, the fried caterpillar pupa sold by street vendors as a delicacy. The middle-aged lady had returned in time to loudly exclaim that she, too, could not tolerate the thought of eating such a thing. Everyone laughed at that.

After an extensive meal of smoked fish and rice served with so many side dishes of pickled this and cooked that, I felt that I had just eaten at a Korean banquet. I ate well, even timidly asking if there were a bit more kimchee. Mun-nam had beamingly pointed this out, saying, "See, I told you he ate Korean food." During the meal, we drank warm tea, but afterward, a bottle of soju suddenly appeared. All the men, me included, had a little poured into their teacups as somebody broke out a packet of harsh Korean tobacco for those who wanted to roll cigarettes. The patriarch packed his long-stemmed pipe and soon an acrid smell wafted in the air as he puffed contentedly.

While the women attended to cleanup and other household duties, Mun-nam discussed family affairs with two of the men and the old gentleman. It would have been unseemly to offer assistance to the ladies and I knew that the family discussion was private business, so I dozed contentedly against a pillar supporting the porch roof.

After a little more than an hour, about midafternoon, Mun-nam roused me to say that it was time to leave if we wanted to get back to the Ville in time for dinner. I sought out the family head once again to thank him for the excellent meal as well as for allowing me to visit his impressive farm. Putting our shoes back on, we started down the lane back to the highway. Mun-nam was confident that we could flag down a taxi at the highway to get the rest of the way into Suwŏn for the bus back to Osan. He was right and the rest of the trip was uneventful but for the up and down travel over those hills.

A couple of days later, Mun-nam asked me to accompany him to meet his landlord, an odd request I thought, until I realized what such a meeting could mean for me. I had mentioned to Mun-nam some weeks back that, if he ever found a nice room for me to rent, I would appreciate him letting me know. I had told him about the various exploits that my work buddy, Kent, had experienced by virtue of having his own place off base in the Ville. Mun-nam had laughed and said my idea of renting my own place had merit.

The landlord's house had at least four rooms with a small courtyard on one side visible from a narrow window in the main room where Mun-nam and I had been ushered once we had removed our shoes. When the landlord entered, I started to rise out of respect, but he said to stay seated as he joined us on the opposite side of the low table in the middle of the room. I noticed that he wore the type of socks favored by Japanese, the kind that had a separate pocket for the big toe. In looking at him closely, I thought that the man looked more Japanese than Korean, something that I would definitely mention to Mun-nam once our business was concluded.

The landlord began by asking me how I came to be interested in Korea and how I was able to speak the language. I told him that I had been to Korean language school in the States as part of my military training. Keeping it short, I concluded by saying that I thought that it would be a waste of my studies if I did not practice it in the Ville.

He grunted in the way that older Korean men do to indicate understanding, which can also convey approval. He said that he had a large room to rent almost across the street from where Mun-nam and his family lived. It had a Korean style kitchen with one high window while the room itself had two high windows, one on each of its exterior walls. He said that he would give the key to Mun-nam who could show the room to me.

Then the conversation took a totally different turn. He inquired in a less businesslike tone whether I hunted. I replied that I hunted squirrels when I was younger. When he asked if I used a shotgun for that, I answered that only bad shooters used a shotgun and then realized that I ought to soften my harsh answer a bit, adding truthfully that, "Of course, hunting birds is different. For that, only shotguns are allowed."

He smiled before turning to call for someone in another part of the house to bring him his Remington. I knew that Koreans could not own handguns or rifles but that shotguns were permitted. Indeed, his gun was an old but well-maintained Model 870 pump that was missing the hinged metal guard to the magazine feed opening. The landlord pulled the missing piece from a bag tied to the trigger guard to show me that the left pivot arm was broken off. He stated that he would pay me for the part and its mailing cost if me if I could get a replacement.

I was confident that I could do so. I described how I would write to the company and include a drawing of the broken part to ask for a speedy replacement since hunting season was fast approaching in Korea. He expressed his gratitude for anything I could do.

Mun-nam and I then left to look at the room, which was indeed across the street only two buildings down from his place and on a corner of sorts since a small path went along one side. By American standards, it was quite crude. The door was sheet metal with a welded-on hasp for security and the walls were wood-framed and filled with thatch that had been plastered with stucco and coated with ochre paint. The windows were placed very high and, although they were quite wide, they would be difficult for burglars to use. A latch from the inside secured them. The floor was raised roughly two feet above the ground level kitchen and it had wall-to-wall vinyl on the floor as a sealant for the heating system running under it, which was fed by the kitchen stove.

Mun-nam strongly urged me to not heat the room using charcoal briquettes in the kitchen stove because of the dangers of carbon monoxide poisoning leaking up from under the floor. I agreed although I pointed out that I would need something for the frigid Korean nights during the winter. I was also concerned about not having a toilet or even an outhouse.

Mun-nam said that he knew where to get a true heating stove and how to get a chimney system installed in the room, something that would be safer than using the under floor heating system. As for the toilet, he was certain that for just a couple of bucks a month, his wife would be willing to handle chamber pot duties, along with providing a half-gallon or so of potable water as needed every day but Sunday. I could just add that to the rent I would be paying him for delivery to the landlord.

It was a deal! From a nearby local furniture store, I bought a cheap roll-up Korean double mattress, complete with sheets and quilting, and a large cupboard that came in two pieces, a much smaller version of an American dining room sideboard and hutch. A low table and a gooseneck lamp completed my decorating. There were already some pegs on the wall common with the kitchen where I could hang clothes.

Mun-nam's wife did provide a chamber pot in exchange for one month's advance rent and a key to the new Master Lock that I placed on the overlapped hasp on the door and jam. Since a sliding oiled-paper door separated the main room from the kitchen, I decided that the far end of the unused kitchen could be curtained off to serve as my comfort station.

Only one day after I moved in, it became clear that I could not totally divorce myself from the barracks. First, I had no shower facility, no way to shave, no one to do my laundry or shine my shoes. It was a small compromise to accept the fact that on nights I spent in the Ville, I would have to get up early enough to do the Four Esses in the barracks and get fresh clothes. It seemed to work for other guys, and I would make it work for me as well.

A week or so after I had my routine all figured out, I got a package delivery notice in my letter slot at the mailroom. It turned out to be the replacement part from Remington Arms. The company was nice enough to send the part to me without charge, a courtesy on low-cost items that the company said it routinely extended to all American military personnel on active duty and overseas. Holy hardware! Even though I would have been reimbursed, this was speedy service with distinction. I got in touch with Mun-nam at the hospital so that we could deliver the part to his landlord. I took the opportunity to bring up the topic of the landlord's ethnicity.

I began by pointing out that I had observed the type of indoor footwear the landlord had been wearing and continued by saying that he looked as though he might be at least part Japanese. When Japan had occupied Korea from the beginning of the 20th century until the end of World War II, Japanese soldiers had coerced many Korean women into being prostitutes, which they labeled "comfort women," for the Japanese occupation forces, and some Korean women, out of financial necessity, served as mistresses of the Japanese. I knew that some of those women had borne children from those relationships.

Was his landlord one of those, I wondered? Mun-nam looked at me with a scowl to declare vehemently that this was a subject that was absolutely to never be brought up. I apologized immediately, knowing that I had stupidly blundered into a forbidden area. After several long seconds of silence as we walked to his landlord's house, Mun-nam said softly, "This is something that no Korean wants to discuss. Please understand that." I promised that I would never bring it up again to anyone.

When Mun-nam and I told the landlord why we came to see him, he was pleased to hear that the part had already arrived – and greatly surprised that there was no charge for it. He was impressed that the company extended such benefits to its military customers. He actually inclined his head and shoulders slightly to me in gratitude. I told him that it had been a pleasure for me to be able to do something for him.

After running his hands over the new part for a few seconds, he retrieved his gun and then a small bag of tools. Mun-nam and I watched as, within just a few minutes, he had the receiver opened up, the new part installed, and the gun put back together. Mun-nam and I were about to depart when the landlord asked us to drink some liquor with him. It would have been a colossal insult to refuse his hospitality. After downing his shot, the landlord asked me if I had ever hunted pheasants in Korea, that the Korean birds were considered quite a trophy.

To be polite, I said that I had not had that opportunity yet, although I had heard a great deal about the famed Korean golden pheasant. Well, my big mouth got me into it once again. The landlord smiled and, glancing at Mun-nam as if to gauge his reaction to what was about to follow, he continued that shotgun shells were extremely expensive in Korea. After a short pause, he informed me that an American military man could get a Korean pheasant-hunting license for less than $40, and that license would entitle the licensee to get a shotgun from the base USO. Further, the loan of the gun was not a rental; it would be free of charge so long as it was returned in the same condition.

I still didn't see where this was going, but I saw that Mun-nam was smiling, so I didn't worry about it. The landlord then came out with his proposition: I will pay for your hunting license and as many boxes of shells you can buy if you take the free hunting safety course. You can then borrow a shotgun from the USO. A group of us will take you along hunting where few people know there are plenty of pheasants. You'll have fun getting a bird, and we'll save money getting ours.

Holy shooting match! I hesitated only a second before grinning widely as I agreed. If this turn of events was a surprise, I was downright shocked when the landlord pulled out a bundle of what appeared to be nothing but U.S. twenty dollar bills – not MPC, those Military Payment Certificates – and peeled off five of them for me. No serviceman in Korea – and certainly no Korean citizen – was allowed to have U.S. currency, yet this guy had a shit load of it. The bills had been folded over only once and, since it was close to an inch think, I later calculated that it must have amounted to about $2,000. I knew that being a landlord in the Ville was a good racket, but I could not begin to imagine where those greenbacks came from and how he had amassed so many of them. As it was, I would just have to convert the hard currency to MPC, signing a military form attesting that someone had sent me the $100 in the mail – no big deal.

Chapter Sixteen: Two Types of Brothers in Arms

After attending the hunting safety class, one that must have been intended for imbeciles in view of the most basic information that was hammered over and over again, I was able to purchase a Korean upland bird hunting license for $38. However, I discovered that I was able to buy only four boxes of shotgun shells – until the Korean man in charge of ammunition sales smiled at me as he said in perfect English, "I have already stamped your hunting ration card on this purchase, haven't I?"

He hadn't, but I was slow in gathering his meaning until he turned away from me, forcing me to realize that our transaction was over and that I would now be able to come back to buy more shells the next day. This guy must have been a close friend or relative of some kind with Mun-nam's landlord and that was how the landlord knew so much about the procedure for Americans getting hunting licenses and borrowing guns. Eventually, I was able to spend nearly all of the remaining money on shells. Once again, I learned just how important it was in Korean society to be connected.

Plans were made to meet early Saturday morning at the landlord's area where a stake-bed truck would drive us into the countryside for hunting and then pick us up later at a prearranged time. I was excited to be going along with five or six others, including Mun-nam who did not have a gun but could certainly borrow mine. After all, I wasn't much of a bird hunter and I hadn't fired a shotgun in more than a dozen years, the last time being with a neighbor buddy and his dad at some skeet range. The gun had been a .410, not a 12-guage like I was now carrying. If I got a good shot in, fine. But if not, then I could certainly act as a bird flusher. Anyway, just being away from the base and out in the fall weather would be invigorating.

When we were let off, the landlord told us to follow him to the fabled hunting grounds where he just knew there were so many birds, we could not possibly get them all. Initially, we walked in single file along rice paddy dikes until we got to fields planted with Chinese cabbages interspersed with Japanese daikon, those large white radishes. In less than a quarter of an hour, we were in lightly wooded hills.

As we passed by the edge of a small marsh, our presence flushed out a snake that had probably been lurking for small animals such as frogs or mice. One of the guys said that some Korean snakes were deadly and that he detested them, killing every one that he could. As we continued on, we came to a small but steep slope, which slowed us down a bit. I was following Mun-nam who was struggling to keep his footing in the rocky soil of the path up the low hill.

Because we were rather bunched up as each of us slowed for the fellow ahead to proceed, my improvised walking stick inadvertently whacked Mun-nam on the back of his ankle. I thought that he was going to lose his mind. He whirled around, dancing about and looking feverishly at the ground, to holler, "Where is it? Where is it? The bastard bit me! Look for the snake!" I eventually broke in to apologize for having scared him with my stick. Upon hearing this, everyone but Mun-nam and me broke out in sustained laughter.

One of the guys asked him, "Did you make water?" For the rest of the outing, Mun-nam was referred to as "Snake Guy." Understandably, he did not see any humor in the event, grumbling that the others ought to not speak until they have been bitten, threatening to find a snake and fling it at them with his own walking stick. "Just wait for the snake," he warned.

About an hour after we were dropped off, the landlord stopped to have us group around him as he pointed out a line of trees, beyond which, he said, were small fields of harvested wheat. "Over there, the birds will be plentiful," he promised. We fanned out to walk abreast as we left the sparse woods to step into the stubble of wheat stalks. Almost immediately, a pheasant took wing to whirr away noisily before anyone was ready to shoot.

We all looked to the landlord who was smiling in delight. He pointed to his eyes and then gestured out broadly toward the field. We understood that if we missed any opportunities, the fault was all our own, as he had clearly brought us to the right place.

Before we had walked even a quarter of the way across the field, we had flushed five pheasants, four of which were taken down as the shooters considered their shots. The landlord missed, I did not fire due to distance, and Mun-nam did not have a gun. After helping to retrieve the birds, I passed my gun to Mun-nam who hesitantly accepted it as we once again spread out to continue our slow advance across the field. Several more pheasants were flushed and all were brought down in a volley of fire. Mun-nam got his bird and offered me the gun back, but I gestured for him to try again. Given the speed at which these birds were flying, I wasn't certain that I could get one, so why not let a proven shot continue with his run of luck. Besides, that would prevent me from embarrassing myself if I missed.

This continued until we approached the far side of the field that was bordered by another sparse stand of trees. The landlord was at the left end of our formation when a cock pheasant rose up seemingly from under his very feet. It quickly changed direction to fly almost parallel to the line of us. No one tried a shot because of safety reasons – except the landlord. Despite the bird being not far in front of us and being only a few feet in the air, I saw him shoulder his gun and take aim to fire.

My immediate reaction was to yell, "Down!" in English as I dove to the ground. I heard the pellets whine overhead and rip into the leaves of the trees off to our right. When I looked up, I saw that my warning had been understood as the others at my end of the line also were picking themselves up. No one said a word to the landlord for this was his expedition, but it soon became clear that he realized he had endangered us all by his intense focus on the pheasant.

We continued to hunt for another hour or so before turning back for the pick up point. Spirits were high for everyone had gotten a bird but me even though I had fired twice. Two guys, the landlord and another, had bagged three birds each, and all of the others brought down two each for a total of 14 pheasants. Even though I didn't get even a single bird, I had enjoyed myself thoroughly.

When we got back to the Ville, everyone split up to go home with his trophies. I retrieved the borrowed gun from Mun-nam, leaving my unused shells with him for some other time. He asked me to come for dinner the next day, on Sunday, saying that his wife would fix the birds Korean style. I was a bit hesitant to intrude but he insisted, so I accepted.

I brought a chilled case of Mun-nam's favorite American beer, Pabst Blue Ribbon, with me to dinner, knowing that his mother and his wife would enjoy a cold one when I wasn't around and Mun-nam would have some spares for the next time his taste buds cried out for an American pilsner. One pheasant had been cut into pieces for preparation in a heavy broth containing other vegetables cut into chunks. Frankly, I thought it was tastier this way than fried or baked like in the States. Mun-nam's wife was pleased to hear this, but I am not sure that she believed me.

After dinner, I asked if I could examine the fighting spurs of the male bird. Mun-nam retrieved one leg and then pulled out his pocketknife to cut away the top part of the hard covering on the lower leg to expose the tendon. He grabbed the tendon with his fingers and gave a pull as I watched the talons retract. Very cool, I thought. Mun-nam suggested I take it to scare the bar girls with. His wife had a disgusted look on her face, but when she turned away, I thought I saw her crack a smile.

On the way back to base with the pheasant leg hidden in my jacket, I decided to stop off at the Stereo Club downstairs whiskey bar, my favorite drinking spot in the Ville since the days of Lucy more than two years ago. In my mind, Lucy was still associated with the club. As I sat on my preferred stool at the bar, a sweet young thing came over to take my order. I decided to show her a magic trick using the pheasant leg. I asked her, if I made the talons of a dead pheasant clench, would she give me a whiskey without charge.

She consulted with the senior waitress who then called over the others to watch me do my trick. I pulled out the leg and showed it to them, turning it first this way and that, to prove that there were no strings or other hidden things attached. One of the girls hesitantly agreed to let me rub the limp talons over her forearm. At first, she was a bit nervous, flinching slightly each time I touched her with the talons. After a couple of innocent dry runs, I let the leg rest on her arm with the talons across her wrist. The ladies were all keenly looking at the foot as I began a ghoulish chant of nonsense words from Jabberwocky before suddenly pulling the exposed tendon and causing the talons to grab onto the wrist of the unsuspecting young woman.

They all saw it happen and they all shrieked, a high-pitched collective screech that was painful to hear. One of the girls jumped back away from the bar into a low cabinet that stored towels behind the bar, nearly knocking it over. The other four scattered, the young lady who was the victim of my prank actually bolting from behind the bar and out of the club.

When things calmed down a bit after they had returned, I showed them the trick. Even though they saw how I had worked the tendon to cause the talons to clutch and that the foot really wasn't coming back from the dead, none of them wanted to repeat the experience. Instead, whenever they had to pass by me, I was given a wide berth along with distrusting glances. I did not get my drink for free because, they adamantly declared, I had frightened them outrageously.

On my way out, I asked if anyone wanted the foot. The young lady that had nearly knocked over the cabinet told me that I should use the talons to hold myself the next time I had to make water. Only she wasn't smiling.

Out in the lane leading to the main road back to the base, I saw a group of ragtag youngsters playing with a severely underinflated soccer ball. I recognized one of them as being the little guy I had befriended some months ago, and I called him over to show him the foot. After demonstrating to him and the others that had crowded around how to make it work, I handed it over and the beaming lad quickly showed me that he could get the talons to clutch. I had to smile as they all ran off to create mischief with it somewhere.

I had come to appreciate the little kids that played in the alleyways around the American bars. They were just looking to score a little cash or get some sort of redeemable treasure from drunken airmen. Many guys got mean when they were drunk and would kick at or cuff the kids swarming about them like flies. I took pity on them so I tried another tack, one that Archie told me he had used during his first time in Korea.

Trying this out earlier in my assignment back at Osan, I had called over one youngster that seemed vaguely familiar. Then I realized that he reminded me of the little orphan boy character that had been informally adopted by the soldiers in the movie "The Green Berets" of a few years back. Skinny and unkempt, he was wary as he approached me. I asked him if I could trust him, to which he had proudly asserted in his best English that he was "Numbah One trust!" I then gave him a 500 hundred won bill, less than a dollar, to buy a bottle of Bacchus-D and to meet me at where the lane connected with the main road to the base. The kid ran away like the wind and was at the appointed spot with my magic elixir before I was.

He gave me the bottle and change, but I noticed that he had kept the coins as he had handed me only the paper bills. He had retained what he thought was an appropriate commission for the errand, but I looked at him with reproach, saying nothing, and then he did pretty much what I hoped he would do. Slapping the coins into my hand in disgust, but calling me a "Cheap Charlie," he stepped away from me, poised to flee if I made any hostile move. I merely said, "You made a mistake with my change. I want to give you this," as I held out a 100 won note.

To him, that was a lot of money, but he didn't know whether I was teasing or not. I let him snatch it from my fingers. After that, whenever the kid saw me, he would hustle over to say, "You need something, GI? I get it no sweat, fast too!" Other guys thought I was being played for a chump, but I nevertheless made an effort to have enough won in change or small bills to accommodate him. I was certain that he needed my petty cash more than I did, and it was a small enough good deed.

Just now, though, I had given the little scamp a very unique toy that he and his friends would shamelessly enjoy until some killjoy adult wearied of their antics.

Even after including me in the trip to Mt. Song-ni National Park and on the hunting expedition, Mun-nam still wasn't out of things for me to get involved with. Since he knew that I always left our Operations area and was back at the barracks by five in the evening, he would occasionally wait at the barracks entrance to catch me if we had agreed to meet or if there was anything on his mind. This time, what he suggested was truly unparalleled. "I want you to join our union," he said as we entered my barracks space. "Union?" I questioned, "You know that, as an American and a Skivvy-Niner, I can't join a Korean union."

No, no, he explained that what he meant by a union was really what Americans call a fraternal organization. He wanted me to join the local lodge of the Pine Tree Association. As with many things in Korea, the pine tree has great significance. Mun-nam pointed out that the tree represented loyalty and virtue as well as longevity. Becoming a member would be a great honor, for he knew of no other foreigners that had ever been invited. Holy brotherhood!

He told me not to worry about being admitted as the lodge members had already discussed my membership and that I had been accepted by the president. I didn't know what to think beyond saying thank you, but inside I was a bit nervous. Mun-nam must have sensed that, for he reassured me that I already knew most of the members from our frequent adventures involving makkŏlli houses.

Still, this was a big deal for me and I worried a bit. When I asked Mun-nam what was expected of me at the meeting, he instructed me to stand facing the president, bow deeply, and pledge adherence to the principles of the association. Mun-nam added, "The last thing you say is 'If there is anything I can do on behalf of the lodge ...' but stop and say no more. Don't sit down until after the president finishes speaking to you."

I pulled the short speech off, stuttering only once as I struggled to recall the word for principles. I remained in a bow as the president spoke to me in English to say that I was welcome as a new and younger brother but due to being a foreigner and the shortness of my stay in Korea, I could never hold any office. He concluded that my initiation fee of roughly four dollars was payable now. Holy frat boy, I was now a Pine Tree brother!

After the meeting, everyone but the president adjourned to a nearby makkŏlli house where I, as the newest member, was expected to foot the bill. I had anticipated something like that and was properly prepared with a hefty wad of Korean won.

There were a couple of faces that I had not seen before, and after introductions were made, I was questioned as to how I had come to learn Korean and be interested to such a depth in Korea. I provided all the stock answers about having studied in the States and recognizing the utility of using it in the Ville. This time, I added, "Besides, it is fun!" Everyone chuckled.

Despite my improving Korean, it seemed to me that the more I learned and practiced, the more I recognized just how pathetic my language skills really were. Yes, I was learning more and making good progress, but there were still times when I had such difficulty in following conversations that I had to ask what probably seemed like really basic questions. Luckily, my associates apparently had unlimited patience.

At one point, one of the lodge members asked me about my flying job. I really couldn't get into the specifics about that, but after imbibing my share of several pots of makkŏlli, I thought that I would explain how a turbo-prop engine works instead. Confidence running on alcohol, I began in Korean by saying, "Well, you know that a fan moves air by means of its rotating blades. And you know that is how a propeller pulls a plane through the air. Well, now imagine a machine that has a long axle and two fans. They are at each end of the axle and that the axle turns inside a strong tube."

I went on from there, and surprisingly, did an adequate job of describing how a turbo-prop works. From the questions that followed, it would seem that I had conveyed at least some information correctly and that my audience had understood it. Even so, I knew that there was still a long way to go before I was as good as I wanted to be and that I couldn't rest on any perceived laurels.

After we left the makkŏlli house, Mun-nam and I headed toward the intersection where we would split up, he walking the remaining distance to his place and I starting to look for a taxi back to the barracks. We had just gotten to the main road when Mun-nam yelled at me to watch out. When I turned to see what he was concerned about, a big hard fist crashed into my head. Holy haymaker!

I was stunned and could not focus clearly for several seconds, but I did not go down. I was later told that almost immediately, several by-standers, all Korean, jumped in to help Mun-nam prevent any further fighting. Fighting? What fighting? There wasn't any fighting, I just got blind-sided, and then the chicken-shit bastard who had sucker-punched me ran off with his buddies. Mun-nam asked me if I knew the guy. I said that I did not, but that I did know why I was attacked: I was in the wrong part of the Ville.

The Pine Tree hall and the nearby makkŏlli house where we had regrouped after the lodge meeting were located in the part of the Ville where years ago black servicemen were forced to go because they had been unwelcome in the other clubs. That had been corrected by an edict from the Osan Air Base commander – but only recently. Any club that refused to serve black Americans would be declared off-limits. Since the base military police patrolled the Ville, it was not an idle threat. Being off-limits meant no Americans and no Americans meant no revenue.

That should have been a very effective tool for integrating the Ville clubs; however it didn't quite work out that way. Blacks claimed that the other clubs purposely did not have any soul music and that brothers did not enjoy the twangy hillbilly or insipid rock songs those clubs played. They wanted to hear soul – the jazz or R&B that was played at Papa Joe's House, the club in "their end" of the Ville.

Club managers countered that they were only catering to what the majority of their paying customers wanted to hear. In fact, they pointed out that even some whites did not like all of the so-called "white music," and those whites patronized different clubs, depending upon whether the club played mostly hard rock, soft rock and pop, or country and western. The club owners reminded the U.S. military authorities that it was pure economics at work, just like in America. Any well-behaved American serviceman with money was welcome at any time in any club in the Ville.

For a while the base authorities tried to force the Ville clubs into playing jazz or R&B at regular intervals throughout the course of an evening. Clubs obeyed in order to avoid being blacklisted, but they also documented that dance floors went empty and bar sales plummeted as patrons left for more musically desirable environments when unpopular stuff was played. Quite understandably, club owners, business women, and American military members – black and white alike – were not at all pleased with the arrangement and, despite official military records that spoke of success, the effort was quietly abandoned after just a few weeks.

Disappointingly but hardly surprising, hard feelings remained and grudges were nurtured so that, despite all the good intentions, there was little noticeable integration and no lasting resolution of a serious American social problem that had been transplanted to Korea. Consequently, Papa Joe's House in the southern end of the Ville was the club at which black servicemen continued to congregate – but white guys like me were not tolerated in that part of the Ville, not even if they liked jazz.

After attending two more lodge meetings, escorted in and of out the area by several of my fellow lodge members, I decided that such efforts were too great a burden for everyone concerned. I bitterly realized that I would have to relinquish my membership in the Pine Tree Association.

Chapter Seventeen: Living in the Ville

Living in the Ville was a lot different than what I had anticipated. There was the privacy and the independence that I had expected, but there were some unusual aspects that took me by surprise.

In the barracks, guys were always coming by to visit their friends and the traffic of bodies moving through the barracks was just part of the scene. By being in the Ville, I thought that I would have plenty of time to read or study in peace and quiet. That was true at first, but just when I thought that it was too quiet and that I might have too much time by myself, I began to get visitors.

One night after suppertime, one of Mun-nam's friends and a regular of the makkŏlli house gang, Shin Chol-sik, gently knocked on my outside door. I was pleased to have a visitor and I invited him in to see my new abode. I had several cans of Dr. Pepper icing down in a large Coleman cooler and an unopened box of Moon Pies in the cupboard, so I broke them out to offer him a taste of what Americans had for snacks. As I was getting the cans out of the ice chest, Chol-sik noticed the large red-waxed wheel of Wisconsin No. 3008 cheddar cheese on a tray in the cooler and inquired about it.

When I told him that it was a type of cheese, his face lit up, so rather than waiting for him to ask, I suggested we have cheese instead of the Moon Pies as I pulled out a large tin of Ritz from my cupboard. Just like beer and soda pop, the delicate crackers came packed in a large round can to survive the long journey from the States. Chol-sik handed back the still wrapped Moon Pie as he just stared at the cheese. I cut off about a dozen thick slivers from the wheel and arranged them around the rim of a plate, into the center of which I carefully dumped out a pile of crackers. You would have thought that I was presenting a feast. He later told me that Koreans lusted after cheese and that, although he hadn't eaten much, mine had been the best cheese he had ever tasted. At least once a week or so, I could count on one or two of my Korean friends to stop by to check on how things were going – and just perhaps to get a taste of Wisconsin No. 3008.

Life in the Ville was an interesting challenge, as I was closer to living as a Korean than most airmen. But every once in a while, perhaps to be expected, I would do something incredibly foolish. One night in the Arirang Club, a smaller club that I did not often patronize, a severe case of beer – actually, whiskey – goggles that I had developed at another club caused me to try my boyish good looks and military charms on a business woman that was behaving in a rather odd manner – but she looked awfully damned good.

After buying her a couple of drinks, I had been able to convince her to spend the night at my place, but because she would not be eating at her auntie's place that night, we needed to leave the club early in order to get some late evening grub at one of the few restaurants still open. I should have known things were going to turn out strangely from the way she ate. I thought she would burst from all the food she put away, like someone who hadn't eaten a decent meal for quite some time. Then she spent such a long time in the restroom that I began to think that she had deserted me through some unseen back door. Eventually, she returned to the table, looking pleased with herself and saying we ought to hurry.

We made it to my palace just before midnight and I proudly ushered her into my main room. She didn't seem to be all that impressed, not saying much and just looking about here and there, poking at this and that. I thought that it was time for bed but she wanted to stay up and chat, a difference of opinion that she won. By the time we did get to bed, the whiskey was making me sleepy to the point that all I wanted was to log some Zs.

In the middle of the night, a loud commotion awoke me. The woman – apparently unconcerned that she was quite immodestly naked – was hopping about the room jabbering about baby ants. The hitch was that there were no ants. I had no idea what was wrong with her and I really did not care – until she pulled the top of my two-piece cupboard over as she searched for an imagined ant farm behind it. I tried to calm her down but she looked at me as though I was a dumb ass for not understanding that all those ants were bad.

Finally, she came back to bed but only to flail about like a child throwing a tantrum. I got worried enough to ask her if she wanted to go the hospital which was less than a quarter mile away. Her answer was a vehemently exclaimed, "No, of course not! Why would I want to go to a hospital?!" I was stymied for I did not want her to wreck my place, but at the same time, I did not want to throw her out before curfew was over.

Then I realized that less than 100 yards from the hospital was the main police station for the Ville. Even though curfew was still in effect, I was positive that I could get to it without incident. And if some wandering cop caught me before I got there, so much the better, for then I would redirect his attention to the serious problem of some crazy business women in my room. I reached the station undetected and caused a bit of commotion as I entered the lobby, an unkempt American babbling about some deranged lady in his Ville abode.

Once the senior cop on duty understood what my problem

was, he assigned two sleepy patrolmen to investigate what was going on. I took a route back to my place that would not pass in front of Mun-nam's place. By now, I realized just what a disturbance this was going to cause in the neighborhood, and I was starting to feel embarrassed. The two policemen accompanying me questioned me extensively on the way back, getting my name and military unit along with why I was living in the Ville, rather than on base like normal guys.

As we entered the room, the woman recognized that I had brought the police back with me. Rather than meekly explaining herself, she began a tirade, yelling stuff in Korean that I could not understand – but the cops certainly did. Out came the handcuffs and within three minutes of our arrival, the woman was roughly escorted away with their cuffs on her wrists in front of her, hands clutching the rest of her clothes, and her coat draped about her shoulders. Despite her considerable attributes still being visible, she no longer looked so good. One of the cops turned to me to say, "You should think. Beauty is not pleasure. They are not the same thing."

When I told Mun-nam about the experience, he merely said, "I thought that you already knew that. You never flirted with the most attractive kisaeng girls, but only the ones whose personalities seemed to fit you. That is why you have such good times, you and your lady friends fit together in the more important ways." I had to admit that he was right. When I related the entire episode to my work buddies, most of them just laughed at me for being blinded by whiskey goggles. Kent, though, warned me that the police were probably not done with me yet. I didn't know what he meant, but he refused to explain despite my pestering him.

It wasn't more than a few days later, when I was scheduled

for a mission early in the morning, that a furious banging on my outside metal door interrupted my pre-flight crew rest. Clad only in my underwear, I cautiously opened the door, only to have it ripped from my hand and flung wide as four Korean cops burst into my room. When I opened my mouth to inquire just what was going on, I was brusquely told not to speak and to stand with my face to the wall in the far corner of the room.

I could hear noises indicating that the room and its contents were being thoroughly searched as even the vinyl was pulled up from the floor, ruining its seal with the concrete underneath it. After several minutes and following an intense but whispered discussion among the policemen, I was told to get dressed and I then was perp-walked to the very same police station that I had visited some nights before.

Time went by slowly in the tiny room into which I was dumped – no chair, no table, nothing but four walls with a small window high up in one of them, and a naked light bulb dangling from the ceiling. Although I did not have my watch, I could see from the light coming into the room from the single high chicken-wired glass window that it was just about daybreak. It struck me that I was going to miss my flight, a very serious military offense, and that I was in deep shit trouble. After what seemed like an interminable time, two other cops pulled me up and pushed me into another room where I was grilled repeatedly about my identity, why I lived in the Ville – and drugs.

It was roughly mid-morning when I was escorted back to my room to get the rest of my clothes and personal effects before being walked to the base by a friendly plain-clothes interpreter who had been assigned to my case. He had proved useful in helping me understand about the various drugs that were making their presence known in Korea. It seemed that Americans brought their bad habits with them, even to remote assignments like Korea, and that the local criminals were taking advantage of that to make money.

It had eventually become clear to the police that I was just an innocent dumb ass American that had stumbled into a pattern of behaviors that raised their suspicions. The flash point had been reached when I had associated with the bizarre business woman from the Arirang Club who was now in jail awaiting trial for using a drug, the name of which I did not catch.

We had been conversing in Korean as we walked to the base but his last words to me were in English. "Be careful. Even monkeys fall out of trees." What the hell did he mean by that, that I was only as smart as a monkey? Maybe he meant my poor choice of a female companion, even though I saw myself as an experienced Ville rat by then. Perhaps he meant that the police had made a mistake and that the narcotics raid was unjustified. Later, my old friend Archie explained that it was an age-old Korean proverb cautioning that even experts make errors, and that any one – or all – of my explanations could be the meaning behind the interpreter's admonition. He laughed at my consternation as he said, "That's Korea for you, jeep!"

My immediate problem, though, was how to avoid the serious trouble about to befall me for having missed a flight, a court martial offense. My supervisor, Archie, believed my alibi, but his boss, the senior NCO in charge of the flying unit, did not. Chief Master Sergeant Wales was clearly not convinced that the interrogation by the Korean police was the cause of my missing the flight.

Wales was a real dick-head, rarely smiling and always looking as though he were angry at something. The only time I saw him laugh was when misfortune hit someone else. I straight up feared him, for he just seemed ready to go off at the slightest provocation. He could have checked out my story easily enough with the Korean police, but he did not, instead reluctantly accepting Archie's trust in me. I didn't like having to keep looking over my shoulder, so to speak, as I continued at my job in his section. That uncertainty plus the boring work made for just another reason to stay off base.

Much later, I learned that the Korean narcs had raided Kent's place a few days before hitting my room. He hadn't wanted to talk about it – or maybe he had been told not to talk about it – and since his event had not affected any of his military obligations, he had just kept quiet out of embarrassment. Kent said that he would mention it to Chief Wales now to see if that would make any difference. I don't know if Kent ever did bring it up with Wales, but if he did, it had precious little effect, for I never felt any warming of Wales' attitude toward me.

I continued to spend many nights in the Ville, and as the weeks passed, Mun-nam asked me what I was doing for New Years, as big a holiday for Koreans as it is in the States. I learned that curfew would be suspended that night so that people could party until the wee hours and not have to worry about cutting the evening short. While airmen would likely overindulge at the off base clubs, I suspected that Koreans in this part of the country would have private parties with close friends and family. Perhaps in Seoul, revelers would take to city nightclubs by the hordes, but the Ville was more of a country town.

Mun-nam was usually subtler than this as I quickly understood what he was hoping for, and since it was a great idea as well as a logical one, I volunteered to throw a party at my place. At first, I thought of including a few business women, but I soon realized that they would prefer to work the clubs and make money. As Mun-nam also pointed out, business women appealed to Americans, not to Korean men. We both knew that I would not be inviting any of my coworkers.

The guests would be primarily the makkŏlli house gang, plus a few others than I had come to know through Mun-nam, for perhaps a total of ten or so Korean friends. My large room would easily handle that many people but I needed help on the menu. Mun-nam said that nobody was looking for Korean food and what would be the hit of the night would be the American treats that Koreans could never get.

I knew what to buy: lots of hot dogs and the requisite condiments, plenty of pretzels and Ritz crackers, and as much cheese as I could get my hands on. I planned on having several cases of American beer in one corner of the kitchen where it would get chilled naturally in that unheated area – Pabst Blue Ribbon seemed to be the brand of choice for Korean palates. At the last minute, I also put M&Ms on my mental list.

Heating the hot dogs would be a challenge since I wasn't going to use the dangerous stove in the kitchen, but Mun-nam came up with the solution: just cover the flat top of my space heater with aluminum foil for a cooking surface since that would certainly provide enough heat, and it would clean up in a flash. He also suggested that I don't do hot dogs in buns with the messy condiments. I had to think about that before realizing that the solution is to make finger food out the hot dogs by cutting them into pieces for dipping into bowls of condiments. Mun-nam refined the idea by suggesting Spam, a great Korean favorite, instead of hotdogs. Cutting the Spam into chunks and impaling them on toothpicks along with a piece of sweet onion and a wedge of cheese would go over well. I could even make a bunch of these *hors d'oeuvres* ahead of time and replenish the supply as they were eaten. Mun-nam and I were pleased with our creativity.

New Years Day was on a Saturday in 1972 and that meant that Friday, December 31, would be a Holiday. The military brass knew that by Thursday afternoon, everybody's minds would be on partying and that little work would get accomplished after lunch that day. Not long after people returned from their noon breaks, thoughtful supervisors would slowly go through their work areas wishing their people joyful and safe celebrations before gruffly admonishing them to get out of the way – by leaving work. I was gone before Archie had even finished his announcement.

Mun-nam was the first to arrive on Friday, bringing a huge plastic bag of peanuts roasted in the shell that Koreans like to munch on when drinking. I was a bit disappointed not to have thought of those but Mun-nam said that getting all the American stuff was more than enough for me to focus on. He also brought over ashtrays and some of the heavy brown paper used in makkŏlli houses for tablecloths, which would keep spills on my tabletop under control. I had nearly three dozen Spam chunks with cheese and onion bits on toothpicks already prepared, with more to come as necessary.

It wasn't long before the others arrived in groups of two and three. Someone brought a portable radio that was eventually turned to a station playing seasonal Korean tunes and reporting on the festivities in Seoul, roughly 40 miles to the north. However, the major focus, at least in the beginning, was on the long north wall of my room.

Although I had no photographs or pictures to hang for decoration when I first moved in, I did have a stash of Playboy magazines from the barracks. By carefully removing the centerfolds from their staples, smoothing out the creases in the glossy paper, and with the meticulous use of double-sided Scotch tape, I created a gallery of girly pics that captivated my friends, most of whom had never seen any American women, at least not women like *these* and certainly not undressed like *that*!

Holy hooters! There were plenty of questions: Were all American woman that big in the breast? Were they all that beautiful? How was the photographer able to focus on his work? How could I sleep at night with all that titillating nakedness staring seductively at me from the wall? I pointed out that I did not pay much attention to the wall anymore, other than to appreciate the colors that the different layouts added to the otherwise drab wall. Everyone looked at me as though I were out of my mind.

I mentioned that I had begun to wonder about the appropriateness of those centerfolds since most of the young ladies I had enticed back to my playpen did not express positive opinions regarding my art collection. Phrases like "She has milk bags like a cow" and "That is just an American business woman" were two of the more common expressions. Some of the guys volunteered to take the pictures if I ever decided to take them down. After a while, the commotion died down and we all got down to the serious business of having a men only Korean News Year Eve party, starting with a game of Thumper to get our engines started.

No one got sick but everybody got noisily drunk, singing Korean songs and chanting ribald sayings. One of the more bawdy ones, which I understood immediately, was "The boneless commander spits white blood." Mun-nam even wrote out the six Chinese characters for me on a corner of the paper tablecloth. Fortunately, none of the people in the neighborhood complained about our outrageous merrymaking. At the end of the evening, most of the food was consumed and we had gone through nearly five cases of beer.

As my guests staggered off to their respective homes, Mun-nam promised to come back in the morning to help me clean up. Actually, there wasn't that much of a mess beyond a large old can filled with stinky cigarette butts, a big wad of soggy paper tablecloths, and more than 100 crumpled beer cans. Mun-nam asked if he could have the empties for recycling, and I quickly agreed, knowing that he would make a bit of change from the junk metals dealer while I would be relieved of the problem presented by a pile of sour-smelling dead soldiers. I also gave him the leftover cheese to take home with him.

A few days later, Mun-nam reported that everyone raved about my party, saying that they had a great time and that their wives and girl friends were pleased that they didn't get into any trouble as they might have at some makkŏlli house or Korean nightclub – plus it was cheaper. I had to laugh; the whole shebang had cost me roughly $30, only slightly more than I would have spent if I had hit the clubs on my own that particular night.

As he and I relieved some of the more outrageous moments – like when I explained and then demonstrated what "mooning" meant – Mun-nam hit me with another stunner. He said that we were the best of friends now and that I should consider retiring in Korea after my military career was over, saying that with my military benefits and retired pay, I would live like a king. I promised him to think about it, as he went on to lay another bomb on me. Mun-nam said that he had no intention of dying at a young age, but that if he did, he wanted me to marry his wife and take care of his family.

Holy matrimony! I was stunned into complete silence. Mun-nam told me that this was a serious matter and for me to think about it before replying because he wanted me to understand the consequences and responsibilities of my agreeing to that. I was in shock, for this is something that most Westerners cannot fathom. I did not know Mun-nam's wife well at all, and in fact, I doubt that we had ever exchanged more than a few dozen words in direct conversation during all the time I had known her. She was pleasant enough in appearance, but as I now well knew, appearance alone does not make for a good relationship. Holy matrimony, indeed!

A few days after that bombshell, I reached Mun-nam at the hospital to ask him if he could meet me alone at the NCO Club for a beer. We met there right after work and I brought him into the club as my guest. Choosing to sit in a quiet spot and after ordering beers and French fries with mayonnaise – Koreans prefer it to ketchup – I told him that I had been thinking of his request almost constantly, but since I thought that he was going to live a long time, such a marriage would be an unlikely event. He stopped me to inquire, "True, I hope to live a long life, but if I do not ...?"

I asked him what his wife thought about his idea, wondering why he did not make this request to one of his long-time Korean friends. Mun-nam said his wife got angry with him for even bringing the subject up, but after she calmed down, she agreed that if anything were to happen, there was wisdom in marrying me. Rolling around in the back of my mind was the question about romantic love, even though I knew that, for some Koreans, it was a Western concept that did not always fully register with them. Mun-nam and I had talked about that many times over the years that we had known each other. He said that his feeling for his wife were deeper and more important than what I meant when I used the word "love."

He explained that his wife would be a good mate in all material respects and that I would not want for anything in such a marriage. Besides, he smiled roguishly as he said, "If this romance thing is what you want, you could always find a mistress." When I had digested all of what he had said, after using the delay of consuming my beer and ordering another round, I looked at him and simply said, "OK, I agree," wondering at the enormity of what I had just accepted.

Mun-nam thanked me for being such a good friend but then said that he did not want to discuss it anymore because he wanted to get off the subject of his death. I concurred, but I said that he should get home before his wife got mad at me for getting him drunk. As he left, I thought that it was probably far too late for that, since I had contributed to his delinquency on a number of occasions.

In fact, several months before I had rented my room, after an evening at the House of Truth, Mun-nam had left our group, but apparently he hadn't gone home. Since I was heading off with Miss Yang to her place, I was completely unaware of where he went. On my way back to base the next morning, I saw Mun-nam's wife standing by the side of the road with her arms folded wearing a stern look on her face. I knew that she had spotted me and that it would be worse if I tried to avoid her, no matter what was on her mind.

Before I could even offer a perfunctory greeting, she icily demanded in surprisingly good English, "What have you done with my husband?" There was no good answer to that, and I said that I had gotten so drunk that I lost track of Mun-nam and that maybe he had slept at the House of Truth since we were good customers there. I realized that she doubted me, but she hurriedly stepped around me in a rush to confront whatever unfortunate soul might still be at the makkŏlli house at this hour. I knew that neither the proprietress nor any of the kisaeng girls would reveal anything, but with Mun-nam's wife at that end of town, Mun-nam had a better chance of making it undetected onto the base.

Even though he was unaware that his wife was out looking for him that early in the morning and he therefore was not trying to be furtive, Mun-nam somehow managed to get on base without running into his wife. I got permission from Archie for a long lunch hour, which I used to track down Mun-nam at the hospital and relate all that had occurred that morning. He looked worried but thanked me for the warning. I don't know how everything played out that evening when Mun-nam got home, but evidently there was no lasting damage. Korean wives put up with a lot from their husbands, although I was certain that I would forever be seen as a bad influence in his wife's eyes.

Well, I was definitely wrong about that since I was now conditionally betrothed to her. Holy matrimony!

Chapter Eighteen: Harry Goes Haywire

Not everything that was entertaining or interesting going on in the Ville involved Koreans. Airmen were often the source of some very hilarious hijinks and Harry, who was my sponsor when I first got to Japan nearly eight years ago in 1964, was a master at creating things to amuse himself. Although I had heard rumors about one old-time Skivvy-Niner who had hijacked a steam locomotive one drunken night on R&R in Japan, that story was never corroborated by anyone I could trust. Harry, on the other hand, always left a trail of evidence in addition to having numerous witnesses, and I was one of them on many occasions.

Harry was usually involved in one scheme or another to make extra money. Most often, he got away with his conniving, although he would sometimes miscalculate and find himself in a temporary jam of one sort or another. I say "temporary" because Harry had a knack for always landing on his feet, falling into shit but always coming out smelling like a rose. It seemed to me, though, that Harry pushed his luck way too far. Even the most heartless of brass would cut an airman some slack if he were a hard worker and generally not a fuck-up. However, as I saw it, Harry came to their attention in undesirable ways far too often for comfort.

For one thing, ever since the incident on my first trip to Korea when Harry had inserted contraband cosmetics into a pack of noodles for a Korean woman working on base, I suspected that he was deeply involved in black-marketing. During the years that we were officially assigned to Yokota Air Base in Japan but spent the majority of our time at Osan in Korea, I rarely saw Harry with the other guys. He was always off doing something on his own, but just what that something was, he never revealed. Interestingly, when Harry's assignment in Japan was up in the early 1970s, he was able to purchase a brand new Japanese automobile with cash. It is possible, I had to admit, that he saved that money from his regular military paycheck, for he had a well-deserved reputation for being a tightwad. More likely, though, I believe that he had made a killing selling goods from the military exchanges or the stuff brought over from Japan to all the friends of his Korean wife. It wouldn't have surprised me to learn that he was even somehow paying off Korean customs inspectors.

Now, however, Harry's marriage had recently broken up and he was on the prowl. Unfortunately for him, however, his long-time love interest Sun-ja had remained close friends with his former wife and she would therefore not even speak to him. Harry had now become just another Ville rat who drank too much.

One night several weeks after my New Years Eve party, I was enjoying a drink in the whiskey bar of the Stereo Club, my favorite off base club since the days of Lucy years ago. Once again, I was in the collective good graces of the waitresses there, engaging in a bit of flirtatious response to their frequent randy remarks or provocative poses that were intended to accentuate what they saw as their best features. The ladies had evidently pardoned me for the incident about the pheasant talon voodoo trick that had frightened them all so badly.

All of a sudden, the outside door burst open to admit a street urchin, perhaps ten or eleven years old, who was panting from exertion. After pausing to catch his breath, he looked about and asked in Korean, "Is the American serviceman known as the Dragonfly here?" Also in Korean, I responded, "The Dragonfly you seek sits before you."

The kid came over to relay a message from the House of Truth to the effect that an older American serviceman, his engine well started, was looking for me to join him there. The little guy continued that this serviceman was also bawdily entertaining all the kisaeng girls, to the point that the other customers had left to seek out other establishments. Since Korean men are a noisy and rather tolerant lot when drinking, it had to be some commotion going on to force them out of an otherwise perfectly good makkŏlli house. Almost instantly, I was certain beyond a shadow of a doubt that there was only one guy capable of accomplishing that: it just had to be Harry!

Harry was an absolute natural at Korean, for he had achieved a level of near-perfect proficiency in the language from only basic language training followed by a few short months in country. Guys like me had yet to attain similar fluency, even after an additional year at language school and many more months of practical study in Korea itself. Harry had other noteworthy characteristics as well: he had precious few of the common social inhibitions most of us routinely observe, and if that weren't enough, he liked to mind-fuck with people. It was often hard to know when he was serious or just messing around.

In one instance, Harry had managed to alienate a group of four or five guys at once, just by crowding them. He had been taking a class in psychology at the overseas university on base at Yokota in which he learned about how everyone has a concept of personal space. Putting this knowledge to use, Harry had moved closer and closer to each of the men in turn, violating their comfort zones until the guys became bothered enough to mutter excuses about having to go somewhere. Harry laughingly told me about this a few days after he had performed his little experiment, and he bragged that he had gotten an A on the paper that he had subsequently written about it for class.

Well, if Harry were at the House of Truth raising a ruckus, it would be worth going there to observe his latest performance. As I neared the building, the unrestrained laughter of women could be heard coming from within its confines. Since there was no hostess at the entrance to welcome me, I followed the sounds of female amusement coming from the large room in the back on the right. I was a bit surprised at this, as I expected Harry to have been shown to one of the smaller rooms since he was a customer group of only one person. This larger back room was exceptionally well appointed for a makkŏlli house. The floor was of well-maintained linoleum and the beams that supported a wood ceiling were sanded smooth, nicely stained, and highly polished. At roughly 15 feet on all sides, it was a room suitable for a small banquet.

That Harry was in control of the large room really did not matter any longer since there were no other customers around, and the other rooms were dark in testimony of that. I removed my shoes and started to slide the rice paper door open as I heard Harry's voice urging everyone to drink up, that he was getting thirsty waiting for the ladies to keep up with him. He was in fine form that evening, having taken it upon himself to pervert the limited understanding of English possessed by the ladies working there.

As I entered the room, Harry greeted me in Korean as his bastard kid brother. I was amazed to hear him make such a reference to his family, even if only by implication, but I should not have been so shocked as he had often enough told me of his childhood, and I had formed the distinct impression that it had not been a happy one. As for his less-than-flattering term for me,

I was not offended because I knew that was only Harry being Harry – but I also knew that I could not let him get the upper hand in the conversation, or else it would turn out badly for me in the end.

With Harry, limits had to be quickly established or all was lost. My response was to immediately identify him as being an unfortunate soul whose birth did not go well, resulting in a condition that left him capable only of cracking pumpkin seeds with his lower body opening. Harry was flabbergasted that I could muster such an expression with that speed. We had not seen each other for roughly two years, since early 1970 when I left for intermediate language school, and he was unaware of my now on-going efforts to improve my proficiency in the language. I was far better than average now and it surprised him more than just a little bit.

My greeting brought Harry up short – but for only a second or so – and after the briefest of reflections, he chose to ignore my retort. So, pleasantries out of the way, he turned his attention once again to the group of kisaeng girls. I was pleased to notice that his audience did not include my Miss Yang, as it would have been upsetting for me to watch her being corrupted by Harry's vulgar efforts. "The phrase," he then continued in Korean, "is a different way of saying 'How are you?'" except that the English phrase Harry was attempting to teach them was, "Hey, you dipshit!" as he emphasized that the accent had to be on the "hey" and the "dip" of the last word.

It continued like this for several minutes as Harry introduced more crude and even offensive military expressions with rather clever new definitions. I knew that I would have to come back the next night to undo all the damage Harry would have done to the meager vocabulary of these poor ladies. It

- 211 -

would be most unfair to allow them to continue believing what Harry was trying to teach. It turned out, however, that I needn't have worried about that, for I subsequently learned that every one of the ladies knew that Harry was bullshitting them, but since he was a rather charming fellow with such a command of their language, they were all more than willing to suspend their collective disbelief to be entertained by his antics.

At the time, though, I decided not to confront Harry, for even though I was beginning to think that he was somewhat of a sociopath, caring only for his own entertainment without much regard for others, I also saw no value in even attempting to correct his outlandish behavior in front of his audience at the House of Truth – even if I could accomplish such a feat. If all the kisaengs there perceived him as a charming potty-mouth and gifted linguist, who was I to object?

Harry was the center of all the attention, and while it wasn't jealousy on my part, I didn't like being ignored, as it was difficult to get a word in edgewise with Harry so dominating the conversation. I drank a couple of cups of makkŏlli and then made my way out of the House of Truth, leaving him to charm his way into the hearts – and perhaps other parts – of the ladies there. However, by going back to the base that early that night, I missed out on the best part of his performance.

After leaving the House of Truth some time before the midnight curfew, Harry felt that he needed to get to Suwŏn, the larger town that was about ten miles or so up the road from the Ville. The problem was that the intercity busses had already made their last runs for the day and, even if there had been time enough for the trip, he did not have enough Korean money for a taxi. Harry solved this inconvenience by stealing a truck.

Vehicle theft was almost unheard of in the Ville, and some

unfortunate worker had left the keys to a company truck in its ignition, a boon for Harry when he determined that it would nicely solve his transportation problem. Without further ado, he climbed into the cab, figured out the gearbox, and was soon on his way. Everything seemed to be going well, since the truck had plenty of gas and it was not difficult to handle, when Mother Nature made herself known to Harry in the form of a full bladder. Since the old Military Supply Route was a 1950s-era narrow two-lane road with no shoulders on which to pull over, Harry drove into the nearest rice field that seemed to be dry for the season.

Call of nature answered, Harry attempted to resume his journey, only to discover that the field had not been completely dry and that the truck was hopelessly mired in several inches of muck on the right-hand side. There was no way to get free, so Harry decided to sit down and think on a pile of hay at the edge of the field while he contemplated what to do. That is where the Korean police found him dozing just after daylight the next morning.

Harry never talked much about the time he spent in jail other than to say that it was a rather unsophisticated experience. When he was finally allowed a phone call to contact the American authorities as required by the Status of Forces Agreement between the South Korean and U.S. governments, it was not the Osan Air Base Legal Office he dialed. Instead, Harry called a Korean army officer than he had known since he was first assigned to Korea more than a decade previously. At that time, the officer had been a company-grade lieutenant. Now a full colonel, the officer had some juice in the local area. After extensive negotiating and in consideration of no lasting damage having been incurred, the colonel was able to gain Harry's release from jail. Nevertheless, there were a few conditions attached to his freedom. Harry had to pay for the tow truck that pulled the stolen vehicle out of the muddy field, he had to reimburse the farmer for the work necessary to get the field back into shape for planting, and he had to "donate" some cash to both the Suwŏn and the Ville police for their time. The most severe stipulation was that Harry would be shipped out of country as quickly as the military authorities could process the required paperwork. During that time, Harry would be restricted to base, as he had now been determined to be unwelcome by the Korean authorities.

Since all of this took place outside of any U.S. military facility, the brass at both Osan and Yokota decided not to file any charges against Harry. However, he did lose his security clearance for what was determined to be unstable behavior. He would not be able to work as a Korean linguist, and the likelihood of his being allowed back in Korea would be close to zero as long as he remained in the military.

Within days, he was gone, and I never saw him again while he was still on active duty. I did not feel sorry for him because I was certain that, being who and what he was, Harry would never give up his scams, and he would always find some way to work whatever system he encountered for his personal gain. After all, in my eyes he had become nothing more than a latter-day Sergeant Bilko.

Chapter Nineteen: Going and Coming and Going

It was the spring of 1972 and the end of my first official tour in Korea was coming to an end. Despite my military record showing that I had spent only 13 months in Korea, the truth was that, due to all the time I had been formally stationed in Japan but in reality performing duty in Korea, I now had the equivalent of well over three full years in country. Although I had enjoyed my time in Japan prior to the constant trips to Korea, I had developed a deep and abiding appreciation of and affection for Korea: the people, the customs, the food – just about everything in the country. As a result, I was trying to keep an open mind about my upcoming assignment to Okinawa, a Japanese island but now under U.S. military control since the end of World War II.

I didn't spend a lot of time thinking about it though, since Mun-nam and the guys made no secret about planning a big deal for my upcoming farewell party. They wouldn't tell me any details, only saying that all of my Korean friends would be there and that the gathering would be held at a makkŏlli house on the Saturday before my Monday departure in the middle of May. Mun-nam joked that I would have the weekend to recover and rid myself of those undesirable after-effects of the makkŏlli.

The day of the party arrived, and because I had already been released from duty in order to clear my affairs with the various base offices, I had nothing else to do and it was difficult for me to wait until it was time to head for the Ville. Since I was feeling somewhat glum at the prospect of leaving Korea for some small island in the middle of the Pacific Ocean, I was tempted to hit the NCO Club to get my engine started. I realized, however, that would adversely affect partying with my friends if I began my drinking on base, so I reluctantly exercised some restraint.

I never did learn the name of the makkŏlli house where the party was held. All I knew was that it was the first makkŏlli house I had ever visited. It wasn't as nice as the House of Truth where we normally went, but I learned that the nameless place had been willing to provide the goodies the guys had in mind for the party at a more reasonable cost. When I arrived, I was escorted to the large room where some of the gang had already gathered around a long but empty table. Chol-sik, the guy I knew best after Mun-nam and who had been the first to visit my off base room, explained that once everyone had arrived, there would be a small ceremony, so in the meantime we just reminisced about the many adventures we had shared.

Not long after I entered the room, I heard a disturbance outside and although I was curious about that, I knew it would be discourteous to investigate, a breach of people's privacy since it did not involve me. Everyone there noticed my interest, but someone told me to not to pay it any attention because the noise would probably soon go away. It was clear, however, that the noise was things being carried from the front of the building to the rear, accompanied by the mutterings of kisaengs in the hallway to be careful about it. I wondered what was going on, but since I am slow on figuring some things out, I failed to connect the dots. Just then, Mun-nam and the rest of the gang came through the door and greetings were once again exchanged as they took their places around the table. I quickly forgot about the commotion outside the room.

Most Korean men smoked tobacco, but the quality of the cigarettes available on the Korean market was horrid – even the second-hand smoke was harsh. Regardless, Korean smokers had to make do with what was available, and the most popular brands in the area seemed to be Sintanjin, though Chindallae probably was a close second with Unhasu being smoked only by hard-core nicotine fiends. But what experienced Koreans really wanted were American cigarettes, particularly Marlboros. I was aware of this, so out of appreciation for the guys hosting my farewell party, I bought two cartons of Marlboros in the preferred flip-top box as my small contribution to the affair.

When I withdrew the cartons from the paper sack I had been carrying under my arm, you could have heard a pin drop. Holy smokes! All eyes were fixated on the cigarettes as I opened one carton to spread the packs around the table, saying in English the words of my long-ago military basic training instructor, "Smoke 'em if you got 'em!" Everyone laughed, and for a short while the only sounds in the room was the crinkle of cellophane as packs were opened and then the snick of lighters being fired. Soon the relatively sweet smell of cured Virginia tobacco was wafting through the air. It sure as hell beat those acrid-smelling Sintanjins, Chindallaes, and Unhasus.

The house proprietress had evidently been watching, for as soon as the commotion over the cigarettes died, two pots of makkŏlli were brought into our room. As we occupied ourselves in courteously pouring each other's cups, I was aware of plates and chopsticks being placed by kisaengs in front of each of us at the table. A huge platter of pulkogi, the wondrous Korean dish of marinated beef slices quickly grilled over an open flame, soon followed this. As quickly as that was on the table, individual bowls of rice and a myriad of Korean side dishes appeared. It was a damned feast!

After eating, Mun-nam handed me a small cube made of folded paper, saying, "It is delicate so be careful." I gently pulled the paper apart to find a single bŏndegi, the deep-fried caterpillar pupa that Koreans love as a snack. Everyone knew that I found even the idea of putting such a thing into my mouth repulsive, and I realized that this was intended as a joke. Well, the only appropriate response I could think of was swallowing it. After looking at it for only a second or two as I racked my brain for other possible courses of action, I popped it into my mouth and flushed it down my throat without chewing by draining my makkŏlli cup, to the cheers of all in the room. I was unable to notice any taste – but that was precisely my intent.

Then Mun-nam brought out a package the size of an phonograph record album but far thicker, saying that this was from all of them. I carefully unwrapped it, not knowing what to expect. I was astonished to see that it was a scrapbook that had been meticulously put together by hand and that it contained line drawings and commentary about the more interesting happenings of my Korean life. Just a few of my favorites I noted when I flipped through it were my arguing with the manager at the Venus Club, the group of us going "sight-seeing" at the river, my pledging to honor the tenets of the Pine Tree Association at the lodge, and my theatrical rendition of Jabberwocky in the hall at Mt. Song-ni – along with too many others to mention.

I was overwhelmed as my eyes began to water and a lump formed in my throat from the sentiment that threatened to overcome me. There could not possibly have been a better present than this simple scrapbook that documented all the important events with my friends during my months in Korea. I opened my mouth to speak but the words just would not come. I think everyone understood as Mun-nam came to my rescue by saying in English, "Over the lips, over the gums / Look out belly, here it comes!" as he gestured for me to drink up. We then all proceeded to rev up our engines as I enjoyed the best damned farewell party ever.

Monday came and I reluctantly boarded the plane for the flight to Kadena Air Base on Okinawa. I was really downcast, for I felt that a very important chapter in my life was closing. I understood that I could not stay in Korea forever, that everything eventually changes, and that I had to move on, but that didn't prevent me from feeling a powerful sense of loss in leaving Korea and all my friends there.

The flight was uneventful, and as the plane approached the Kadena Air Base runway, I did not get to see much of the island since our approach was from the sea. There was only the expanse of blue-green water until we got over land, perhaps only a mile from the end of the runway. First was a sandy-looking beach, then innumerable clusters of houses close together bounded by a wide four-lane highway that was just outside the perimeter of the base, and finally the bump as the landing gear made contact with the concrete airstrip.

The sense of loss for having left Korea was slowly being replaced by one of curiosity. I had spent time on Okinawa before, since it is the location of the altitude training and certification center for aviators in the Western Pacific theater. The U.S. had maintained control over the island ever since the end of World War II, but I had the luck of arriving on the day that the island reverted back to Japanese administration. There wasn't any great confusion, for this had been in the works for sometime on the island.

However, for the Okinawans, it was a huge victory to be out from under what they saw as the heavy hand of the imperialist Americans. Sentiment against the U.S. had remained high since the end of the war for at least two reasons. It began with the battle for Okinawa, which was fierce and protracted, and countless civilian deaths had resulted from the hostilities. This was exacerbated by the great number of suicides out of fear of the advancing American combat units. This ill will might have dissipated over time but for the fact that too many drunken American servicemen routinely committed too many heinous crimes against the local population. Some of our guys were responsible for rapes, strong-arm robberies, drunk driving homicides, and other stupidities too numerous to mention. From the Okinawan point of view, Americans were nothing more than a bunch of less than human animals.

My sponsor met me at the incoming side of the air terminal and quickly got me squared away in the squadron barracks, and pointed out the various on-base facilities that I would need to check in with. As I was anxious to get to work, particularly in view of what I saw would be a less than welcoming scene off base, I registered with the various support units on base as rapidly as possible and reported for work after only two days.

Before I could even get my desk and work space organized, the word came out: My new co-workers and I would be going back to Korea for a few weeks to help the Skivvy-Niners implement a new program. Having just left Korea, the irony of this was inescapable, the situation being just incredibly ridiculous – so typical of life in the military. I burst into laughter, much to the amusement and curiosity of those around me.

Less than month after I had arrived on Okinawa, I was perfectly happy to be heading back to Korea, for Okinawa was not my cup of tea. While the work at my new unit would be an interesting and rewarding challenge, being stationed on a small island with an unhappy native population was the pits, not at all similar to mainland Japan and totally different from Korea. Anyone who says that Asian countries are all alike doesn't know his damned dick from a daikon.

What made my return to Korea even more unusual is that I was one of only two Korean linguists among the group who had spent any significant amount of time in Korea. With the exception of my new boss, who was not a linguist, all but one of my new associates were short on experience, and they would be seen as "green beans" by the ladies of the Ville and as "jeeps" by the experienced Skivvy-Niners. Consequently, many of them looked to me for information and guidance on Korea. Holy Ville rat! I was seen as an old hand by these young rookies.

When we got to Osan and after we had dumped our baggage near our assigned bunks in the Skivvy-Nine barracks, we wangled a ride to the Operations Building to be briefed by my old nemesis Quentin, the dim bulb that my friend Archie and I had embarrassed to the point that he vowed to put our airborne asses out of business. Even though that had been roughly four years ago, he was grinning widely as he pointed out that he was managing the new program, thinking that since we airborne guys were being assigned to his ground-based project, he had achieved his objective. I told him not to bust a nut quite so fast, that we would be gone in a month, back to flying while he was just another version of an extinct flightless bird. He probably wasn't smart enough to catch my play on the word "dodo," but he was certainly not amused by my retort – and he did stop flapping his lips about his position.

The project work was boring and it was under horrible working conditions, cramped and dark and cold and noisy – somewhat like being on an obsolete mission aircraft but without the sense of adventure – or flight pay. However, we sucked it up for eight hours every day, looking forward to spending many evenings in the Ville with me leading tours and offering pertinent nuggets of useful information as the occasion arose.

I contacted Mun-nam right away to let him know that I was temporarily back and we managed to squeeze in a couple of evenings at the House of Truth with the old Korean gang. When I explained how new to Korea most of the guys were, Mun-nam thought it would be a good experience for them to visit a makkŏlli house. I thought the part about introducing the rookies to a makkŏlli house would be an entertaining as well as a necessary piece of their education about Korea, but I wasn't convinced about green beans being able to handle makkŏlli.

Mun-nam eventually saw the wisdom of the new guys sticking to beer and he agreed to set up a catered party at the same makkŏlli house that had hosted my farewell gathering only a little more than two months previously. After totaling the cost, it worked out to less than $7 per guy, including tips for the kisaengs that would be serving us, about what a night of drinking in the Ville might run. I told Mun-nam that in exchange for all his work, he could attend as my guest. His command of English in addition to his sense of adventure and engaging personality would add to the festive air. He could certainly explain the finer points of Korean culture that I didn't know.

The party went off without a hitch and all of the young jeeps had a fine time but for one who got so drunk that he began to cry over some former girl friend back in the States. We later fixed him up with a more-than-willing business woman from the A-Frame Club and his tearful complaints soon stopped.

In very short order, Quentin's new program was successfully launched, and we all returned to Okinawa and back to flying. I kept in touch with Mun-nam through letters – it was a good way for me to maintain my reading and writing competencies – and in addition, every so often, there would be a conference or some similar activity at Osan that required my presence. Mun-nam and I maintained our close friendship in this manner, even though it wasn't like being stationed in Korea – but it was better than nothing.

I gave up on trying to form any friendships with any Okinawans, instead focusing upon my work in the beginning, and then eventually starting to take college courses in the evenings to work on my bachelor's degree. Through minding my desk job, flying missions, attending classes, and completing homework, I stayed busy and my time was well occupied for the next few years.

Chapter Twenty: Another Vacation in Korea

Five and a half years had passed and the end of my long tour in Okinawa would arrive in a very few months. Since it was the winter semester break, I didn't have any classes. I had been taking college courses after work for the last few years and, what with academic credit for my language programs courtesy of the Air Force, I was now a first semester senior. I was full of myself and felt that my shit definitely did not stink.

It was time for a vacation, I thought, and what better place than Korea. It had been a while since I had spent even a few days there, preferring to let others go to the conferences while I focused on my education. As I thought about all the time I had spent in Korea, I realized that I had never taken the opportunity to visit some of the sites of ancient Korea since none of them were near the base.

I made plans to visit a professor who was now teaching in Korea. The Department of Defense had contracted with a major stateside university to send adjunct professors to various military posts all over the world. Some of the larger military bases had enough professors to offer a wide range of courses, almost like a small college. Kadena Air Base was one of those. An airman could actually complete a liberal arts bachelor's degree by taking these courses on base even while overseas, and that degree would be fully accredited and accepted throughout the States.

That professor from whom I had taken a couple of courses was now at Osan. Despite the difference in our levels of education, we had struck up a friendship based upon having a few significant things in common. We were roughly the same age and single, and he was prone to partying when not occupied with teaching or grading papers. He also had an interest in learning more about Asian cultures, which was one of the reasons he asked to be assigned to Korea after being on Okinawa for only a couple of years.

During class breaks, I had told him a number of stories about the Ville, and he was interested in learning more. When I mentioned the rich history of Korea, he became even more fascinated. Once he was in Korea, he had made the rounds of all the museums and cultural exhibits in Seoul, but since he did not speak Korean, he was seen as just another American and he did not experience Korea in the way that I had. Further, he did not know his way around the country – he needed a guide, and I was happy to fulfill the need since I would be able to visit the ancient sites as well. We made plans to meet in Osan just before the end of December 1977.

There was another reason to go to Korea. I hadn't visited my buddy Mun-nam in a several months, and I heard that he and his wife had another toddler, a daughter. Because the trip would start just before Christmas, I could drop some American-made presents off for Mun-nam's family and maybe spend some time with him before heading out with the professor on our jaunt to see as much of Korea's history as we could in ten days or so. I would be returning to Okinawa just after the New Year, and that would provide plenty of time to see the major sights. After coordinating my vacation with both Mun-nam and the professor, it was agreed that I would spend the first day or so in Osan to hang out with Mun-nam and the gang.

The Air Force allows military members and their families to travel on transport aircraft if there is seating available under a program named Space-A, the "A" meaning available. I received confirmation of a seat on a Space-A flight from Kadena to Taegu

Air Base in southern Korea, with no guarantee of being able to fly all the way to Osan. That did not concern me, for all I needed was to get over the water and into Korea. I was confident that, given my language skills and an adequate knowledge of the country, even if there was no room on a continuing flight, I could get to Osan from Taegu one way or another.

My seat was on a C-130 four-engine turbo-prop, but because the aircraft was dedicated to hauling freight between various Pacific air bases, it was not designed to carry passengers. The only seats available were pull-down webbed affairs, sort of like cheap collapsible picnic chairs, that were normally folded up against the exterior wall of the cargo space to make room for pallets of goods strapped down on the floor. It was a not a comfortable arrangement, and it was cold and noisy as well. Don't gripe, I thought to myself, because it will get you to Korea.

Flight departure was delayed due to some mechanical problem. There were two other younger passengers with me who started to have second thoughts about boarding the plane, even after whatever problem to be fixed was handled. I told them that I had over 1,700 hours of flight time as a crewmember in a similar C-130 and that I thought that it was one of the safest aircraft in use today. That seemed to calm them down enough that the two stuck with their plans to take this flight.

Once airborne, I tuned everything out and promptly dozed off. One thing that being in the military teaches a guy is to sleep when he can. Civilians often don't appreciate that ability, and they marvel at my knack to go to sleep at a moment's notice. Too bad for them, I always thought. All of a sudden, I came to full alertness with a start. Something was not right, for the noise of the propellers was louder than normal. The noise went away as quickly as it began and I realized what had happened. One of the turbo-props had gotten out of sync with its neighbor, causing the racket, a problem that the pilot had solved by shutting down the turbine and feathering the prop. I looked out of one of the small left side windows and, sure enough, Number Two propeller was feathered and no longer rotating.

This posed no danger to us, for although one engine was shut down, we still had three, and we could get safely to Taegu on only two. However, that did mean we would not be riding this plane on to Osan, at least not today. I quickly began to form a Plan B. Taking a taxi from Taegu to Osan was out, for even if I could get a driver willing to drive the distance of well over 125 miles, the cost would be prohibitive. I didn't think that a train was the answer because Osan still didn't have any rail service that I knew of. The only mode of transportation to Osan remaining was an intercity bus. I quickly explained the situation to my fellow passengers since they were also traveling to Osan.

I informed them that I could speak the language and, if there were buses to Osan, we could likely get seats for a reasonable cost. Since they were being assigned to Osan, they were traveling on Uncle Sam's dime, and no matter the cost, they would be fully reimbursed, so they agreed to follow my lead. We would take a taxi from the base to the Taegu city bus station and inquire about a bus to Osan. If there wasn't one, we could always return to Taegu Air Base, get a room for the night in the Transit Hotel, and take the next flight to Osan.

We landed and, as I knew he would, the pilot announced that we would all have to deplane as aircraft mechanics worked on the propeller synchronization problem. The loadmaster told us to take our baggage with us since we would be remaining overnight at Taegu, and that we would not be going through Customs until we reached Osan. As I thought about this a bit more, I realize that this was really working out to my benefit. While the bus trip to Osan would certainly take a lot more time, I wouldn't have to go through Customs at Osan. Since this was a cargo flight with a final destination of Osan, both the military and Korean officials assumed that people needing to go through customs would do so at their destinations, not at any intermediary stops. Passengers were not expected to be getting off at Taegu so no Customs agents were on duty.

I really hadn't worried about Customs at Osan because I was confident that I could explain that the gifts I was carrying for Mun-nam and his family were really for an airman and his family living at Osan. It might take a bit of convincing but I thought I could pull it off. The mechanical trouble, however, eliminated that issue altogether. Despite the plane being broken, I thought that the trip was starting out well.

All three of us grabbed a quick bite at the air terminal cafeteria before hopping a taxi to the Taegu city bus station. When we arrived, I quickly looked for the ticket windows to see which one sold tickets for the Ville. There was no such window. Hmm, what to do? I got in line to talk with a ticketing agent. She was surprised to hear an American speak Korean and it took her a few moments to understand what I was saying. It turned out that there was no bus service to Osan, either. I had a momentary sense of things going awry; however, I learned that in the five and a half years I had been gone, the old two-lane MSR – Military Supply Route – from Pusan on the southeast coast to the capital of Seoul had been replaced with a modern four-lane divided highway capable of moving high volumes of automobiles and trucks easily over the mountains and through the valleys at very high speed.

The ticket agent pointed out that the express buses to Seoul would pass right by a highway interchange just a couple of miles outside Osan. I asked her if the driver would stop at the side of the road if we tipped him well. Her response was for me to ask the driver myself as she pointed me in the direction of where he would be preparing the bus for departure in less than an hour.

I located the bus driver, an older Korean man probably in his early forties. When I explained what I had in mind, he readily agreed, saying that his older brother had served with an American combat unit during the Korean War and had nothing but good things to say about GIs. Well, it couldn't get much better than that, so we went back to the ticket window and got our tickets. Holy road trip! We were back in business.

When the driver reached the Osan interchange, he pulled over on the wide shoulder and got out to extract our bags from the luggage storage under the bus. I could see the toll booth at the Osan entrance to the highway just a couple of hundred yards away. Even with our heavy bags, the walk was a piece of cake. As we approached the tollbooth, both the toll taker and the Korean policeman assigned there stepped out to watch us. I addressed them in Korean, explaining briefly what we were doing, eventually asking if one of them would be so kind as to call us a taxi.

With good humor, the toll master went in to take care of that while the cop wanted to know how we came to speak Korean. I explained that the other two GIs worked for me, and that only I spoke any Korean. That seemed to satisfy him and it wasn't long before we saw the headlights of a taxi turn off from the old MSR and onto the road leading up to the interchange tollbooth. Within fifteen minutes of having left the warmth of the long distance touring bus, we were in the Ville. I told the driver where Mun-nam's house was and explained to my fellow travelers that I would be getting off there. I gave them my share of what the fare should be when they would get to the main gate of the base, which was less than ten minutes away.

Mun-nam was surprised to see me, for through his connections on base he had learned that my plane had been delayed at Taegu. I told him that he should have remembered how resourceful I was in getting what I wanted. He just laughed and agreed with me as he ushered me into his new digs. He and his wife had moved up in the world a bit. Now, they had two rooms attached to a new beauty parlor that his wife ran during the day. Mun-nam said that I could sleep on the large couch in the parlor if I desired and I accepted with gratitude.

Then I said that I had gifts for the children and maybe something for the adults as well, if could spread out my A-3 flight bag on the floor. Knowing that boys are rough on things and that this was particularly true in a environment like Korea, I had purchased two strong metal Tonka toys, a dump truck and a bulldozer, for Mun-nam's son who was now about six years old. His daughter was less than two years old and she would have to grow a bit in order to completely appreciate the doll that closed its eyes when on its back, as well as all the clothing accessories that came with it.

For Mun-nam's wife, I had purchased what I knew was a very popular perfume with Korean wives on Okinawa: Windsong by Prince Matchabelli, and for his mother I had a package of six multi-colored pure silk scarves with various patterns. I noticed that Mun-nam was looking into my bag, probably wondering what was in there for him. I had saved that for last, tantalizing him a bit, before pulling out a boxed quart of scotch, 32 ounces of Johnny Walker Black Label. His eyes lit up as he weighed the merits of drinking it himself versus selling it on the black market. Either way, he seemed pleased with his gift – as did the others.

It was late, but Mun-nam's wife offered me a bowl of leftover rice with kimchee and some side dishes, which I scarfed down hungrily. People had to work the next day, so we all turned in. The couch in the beauty parlor was quite acceptable, for I had slept on worse things in my military career. The next morning after some hot tea, I accompanied Mun-nam on his way to the base. I intended to meet with my former professor and get a big breakfast somewhere, preferably not at the chow hall.

When I inquired at the Officers Quarters front desk, the clerk rang his room but there was no answer on the telephone. I figured that the professor had scored in the Ville last night and had yet to make his way back to base, so I got permission to leave my bag there behind the counter and I went off to the NCO Club for breakfast. When I entered the club, the first person I saw was Ruthie. She was standing with her back to me talking to an attractive Korean woman in her late 20s sitting at one of the tables, presumably a wife of some guy. The woman looked familiar and she stared at me for several seconds before turning away as Ruthie came over to take my order. She reminded me of Lucy, but I remembered Lucy as being a bit shorter and somewhat heavier. I was curious about the woman but I knew better than to ask Ruthie who would likely tell me to not mess with the wife of another man.

After breakfast, I went back to the professor's place. He was looking worse for the wear and he explained that he had partaken of too much cheap booze in the course of the evening. I thought nothing about that for I had done the same on too many occasions to mention. It was too bad that I didn't have any

Bacchus-D on me to help him out. Anyway, we made plans to take a taxi up the road to Suwŏn to catch the bus for Taegu and then transfer to another for the trip to Kyŏngju.

I had pointed out to him that there were a number of historical sites in the Kyŏngju area that dated back to the time of the Three Kingdoms period in Korea. I had studied them during my language training and of course had seen pictures, but I had not actually been on site. Now I had that opportunity.

We left the next morning and arrived in Kyŏngju without incident, merely tired and achy from being cooped up in a bus for a large portion of the day. We found a restaurant near the bus station and got a quick Korean meal along with a couple of beers. Mun-nam had given me a bit of advice on where to look for sleeping arrangements – he had suggested a Korean style hotel for its prices, rather than a Western one which would be much more expensive.

Mun-nam was right, the hostel was quite cheap, particularly so since the one room was big enough for both of us, and it came with two separate sleeping pallets plus a folding screen to offer a bit of privacy if desired. I wasn't sure but I thought that the professor would have preferred something more Western. Even if he did, he did not offer to pay for any upscale accommodations and so the hostel is what we accepted. That night, the professor got quite drunk in a nearby bar while I held back since I did not want to go around sightseeing with a hangover that even Bacchus-D wouldn't cure.

The next morning, we got up late and had an early lunch before heading to the nearby Pulguksa Temple grounds. I found it to be absolutely fascinating and used more than two rolls of film in photographing the buildings and structures that dated back as far as 1,200 years ago. The professor, however, seemed to be stuck in the days he spent on Okinawa, for he tried conversing with the Koreans in Japanese. I warned him that Korea and Japan were not on the best of terms because of the harsh treatment Koreans received during the Japanese occupation from the turn of the twentieth century until the end of World War II. It didn't register with him and I felt continually embarrassed as he spouted a language that older Koreans would recognize with distaste, if not actual hatred.

There was enough to occupy our time for most of the day and we stayed until late afternoon. After another inexpensive Korean meal, the professor wanted to pick up some women. I pointed out to him that this was not a camp town, that we would find it difficult to coax any sweet young things to be with us, for if they were seen with foreigners, their value to Korean men would be considerably diminished. It wasn't a racial or cultural thing on the part of the girls; it was strictly economics at work, and few people are more practical than Koreans. The professor was pissed because he thought that my ability to speak Korean would result in him getting laid at a cheaper price. I didn't like the thought of me being his pimp, but I let that go. Neither of us was getting anything that night – and that was just fine with me.

The next day, we intended to do a pilgrimage up to the summit of Mt. Toham, the site of Sŏkkŭram, a man-made cave built with its entrance facing to the east and containing a statue of Buddha. I had been taught that the Buddha originally had a ruby affixed in its forehead such that when the morning sun arose out of the East Sea – the Sea of Japan as it is referred to by the Japanese – its rays struck the ruby and were diffused to cast a rosy glow throughout the chamber. I wanted to see that, and climbing the mountain is what Buddhist travelers were expected to do.

In fact, we arose far too late to be at the mountaintop in time to see the first rays of the sun, but I was not eager to climb the mountain in the dark in the first place. We decided to just do the climb of over 2,000 feet and see the grotto with the benefit of daylight. Since we would be leaving for the port city of Pusan at the end of the day, we took our packs with us to avoid spending another night at the hostel.

Not far into the trek up the mountain, we both realized our mistake. We could have checked our baggage at the bottom of the path up the mountain but we thought, being Americans, we could make the trek without having to pay for storage – a bit of arrogant stupidity on our part. However, we had a bit of luck, for halfway up the mountainside was an enterprising young man with a refreshment stand. The prices he charged for ice-cold drinks reflected the effort involved in lugging cases of beer, soda pop, and ice 1,000 feet or thereabouts up a narrow, twisting, and rugged path. For a small fee, he would safeguard our stuff until we returned on the way down. He probably figured on making another sale of liquid refreshments to those dumb ass Americans as well.

So on we went until we crested the mountain. I was quite fatigued and the professor was not in the best condition either. After all, a two thousand foot climb is the equivalent of some four thousand stair steps. I didn't know many people that can do that. The last few feet were the toughest, but the surprise that awaited us was crushing. We pushed through a tangle of brush and debris at the top, only to step into a large paved parking lot filled with tour busses and taxis. We had struggled up the mountain only to realize that a crush of tourists had beaten us – and they had done so in complete comfort. That ruined some of the value behind our spiritual pilgrimage.

After a few moments, I began to see the humor in this, but not the professor. However, my amusement rapidly evaporated when it dawned on me that we would have to walk back down the mountain in order to retrieve our packs from the refreshment stand at the halfway point. Even so, I salvaged some of the pride lost from foolishly hauling our stuff halfway up the mountain by congratulating myself on having made a spiritual trek, a true pilgrimage, just as any Buddhist devotee would have done. And the distant view of the East Sea from the mountaintop was indeed incredible. The manmade cave with its great statue of Buddha was impressive as well, although I soon realized that the story about a ruby capturing enough of the morning sun to cast a rosy glow about the cavern was likely just one of those legends that doesn't bear up under much scrutiny. In any case, there was no ruby.

The ordeal of going down the mountain was much harder than you might think, because muscles are normally used to rapidly push weight up, not to slowly lower weight down. After another Korean supper and a couple of beers, we turned in, very tired and beginning to feel some soreness from all the exercise and having decided to spend another night at the hostel anyway.

The next morning, we caught a bus for the port of Pusan. I had read about how a Korean naval commander, Yi Sun-shin, had used the famed Korean turtle ships in defeating the Japanese navy and thus turning back the last in a series of Japanese invasions of Korea in the late 1590s. I had visited the exhibit on Admiral Yi in the museum in Seoul, but since we were near Pusan, I wanted to see the statue erected there in his honor. The professor wanted to go to Pusan for another reason: he figured that as a major port city, Pusan would have a wild and decadent waterfront, particularly during the evening hours, suitable for accommodating the wants and needs of visiting mariners. In that he was correct.

After arriving in Pusan in early afternoon, we visited the park with the statue of Admiral Yi and then got rooms in a medium-quality hotel, the professor being tired of sleeping on pallets on the floor. As we checked in, I was appalled to hear the professor blatantly inquiring as to where the entertainment girls were. I was equally astonished to hear the desk clerk respond without missing a beat that the hotel had a fine whiskey lounge on the top floor and that he was certain we could find whatever type of girl we wanted from among the "hostesses" that would be there. I jumped in to ask in Korean whether those "hostesses" were kisaengs. He assured me that the young women were not; the ladies were available for "appointments" with guests wanting their kind of service. Holy hookups! This hotel had its very own whorehouse on the top floor.

As we rode in the taxi to a restaurant recommended by the hotel concierge – the professor wanted American food – I engaged the driver in a bit of conversation. I was not particularly enamored of picking out a bedtime partner from a stable of consorts offered by any hotel. In fact, since I did not know my way around this town at all, I was inclined to exercise a bit of patience until I was back in the Ville. Although I no longer knew any of the young ladies there, I did know the lay of the land, so to speak.

The taxi driver explained that most American visitors go to Texas Street near the waterfront. "Texas Street"? Why in hell is a thoroughfare in Pusan called "Texas Street"? The driver could not answer that, but he insisted that it was the place where all the sailors celebrated when they got off their ships. There were bars, girls, shops catering to foreigners, restaurants, more bars, and more bar girls. The driver offered to take us there and run up and down the street once for under $5, just to get a feel for it. I agreed and told the professor what was happening. His face lit up like a starving man smelling food.

Texas Street ought to have been named "Sleaze Avenue." Even in the late afternoon sunlight, it was unadulterated coarseness. I hadn't seen anything liked that since the one time I visited a border town in northern Mexico so that I could say that I had been there, or when my sponsor Harry took me to the Japanese "art theater" right after I got to Japan. There were restaurants and tailors and souvenir shops, all right. But the number of bars reminded me of the small town just outside Yokota Air Base in Japan. There must have been over two hundred drinking establishments. Not many business women were visible, but the ones that were lounging in doorways or hanging out windows looking for customers appeared mean and angry – and they weren't that attractive. Without consulting the professor, I directed the driver to proceed to the restaurant.

The steaks were tough and overcooked and the vegetables were merely lukewarm. All in all, it was a most unsatisfactory meal, but I am convinced that the hotel concierge would get a kickback for having sent us there. This wasn't a case of Koreans ripping off Americans; it was a case of a business ripping off unsophisticated visitors of any nationality who were highly unlikely to ever return anyway. It didn't sit well with me, though, as the professor and I split the bill. I said that I would get the tip, which I did – a single 100-won note, worth about 12 cents. To hell with them, and I hoped that the cook had to use a pheasant talon when he made water.

Neither of us wanted to patronize the hotel-endorsed flesh-peddling lounge on its top floor, so we took a taxi to the hotel but walked around the area looking for drinking establishments more to our liking. We found a few, but the first two had no ladies in residence and we quickly moved on after only poking our noses in. The next bar suited me just fine. It was an upscale version of one of the clubs in the Ville and there were several young women hanging around looking for business.

I told the professor that we needed to sit at the bar for a bit to see how things played out. I ordered a scotch for the professor and a whiskey for me. It wasn't long until two of the more adventurous ladies came over to chat with us. Both wanted us to buy them high-priced lady drinks – likely to be iced tea rather than booze – but I declined, saying that was what bar girls in Japan did to make a living. The professor joined the conversation – in Japanese. The young ladies looked perplexed, wondering why someone obviously Caucasian would choose to speak Japanese to them in Korea. I quickly explained that the professor had last been assigned to Japan and that he was mentally stuck on his first foreign language.

One of the women remarked that she was born well after the Japanese occupation but that her parents had often condemned the Japanese for their brutal treatment of Koreans. In a harsh tone, I told the professor to stick with English even though the other woman admitted that they often entertained visiting Japanese businessmen. Crisis averted, the four of us chatted about this and that until it was time to make further arrangements. Expensive by Ville standards, the two beauties agreed to spend the night with the professor and me at our place.

As we entered the hotel and waited for the elevator, I noticed the desk clerk glancing at us and hurriedly making notes. I knew that no good would come of that even though I didn't know exactly what was going on or how it would turn out.

The next morning when we checked out, the bill showed charges for two extra guests – and we were in no position to argue. The young ladies were indeed extra guests without a doubt, since they clearly had not come from the top floor hotel lounge. The professor was about to throw an Ugly American fit, which would serve no purpose beyond irritating the smug manager who had come out of his office to face us. I was in the habit of carrying a US $100 bill in a secret compartment of my wallet for emergencies, and this situation certainly qualified. It wouldn't cover the entire amount of the extra charges but it was in hard U.S. currency, a fact that would add considerably to its face value. I had taken the manager aside to get him away from the professor and admitted that I did indeed understand his position. I then pulled out my wallet to extract the greenback, and when I saw his eyes flash, I knew we had a deal. I would replace the Benjamin in my wallet when I got back to Okinawa.

I was pleased to have escaped what could have been a truly sticky situation with as little fuss as we did. The professor, on the other hand, still wanted to make a scene until I finally convinced him that there was no way we could have won that argument. He protested that we were Americans and that we should not allow ourselves to be treated that way. With disgust, I pointed out that at the moment we were not in America and that he had no idea what a Korean jail was like.

Finally, the professor stopped ranting enough to agree that it was time that we find the Pusan bus station and purchase tickets back to the Ville. He wasn't impressed with the Osan highway interchange exercise that we would have to endure, but he reluctantly acknowledged that it was the best way to get back to Osan.

Once we were on the bus and it was underway, I turned away to nap during the long ride back to the Ville. Before I fell asleep, I began to wonder about the value of a PhD, if the only thing that amount of education did was to make a person arrogant. I no longer saw the professor as an exalted wellspring of knowledge, for he was just another self-centered oversexed American dick-head to the core. I saw this part of my vacation to Korea as a failure and I was looking forward to spending the rest of it with Mun-nam and the gang before my return to Okinawa.

Chapter Twenty-One: The Return of the Dragonfly

By August of 1980, I was back in Korea after two years in the States following my years on Okinawa. During that time, I had earned a bachelor's degree in Asian Studies, and I also had garnered two more promotions. I was now a senior NCO and I would have my own section of people to supervise at Osan. That was all fine, but Korea had changed. Although I had made a number of short business trips to Korea and as well as spending some vacation days there over the years, it had been nearly eight years since I had spent any significant amount of time in country. It would take some getting used to the differences.

For one thing, there were American women all over the place. Freedom's Frontier, as Korea had often been labeled due to the tensions between the North and the South, had evidently become much less risky, at least in the eyes of the politicians. As a result, the Air Force allowed its career personnel to bring their wives and families along with them when being assigned to Osan. Of course there was a catch, since if an airman did bring his family to Korea, his tour of duty was no longer just thirteen months but two and a half years. For some guys, having their families accompany them was worth the increased time in Korea. For others, though, Korea remained too primitive a place by their standards – or perhaps they actually wanted the time away from their domestic obligations – and they chose to do an unaccompanied tour that was now only twelve months.

In the larger scheme of things, though, and more important than having American wives and family at Osan, female members of the military had finally been allowed to join their male counterparts in nearly every Air Force occupational specialty. The impact of this was that the Skivvy-Nine

Operations Building was no longer a bastion of males that could freely express ribald humor and engage in bawdy practical jokes. Even the Orderly Room that handled the non-operational administrative duties for the unit had women assigned there. I was not at all opposed to that, but it certainly was a change – and I would have to watch my language very carefully from now on.

When I had gotten off the plane at Osan, I was looking forward to seeing my military sponsor, as I had known him from my days at Yokota, my first overseas assignment more than a decade ago. Unfortunately, he was not there to meet me when I cleared Customs at the air terminal; he was in Rehab for alcoholism, and the person in charge of the Skivvy-Nine sponsorship program had failed to designate a replacement. Fortunately, I still remembered my way around the base, so I just grabbed a taxi and went straight to the Orderly Room.

I arrived there still slightly miffed that a sponsor had not met me to provide the informal "heads up" briefing that career people expect when arriving at a new unit. Instead, I was forced to present myself like some low-end salesman making a cold call on some unsuspecting customer. One of the clerks behind the counter, a female junior NCO, quickly realized that I was a new assignee and greeted me with a beautiful smile. I had been mentally preparing to lodge a complaint about no one meeting me, but those thoughts rapidly vanished as I found myself captivated by her presence. It wasn't her beauty, although she certainly a long way from being ugly; it was her personality. We engaged in an inordinate amount of small talk as she helped me fill out all the necessary paperwork. It seemed to me that she was very friendly in addition to being quite the touchy-feely type. Either she was a big flirt, or ....

Fortunately, I quickly realized that I had better assume a more professional demeanor as we continued with the business of getting me set up yet again in Skivvy-Nine. At one point during the process, she glanced up to greet a Korean man entering the room, a Mr. Lee by name. I did not immediately recognize him as the former houseboy that had so kindly extended a dinner invitation to me when I first visited Korea with my friend Buck sixteen years ago. Mr. Lee was now in charge of all the houseboys for Skivvy-Nine and, as such, he was an official member of the squadron administrative staff, even having his own desk in the Orderly Room. We had crossed paths a few times during my various stays in Korea and he did remember me. Now we shook hands as I congratulated him on his success.

Another change that had occurred in the years I was away was that the barracks were no longer open bay style of bunks with their head ends against the wall and separated by large standing lockers. Each barracks wing had been divided into four rectangular rooms of about 10 feet by 15 feet, plus a private entry area, a clothes storage area, and a shared bathroom between each pair of rooms. Depending upon rank, rooms were occupied by two junior personnel or one senior person. As a senior NCO, I was assigned a private room in a barracks housing only those of similar rank. I was a bit disappointed to not be in a Skivvy-Nine barracks even though I recognized that having a single room was a case of rank having its privileges, and that it was not a trivial benefit.

I wasn't in any hurry to hit the Ville in view of the fact that Mun-nam was no longer in Korea. After his mother had died, shortly after my last visit more than two and a half years ago, Mun-nam and his family had somehow obtained visas to emigrate to the States. Although we had stayed in contact through letters and Mun-nam had even called me once from his new home when I was also in the States, I had been unable to visit him due to the distance involved and my frequent military travels. I was glad that he was able to realize his desire to get to the States, but the Ville would not be the same for me without him.

Some things in the Ville hadn't changed, though. Souvenir shops and restaurants offered the same sorts of things they always had, and tailors and cobblers continued to hawk their goods to potential American customers. Airmen still got drunk and business women continued to entice them with their charms, while makkŏlli and soju continued to be the drinks of working-class Koreans.

Now, however, there were sidewalks and sewers and well-paved streets. I was shown all of this and more on my official tour of the Ville conducted by the top squadron leadership, a recent practice to ensure that newly arrived supervisors became aware of the environment that their subordinates would be dealing with when off duty. I didn't tell them that I could give them a far more informative tour of the real Korea that would shock and amaze them. As it was, I diplomatically kept my mouth shut for once and noticed how young the business women seemed – or was it me, now entering my late-30s, just getting older?

After establishing myself at work and arranging my room in the barracks, I spent a lot of time in the Skivvy-Nine lounge next to the Orderly Room in order for people to get to know me and for me to know them. There is no better way to learn about people than mingling with them when off duty. I made certain, however, not to interfere with their pool games, dart contests, or social interactions. I was just being there, becoming acquainted with my new squadron mates.

One night in the lounge shortly after my arrival, I saw Linda, the clerk that had processed my paperwork to get me established with the squadron, as she finished working late in the office next door. She was looking for a seat and I motioned for her to join me at the bar, flippantly offering to buy her a cup of coffee. She hopped onto the stool next to me to reply with a wide grin, "They don't serve coffee here, but I'll drink a beer with you." I thought that was a rather flirtatious response since she had maintained her hand on my bare forearm as she spoke. We finished our drinks and, since Linda had scarfed down a cheeseburger with fries delivered from the Snack Bar, I excused myself for the NCO Club to learn what they had as the dinner special that night.

After eating and back at my own barracks, I made an appearance at the lounge that had been built in what had formerly been the community latrine before individual rooms with shared baths were built. Barracks lounges were hit-or-miss affairs, being left to the occupants of each particular barracks to furnish and improve the area as they saw fit. The senior NCO barracks lounge sported a nicely appointed bar with six stools that had been built by previous occupants. The room also had a felt-covered poker table and chairs, a large couch, a few chairs, and a good-sized color TV console hooked up to a VCR. There was also a large bookcase populated with pulp fiction paperbacks and porn tapes.

I was welcomed by the senior NCOs already there – and then informed that lounge dues were a case of beer or a bottle of whiskey at personal expense each month. That wasn't a big deal since guys could legally purchase far more beer and whiskey than they could individually consume. The goods were then sold back to residents and their guests at reasonable prices with the proceeds used to fund special occasions like promotion parties and other social events. Tonight, however, the older Korean woman, a Ms. Yun, who was tending bar informed me that my drinks were on the house to celebrate my arrival.

When she learned that I spoke Korean, I thought that she would never stop talking to me. Although we never discussed it explicitly, it soon became evident that she had become a single mother rather late in life and that tending bar in our barracks lounge was to supplement her day job as a seamstress on base. She asked for my name as I left, to which I responded by saying in Korean, "You have been talking with the Dragonfly." She took in my offhand remark with undue seriousness, and I would forever be "Master Sergeant Dragonfly" to Ms. Yun.

I got to know the rest of my fellow barracks mates in due course and discovered that they were a sundry mix of occupational specialties. We even had a few senior NCOs from the Army who supervised the soldiers manning the numerous anti-aircraft artillery emplacements defending the base from any aerial attack.

It was actually a bit of a surprise when I realized that Osan was a good social environment. The NCO Club often presented USO shows from the States or great Korean acts from Seoul, the Skivvy-Nine lounge was there for mingling with my work associates, the barracks lounge had my age and rank peers, and there was the Ville if I wanted wilder entertainment. In addition, there was the movie theater, the Service Club, and of course my old friend, the golf course.

I was taken aback somewhat to learn that one of my barracks mates, Xavier, had found an even better way to enhance his particular social opportunities. It was a case of having his cake – in the form of a short tour in Korea – and eating it, too, pardon the pun – by the simple act of flying his wife in from the States to join him. Xavier had only recently married, perhaps his second marriage, and he was unwilling to spend a year separated from his new wife. Since he was close to retirement, the length of a family tour in Korea would interfere with his intent to leave the service at the end of his twenty years. The solution was to bring his wife over at his own expense to live with him in his small room. They used his small quarters as their private retreat and spent much of their time in the barracks lounge, at the movies, or the like.

To everyone's surprise and relief, Xavier's wife had rapidly adapted to the rowdy and bawdy behavior that went on in our lounge, to the point that most of us often viewed her as just another guy. She even critiqued the porn tapes, scoffing at the improbable boobs and the faked passion – but right after the porn tape reached its predictable ending, she and Xavier would quietly disappear to their private room. In effect, the barracks lounge became their living room. In addition, everyone certainly appreciated the accomplished cooking skills she brought to our social events. Of course, the brass would have strongly disapproved of the arrangement; however, as senior NCOs, all of us knew when and how to bend the rules for the general welfare of the troops, particularly when Uncle Sam wasn't being harmed. The houseboys certainly weren't going to make a stink, for they knew who it was that paid their salaries, and Xavier more than likely paid his houseboy a little extra to handle the additional laundry.

Late one weekend late afternoon as I was in the barracks lounge reading a book, Ms. Yun asked if she could speak with me about a personal matter. I cautiously replied that she could, but she wanted to talk privately in my room. I was hesitant in being alone with her simply because I had no idea what she wanted. After several false starts in Korean that I was barely able to follow, she was able to get across to me that her daughter had dropped out of school several months ago and now had just turned 18. The daughter was quite pretty, according to Ms. Yun, so she would probably soon have boy trouble and maybe even get married to some poor laborer in the Ville. Ms. Yun had bigger and better plans for her little Myŏng-tal.

She asked me to teach her daughter how to sexually please Americans so that she could entice some airman to marry her, after which the daughter and her husband would return to the States with Ms. Yun as part of their extended family, presumably to a better life. Ms. Yun had heard that Americans tended to have larger penises than Korean men and that all military men enjoyed receiving oral sex. She explained that Korean women normally weren't down for that. However, if her precocious Myŏng-tal were to develop skills in those areas, she would be able to capture the heart of some serviceman who would marry her. I was thunderstruck by both the depravity and the practicality of her thinking. Setting aside the moral and cultural issues, I had to admit to myself that the plan – if properly implemented – would have a very good chance of working, for even though her daughter was very young and extremely naïve, she was indeed a beauty.

Now it was my turn to have difficulty with words. I could not outright refuse Ms. Yun, for that would be a tremendous loss of face for her, in light of the seriousness of what was being offered – not just her daughter, but her daughter's virginity. I also knew that I could not possibly do what she expected. I admitted to Ms.

Yun that her daughter was truly a stunning young lady but that I would not be able to instruct her in American carnal arts, simply because I was involved already with another woman who was wearing me out. I had nothing left for another woman, no matter how desirable.

Ms. Yun reluctantly accepted this, saying that she understood, before asking me if my lady friend was an American military woman. I lied that was indeed the case. Ms. Yun remarked that from what she had heard, American women seemed to enjoy sex more than Korean women. I did not tell her that I certainly did not find that to be true, but I had created an excuse that worked, and I wanted to end this conversation as quickly and cleanly as possible. Besides, I always felt that virginity was an overrated – highly questionable – virtue.

I had just turned down what some men dream about, and the conversation had put me in the mood for some female companionship, so I wandered over to the Skivvy-Nine lounge. Now that women were fairly well integrated into most Air Force units, I had discovered that there was always some level of social activity between the genders. As long as a few common sense rules were observed, no one seemed to have much of an issue with it. I had already learned of several such relationships, a couple of which were rather long-term and seriously romantic affairs, while others seemed to be less formal and more of a friends-with-benefits relationship. There were even a very few women who played around quite a bit, openly establishing themselves as being in the game for whatever gains could come their way.

I thought about Linda, the clerk that had seemed so friendly when I checked in to the unit and who had later shared a drink with me a few nights after that. She was not in the lounge when I entered, but I had a whiskey at the bar, hoping that she would show up. She didn't come in by the time I had finished my drink, so I decided on the NCO Club for dinner. When I returned to the Skivvy-Nine lounge a little over an hour later, Linda was sitting at one of the tables with her roommate, one of the women in a long-term friends-with-benefits relationship. Linda waved me over to sit with them.

The roommate was playing darts with her boyfriend as a teammate. Every few minutes she would leave us as her turn to throw came up. This gave Linda and me many chances to talk, but I am often very slow in making my move in such circumstances. As the evening wound down, most of the people were leaving, although Linda stayed behind to talk with me. It was clear that we liked each other, at least to some degree, and soon only the bartender remained. I knew that I needed to make something happen or it would forever be too late. I asked Linda how her roommate and her boyfriend ever got together, since they were roommates. Linda looked at me with a mischievous grin before admitting that she often slept on the couch in her barracks lounge to give them privacy.

Without thinking, I said with all sincerity, "Well, that is just not right, you need a better place to stay – why not my room?" As soon as the words had been uttered, I realized that I was running the risk of offending Linda. I wished that I could take the words back as I saw her take a deep slow breath. As I hastily began to form an apology, Linda let her breath out in a long exaggerated whoosh to say, "Geezus, I thought you'd never take the hint! I've been waiting ever since you bought me the beer that night." With that, she kissed me. Holy hot lips!

The lounge was closing, so I bought a six-pack of beer to stock my small refrigerator. Linda and I then walked arm in arm to my room for a delightful night followed by a late breakfast together at the NCO Club in the morning.

I eventually took Linda on tours of the Ville, which she had rarely visited, to show her all the places where I had hung out so many years ago, parts of Korea that most Americans never see. On one of those excursions, Mom of the Camellia House, my makkŏlli house retreat of long ago, had evidently recognized me despite several years having gone by, for she had stopped me on the street to rebuke me with some indignation for preferring American women now that I was older.

Linda was more than a bit curious about my conversation with a Korean woman who was obviously at least two decades older than me but who nonetheless seemed to know me well. I reluctantly summarized the brief exchange as Linda got a rather amused look on her face. She had chuckled, saying that obviously I had better taste these days.

One late night when Linda and I were in the Skivvy-Nine lounge, a junior airman rushed in to say that the base commander had just pulled up in his chauffeured car and appeared to be heading for our lounge. None of us were impressed, and we continued with whatever we were doing – drinking, shooting pool, or throwing darts. The general did indeed enter the lounge as his driver called the room to attention. Before we could react, however, the general told us to stay as we were. Since all of us were slow in responding anyway, the only change in our postures was everyone turning to look at the general who was still wearing his billed garrison hat.

The bartender quickly rang the gong at the end of the bar, signaling that some dumb ass had worn a hat inside. Military regulations require that headgear be removed upon entering buildings. I did not see who it was that loudly proclaimed, "He buys the bar a round!" but I knew that this was serious, for if the general refused to follow a well-honored Skivvy-Nine lounge tradition, things would go badly. The general thought about the situation for perhaps one full second – which seemed like an eternity at the time – before reaching the same conclusion. He pulled $20 out of his wallet with a grand flourish and then respectfully placed the bills on the bar before leaving the lounge as quickly as he had entered. He had spoken only the three words, "As you were," before reconsidering his impromptu visit. The general must have heard the raucous laughter and hoots of derision that erupted as he made his way back to his car.

I later heard that our squadron commander received a phone call from the base commander in which the topic of conversation was the *esprit de corps* that had been so boisterously demonstrated the previous evening by a bunch of Skivvy-Niners in the lounge. No one could figure out whether it was a criticism or a compliment, but nobody really gave a rat's ass one way or the other, for we had intimidated the brassy bastard into buying a round of drinks for the entire bunch of us. Every time that Linda and I were reminded of the incident, we had to laugh as the bizarreness of a bunch of low class enlisted swine intimidating a general.

Other things also made her laugh like a little kid. One night as winter was beginning to send a deep and dry Siberian cold spell our way, the vintage oil-fired heater in my barracks gave out. One of the guys made a call to the maintenance squadron in charge of such things, only to be informed that it would be several hours before a crew could get to us, the numerous operational emergencies taking precedence over residential problems. Linda's roommate was entertaining that night, but now Linda and I had an additional – but totally unnecessary –

reason to stay close for warmth.

I had ordered a custom fold-up double-size mattress from a Korean bedding shop, the one that had furnished my one-room off base retreat so many years ago. It looked like a collapsible Japanese futon, although I refrained from using that term, with the added benefit of it being able to serve as padding for a couch when folded over a frame I built with the help of my houseboy. This replaced the standard single-sized military bunk normally in the room, which the houseboy had stored away. As the temperature inside dropped in response to the chill wind blowing outside, Linda and I unfolded the bedding and got under the covers to cuddle.

I knew we had enough blankets to survive the lack of heat comfortably, but I hadn't reckoned on the extremely dry Siberian air being so conducive to static electricity. When she moved about, Linda noticed that she created little sparks by rubbing against the covers, and I certainly detected them as she ministered to a very sensitive part of my male anatomy. She thought that it was hilarious as she then went to great lengths to create more and larger sparks. I decided to reciprocate in kind, and between the two of us, we ultimately generated our own *aurora borealis* that night.

Not every social encounter between the genders in Korea was pleasant or entertaining. Many marriages between Americans and Koreans don't work out, for two very basic reasons: the cultural or social differences, and an inability to communicate effectively on important matters. One junior NCO I knew, a Skivvy-Niner named Thornstaff, had married a very young and extremely unsophisticated Korean business woman. His wife knew practically nothing about American culture and Thornstaff was forced to constantly deal with her lack of knowledge and social limitations in order to make her feel less uncomfortable. She was indeed attractive, but I still failed to understand why he decided to marry her.

One night I had gone to the NCO Club for dinner only to find that the main ballroom was nearly full, probably in anticipation of a USO show from the States scheduled to take the stage later that evening. Off to the side of the ballroom, was a smaller and quieter place, often used for private parties, where people could eat. Normally, I didn't go there so as to leave those tables for families, but that night I had no other choice. As it turned out, the side room was almost full as well, but I noticed Thornstaff and his wife about the same time they saw me. He invited me over to dine with them and I gratefully sat down, pleased to be able to eat without further worries about seating.

They had just ordered but the efficient waitress hurried over so that I could quickly make my selection in time to be served with them. Thornstaff had ordered steak for his wife and fried chicken for himself, and I decided on the meatloaf. Our dinners arrived and I dug in, paying little attention to the others until out of the corner of my eye, I noticed that Thornstaff was using his own knife and fork to cut the steak for his wife. I must have been staring, for he matter-of-factly explained that she did not know how to use Western utensils. I redirected my attention back on my own grub, but I could not get that vision out of my mind as I wondered how this poor creature was going to adapt to life in the States.

I casually mentioned this later to Linda, who remarked that she felt that it was Thornstaff who was lucky to have found someone to marry him, as she thought it was he who was the poor creature. Linda felt that he was not very masculine. She then related another story about an extremely macho guy, an event that had occurred before I arrived. His Korean wife argued with him constantly about the time and money he wasted on drinking at the NCO Club after his shift before going home to her. Their relationship had deteriorated to the point where he verbally and physically abused her out of frustration with her nagging. When he went back to the States at the end of his tour, she chose to remain in Korea. They would be divorced eventually and she would then lose all of her base privileges, possibly reverting back to being just another – and older – business woman in the Ville.

I thought about that and the fact that I had come across some really nice Korean women over the years. Ok-ja – and Lucy too, for some reason – readily came to mind, but Ok-ja had refused to get involved with me, and Lucy was married. My reckoning at the time was that none of the others would have made a good life-long partner for me, and I congratulated myself for not having gotten myself into such a situation.

Chapter Twenty-Two: Some Unpolished Brass

Most career enlisteds, despite occasionally griping about officers, truly appreciate leaders that are worthy of following. Skivvy-Niners were no exception, and every one of us knew how to deal with the brass when those senior officers performed in the proper manner; that is, they actually led by principled example and thoughtful inspiration, rather than by caprice and dictum.

Although all of the lounge occupants had enjoyed a good laugh at the expense of the base commander who had walked into our squadron lounge late one evening, some of us eventually came to realize that the general actually deserved our respect and admiration. First of all, he had honored our tradition and he did not try to avoid any accountability by pulling rank. I doubted that the $20 meant much to him, but the act of buying us all a round of drinks was, at least in my mind, a real class act. I also later concluded that, because of the congenial manner in which he had dealt with our challenge, the general hadn't left the lounge out of defeat or even in embarrassment, but rather because of the realization that his presence had not been needed. It became a life lesson for me: A good leader knows when to lead and when to get out of the way.

In any career that spans twenty or more years, members of the military can expect to encounter all kinds of officers, and that was certainly true for Skivvy-Niners as well. By virtue of the demands in our field, most of our officers were intelligent and caring leaders. A few, mostly butter-bars, either grew to meet the level of responsibility required of their positions or they were soon ignored – and then mustered out of our field. At the top, however, officers needed to be at the peak of their game right from the start, and this was mostly true. There were, however, a notable few that were miserable failures because of having reach the limits of their abilities or due to their willingness to inflict military chicken-shit upon those under their command.

Now anyone who has spent even the slightest amount of time in and around the military knows that fraternization, specifically between officers and enlisteds, is a huge no-no. There is strong justification behind this, for such relationships compromise the ability to command. Further, the power levels are not equal in such relationships, and officers have inappropriate advantages over enlisteds. It also applies to enlisted personnel having unprofessional relationships with those that they supervise. Strictly speaking, the relationship that Linda and I shared was probably not officially condoned. However, even though I was senior to her by two pay grades, I was not her boss – and she had total control over my military records, anyway. Most reasonable people would say that made us pretty damned equal in power and any relationship would be peer to peer.

On the other hand, recently commissioned and newly arrived Second Lieutenant Underhill, despite obviously having attained a college education, had little common sense. He was a colossal mistake just waiting to happen. We all knew he was bound to screw up, although no one could have predicted how dramatic it would be and what kind of punishment would ensue. Eventually, Underhill did make a fateful mistake in judgment and he wound up being doubly penalized.

It wasn't a case of double jeopardy at all, which most people really don't understand in the first place. To explain in simple terms, the prohibition against double jeopardy merely means that a person cannot be tried for the same crime in the same judicial system. That is applicable in the Uniform Code of Military Justice – UCMJ – system, as well. Sometimes, however, Lady Justice, being blindfolded, administers poetic justice rather than judicial punishment. Underhill became a remarkable example of that.

Despite being an officer, an attribute almost certain to attract a particular category of women, Underhill exercised very little discretion in his personal affairs. Soon after being assigned to duty in the Operations Building, he happened to observe one of the Skivvy-Nine women who was in play for whatever would benefit her the most – emotional or sexual gratification not necessarily being her highest priorities. Jessica was not any Einstein, but she was smart enough to recognize a sure way to profit from her native gifts.

She had an exceptional pair of breasts that she was not at all opposed to displaying as much as military decorum allowed while in uniform. As it turned out, the many electronic devices in one part of our work area often made for an abundance of heat buildup that contributed to her self-promotions. Air Force regulations notwithstanding, operators had long-standing informal permission to remove their outer work shirts when temperatures climbed, as long as their upper bodies remained covered with a military-style white undershirt. Females were expected to wear brassieres as well.

Jessica was well aware that she possessed a pair that most men were quite interested in seeing, so she made certain to wear the thinnest of tee-shirts as well as the filmiest and flimsiest of bras. Seeing Jessica as she moved about her workstation was like watching great ocean swells gently undulating across the surface of the sea. Underhill – as one who thought about such matters with only his other head – was quite understandably captivated, and he really was compelled to follow wherever his johnson pointed.

What Underhill failed to consider, though, was the risk of such a relationship. For starters, the squadron commander, an aging colonel notorious for his strict old-school ways, would certainly disapprove most vehemently. Perhaps our commander was pissed because he realized that he would never make general. There were other risks as well, and Underhill ultimately paid for his indiscretions in a rather unusual way.

Terry, one of my coworkers, was taking inventory of materials stored in a large closet at the rear of the operations briefing room. The closet was originally designed to house a rear-projection display system for use in briefings, but that rear area also served as a much needed storage closet for many of our smaller and less-frequently used supplies. Terry heard the briefing room door open and the voice of our commander ordering someone inside. Before Terry could announce his presence, the commander launched into a tirade of abuse directed at someone Terry soon realized was the poor unthinking Underhill. The commander said that he was able to easily identify Underhill as the only second lieutenant in his command who had contracted a sexually transmitted disease – gonorrhea. It seemed that, despite some efforts by the base medical facility to conceal individual identities when reporting medical statistics to squadron commanders, this time the effort had been inadequate. Underhill was chewed out for being "unclean" and therefore bringing shame and embarrassment to Skivvy-Nine.

What a load of chicken-shit! Hell, at any given time, the odds were high that at least one enlisted person in our unit had the clap, but officers were somehow expected to set an example of "clean" behavior. The commander continued his diatribe in the manner of an Old Testament patriarch outraged by a family member who failed to uphold some ancient biblical law. The punishment Underhill received was a lowered rating on his annual efficiency report, which was a permanent part of his military record. However, it was not for fraternization – a guy stupidly dipping his pen in a subordinate's inkwell – because the dumb ass commander was not smart enough to connect some rather obvious dots. As it turned out with regard to that statistical one enlisted person with an STD at any given time, it was Jessica. Indeed, she was the one who gave the clap to the lieutenant, a dose of Mother Nature's poetic justice for failing to use a condom.

Incongruously, an authorized outlet for sexual tension did exist on base and it had the unconditional, if only implicitly expressed, blessing of all the brass. In addition to the normal recreational facilities available on any military base, there was the Steam Room next to the base gym, a concession operated by young and attractive Korean women. Famously referred to as the "Steam and Cream Parlor," it was an officially sanctioned sexual outlet for anyone willing to pay a few bucks above and beyond the price of a regular steam bath and massage. It was impossible that any of the brass remained unaware of the extra-curricular activities that were routinely provided there.

In the beginning, I had felt sorry for Underhill, but after one close encounter of an unwelcome kind, I realized that he was just a dick-head butter-bar with little chance of improvement. In our jobs, we generated a lot of classified waste material that needs proper disposal. Every so often, airmen were selected from a duty roster to perform burn detail. Unlike the ignorant

U.S. State Department, the Air Force first cross-cut shredded the classified waste and then burned it in a furnace designed specifically for the task of handling high volumes of waste effectively and efficiently. It was my turn to supervise the burn detail.

Supervising a burn detail was quite boring until the very end of the duty, when it became dirty. Usually a couple of junior airmen did the work of carefully loading the hopper of the shredder to keep it from churning needlessly due to an inadequate supply of material to chew through as well as not creating a massive paper jam from feeding too much material at a time. Once the paper waste was shredded into bits, it was carried into the burn chamber by air from a high-speed blower. The forced air was not only the carrier of the shredded material but it also served as the primary oxidant for the combustion, sort of like a bellows for a blacksmith. The whole contraption functioned like a miniature blast furnace. The process generated enough heat to melt paper clips and staples, which puddled in the bottom of the burn chamber.

My job was to ensure that all classified material was accounted for when we started and that everything had been completely incinerated at the end. As a final security check, I had to wait until the air blowers cooled the burn chamber down so that I could stick my head inside to inspect it. There was always some amount of soot, but there never were any bits of paper left. Regardless, the burn chamber had to be checked anyway. At the bottom was usually an irregularly shaped mass of melted metal that gleamed brightly. It would make a good paperweight, I decided, since it looked like a gigantic nugget of polished steel, a really nifty-looking glob that would make a nice souvenir.

The final certification needed to be performed by an officer, and I had been saddled with Underhill, who had a different perspective. First, he tried to convince me that there could be bits of classified paper imbedded in the core of the nugget. I openly ridiculed that idea, so then he insisted that he needed to get approval of the commander for me to remove anything from the burn room. Until the commander approved, Underhill said he would have to confiscate it as some potentially classified residue. I knew that he was a lying piece of shit, but he pulled rank on me. Realizing that my argument was lost, I ungraciously tossed the nugget in his direction, hoping that he would not be able to catch it, but he reacted more quickly than expected, making the grab just before it hit the floor.

Several days later, I happened to see my nugget serving as a paperweight in the top tray of his in-basket. I boldly entered his private space and snatched it up without any compunction whatsoever. Even though I am certain that he quickly figured out who had taken the paperweight, he never had the balls to confront me over it.

I started to feel the need to get away from the Operations Building for a spell. Winter wasn't over but there was a break in the weather for the next few days, and to take advantage of that, Linda and I made plans for a long weekend getaway in Seoul. I wanted to show her a couple of the museums and she wanted to do some souvenir shopping since her assignment was coming to an end. We figured that we ought to be able to do all that in three days, so I made reservations for a large room with a view of the city at the Naeja Hotel, a U.S. leased and operated R&R center for military personnel in Korea. The accommodations and service were the best either of us had ever experienced in our lives up to that time and we both enjoyed being away from Osan to the fullest.

On the way back to the base from Seoul, Linda had the window seat in the bus and I was dozing in an attempt to get some sleep – R&R is really a misnomer, for no serviceman ever goes on vacation to *rest.* I was just about asleep when Linda poked me in the ribs with her elbow and excitedly pointed out the window to the rice paddies along the highway. The temperature had dropped below freezing during the night and there was a thin layer of ice covering the rice paddies where wind hadn't disturbed the water surface.

Out in the rice paddies were several Korean men with their pantaloons rolled up above their knees. They were planting some form of winter rice in water than could not have been much above freezing. Linda marveled at their willingness and ability to endure such harsh working conditions. I agreed that those guys were real men, doing what was needed to make a living for their families.

Just before the bus reached Osan in late afternoon, it began to snow – really snow. The break from the cold was over as the weather forecasters were predicting snow for the next two days, with Osan getting perhaps as much as several inches altogether. That night in the Skivvy-Nine lounge, someone came up with the idea to make a snowman. I chimed in with a couple of ideas on how to make something a bit more interesting. After some discussion, the Snow Bitch was born in the minds of the depraved. After laying out the form of a woman on her back in the middle of the street, we added an old string mop head for her locks, two peanut shells for nipples, and a bunch of steel wool for pubic hair. Everyone had to agree that we had posed her in a very seductive pose with one leg canted open invitingly.

As the evening wore on, each person arriving in the lounge commented favorably about our creation – our art was appreciated by all but one. According to the leader of the snowplow crew on duty that evening, a female officer had driven past our Snow Bitch and had been offended enough to demand the plow make a short detour up our street so that the Snow Bitch would be wiped out. We were still in good spirits since the plow driver reported that he enjoyed running the tip of the plow wedge right up between her legs.

We decided that we were not done, that we still wanted to create something new and different so we continued our degenerate thinking. This time it was in the form of a very human-looking snowman, but one with a very noticeable attribute. We felt that the snowman would have had a very favorable reaction to our Snow Bitch, if she had continued to exist. With that in mind, we built the snowman over an inclined broomstick, the result of our efforts being that the snowman sported a rather impressive display of interest in the opposite gender. As the snow continued to fall, our last creation became more and more realistic. Even some of the ladies remarked admiringly about the snowman's exceptional attribute. Linda accused me of being debauched, pausing before adding with a smirk, "but in a good way."

The next morning, as the female officer who had complained about the Snow Bitch passed by the Orderly Room on her way to work, she was greeted by our Snow Dick that was sporting evidence of his pleasure in seeing her. Unlike most of the women in Skivvy-Nine, the officer was not amused. She got out of her vehicle to enter the Orderly Room, demanding that Mr. Lee, the houseboy supervisor, knock down our obscene creation and retrieve the government property broom handle. Some of us began to wonder why a stupid college education seemed to turn people into Puritans.

New Years was fast approaching and since Skivvy-Niners do parties right, we had rented one of the newer clubs in the Ville for the complete evening a day before the actual end of the year. We had wanted to hold the party on New Years Eve itself, but no club that catered to the American military was going to give up that prime date for a relatively calm party. Since it wasn't the official holiday, the midnight to 4 AM curfew would still be in effect, but a big difference was that the bar agreed to stay open all night long, the only requirement being that those staying after midnight had to remain inside the bar until curfew was over. This was a handy excuse for hard-core partiers to continue their excesses for four more hours.

Linda and I arrived at the party after a great meal at the NCO Club. Neither of us wanted to get totally bombed, since drinking on an empty stomach or when blood sugar is low results in a quick drunk – and an equally quick spin, crash, and burn that ends participation in any festivities. I had introduced her to Bacchus-D, something she thought ought to be exported to the States. We each downed a bottle before going to the party, and I had stashed two more bottles in my coat pocket for later.

As we entered the second floor club, I was very pleased to note that the squadron houseboys felt welcome enough to show up. Inviting the houseboys was a statement that we airmen appreciated all that they did for us and that they were not seen as just servants. In fact, my houseboy Mr. Ch'oe and I had developed a good relationship, once he realized that I was a fanatic about Korean language and culture. He felt comfortable enough with me to occasionally ask for one of the Dr. Peppers that I always had stockpiled in my small refrigerator. It was Mr. Ch'oe who had helped me a great deal in turning my Spartan barracks quarters into the warm and welcoming retreat that

Linda and I enjoyed, so I was happy to provide him with an occasional soda.

Since she had taken a liking to Mr. Ch'oe as well, I pointed him out to her as we walked to the bar. I called out to Mr. Ch'oe and wished him a happy new year in Korean as I bowed my head slightly in deference to his age. He seemed pleased he was respected enough that an American would acknowledge his presence. Linda also waved to him, and he smiled even more broadly as she hollered out the standard Korean greeting, "Are you peaceful?" Everyone liked Linda, and unfortunately that included Lt. Underhill.

Not long after we got our drinks – beer for Linda and whiskey for me – Mr. Ch'oe came over to invite me to visit with the houseboys for a while. I felt honored that he would want me to site with his peers and I told Linda that she would be on her own for a while. She laughed and said that she would not be alone for long, as she flicked her eyes in the direction of a noticeably drunken Underhill who was now lurching in her direction. I wasn't pleased about that, but I did not want to make a scene at a squadron event, and certainly not with an officer. However, if he got out of line, all bets were off. I wasn't being possessive, but I wasn't going to have my date for the evening slobbered over by some overpaid bag of bullshit like Underhill. I told her to send for me if she felt the need for a rescue. She said with a smirk that she always had a thing for a guy that helped a damsel in distress.

Sitting with the houseboys required introductions all around, after which I got the inevitable questions of what did I think of Korea. I gave all the standard answers, but then turned the tables by asking each of them a bit about themselves, like did they have families, were they from this area, how long had they been with Skivvy-Nine, and what did they really think about American service members. This last question always generated quite a bit of laughter, but whether the laughter was out of embarrassment or from amusement, I never figured out. We discussed the merits of American beer versus Korean O.B. or Crown – American being the clear preference. It was the same with smokes, and I had once again thought to bring a carton of Marlboros in the flip-top box under my coat for such a contingency.

After more than a half hour with Mr. Ch'oe and friends, I wanted to get back to Linda, but when I looked around the club for her, I saw that she was in a heated discussion with Underhill. I gave Mr. Ch'oe an apologetic look and explained that I had some business to handle. Mr. Ch'oe advised me to be diplomatic, since Underhill was an officer. I agreed but pointed out that a drunken son of a dog was still a dog, no matter what his rank was.

I got to Linda's side just as Underhill slid off his bar stool into a crouch and vomited all over his pants legs and shoes. I thought I had seen Linda push him away, or maybe it was a feminine fist to the gut. Either way, when Underhill was finished heaving, Linda bent down to tell him that he ought to stick with his own kind and that he needed to learn what it meant to be a gentleman. I looked at her quizzically, but all she said was that Underhill made a rather clumsy and crude pass, and that if he made any trouble for her later on, she could use some witnesses to testify about what really happened. Two guys near her spoke up immediately to say that, if they were asked, their statements would demolish Underhill's career if he were stupid enough to charge Linda with anything.

One of the junior employees of the club had been given the

unpleasant task of cleaning up Underhill's mess. Two other squadron officers had rapidly escorted him out of the club and into a taxi with instructions for the driver to go directly back to the Bachelor Officers Quarters without any diversion.

Just about a half-hour before curfew, our squadron commander went around to the officers as well as the senior NCOs to remind them that curfew started at midnight. We were all smart enough to recognize an order when we heard one, no matter how subtly it was couched. He was saying, "Time to RTB" – return to base. I told Linda that I always got a case of the ass when somebody tried to do my thinking for me. She calmed me down, saying that neither of us had intended to party all night anyway, so why not get a head start on finding a taxi. Besides, we could still get some grub from the Snack Bar if we hurried. Linda was right, so I dropped the attitude and picked up our coats. I shouted a "Happy New Year!" in English to the remaining partiers and repeated it in Korean to the houseboys who obviously all had kitchen passes and were going to make a night of it. Clearly, their wives did not wield the same amount of clout as a commanding officer.

Within a few weeks, Linda went on to her next assignment, back to the States and a base near her hometown. I felt at loose ends without her, but my career was winding down and hers was not quite at the midpoint. It would not have been a good match professionally, but even so it was not easy losing a very good friend – especially one that offered such great benefits.

I was curious to see who would take Linda's place, so I stopped by the orderly Room late one afternoon after work. The Orderly Room always had extended hours to handle the issues of people that worked in the operations area. The first person I saw was Mr. Lee, the head houseboy, pacing the halls with his head down and muttering to himself. I had never seen him so upset. At first, he brushed me off, saying that it wasn't any big deal. I didn't believe that, for I had seen Mr. Lee handle disagreements between houseboys who, like all Koreans, can get agitated when expressing themselves.

When he saw that I was truly interested, he told me that he had expected some sort of celebration that day for his having worked for the U.S. military and Skivvy-Nine for twenty years. It was his employment anniversary, and while he wasn't expecting any retirement ceremony, he had thought that people would congratulate him on such a significant achievement in his life. I was so stunned that I didn't know what to say.

It was an impossible situation: I knew that the Orderly Room tracked the employment of Skivvy-Nine houseboys, but I also knew that no one ever thought much about it after the correct data had been annotated in the correct format on the correct form and then put back into the correct folder in the correct drawer of the correct filing cabinet. In truth, Mr. Lee's expectation was unrealistic from the U.S. military point of view, but that wasn't going to make him feel any better. Nearly all of us liked Mr. Lee and thought that he was a great addition to the Orderly Room staff. Without exception, the houseboys respected Mr. Lee for his impartiality and ability to resolve issues quickly and fairly. In short, he was an extraordinary employee who just happened not to be an American.

I offered to buy Mr. Lee a beer in the lounge, but he declined as I knew he would. After seeing all the troubles that drunken airmen got into, he rarely drank anything. Further, he was totally a family man. At the New Years party, he had made an appearance because his houseboys were there, but he left early to be home with his wife and children. I felt horrible that the squadron leadership had failed to show Mr. Lee that he was held in high esteem and that his having achieved twenty years with Skivvy-Nine was indeed a notable accomplishment deserving of some appropriate recognition.

Even though there was no graceful way to salvage the situation after the fact, I did bring it to the attention of the First Sergeant who dismissed my concern as being misplaced since Mr. Lee ought to be grateful that he had a well-paying job that was not physically demanding, and besides all that, he wasn't even in the Air Force. As a Korean, what did he expect, a gold watch or something? I got similar responses from other senior people in the organization. Holy heartlessness! I fervently hoped that the gods pissed all over their own retirement ceremonies when it was time.

Chapter Twenty-Three: Over and Out

Despite all my activities, I felt that I now had a lot of time on my hands. Work was engaging, if a bit boring when compared to flying duties, but it ate up a good piece of only my weekdays. The Skivvy-Nine lounge had lost much of its appeal since Linda had been assigned back to the States, and I found myself hanging out frequently in the barracks lounge, instead of just occasionally as before.

When I noticed that Yancy, one of the Army guys seemed to never be around the lounge anymore, the others related a sad tale. They reminded me that he had been on leave to the States for a month, but he had returned to Osan a few weeks ago. During his vacation, though, the Army brass had pulled a surprise inspection on his troops manning the anti-aircraft artillery batteries around the base. It had been determined that the level of readiness was inadequate, that Yancy's training and supervision had been inadequate, and that he needed to made aware of his inadequacies in an adequate fashion. Immediately upon his return from the States, Yancy was assigned one month of duty right up next to the DMZ, the 2.5-mile wide De-Militarized Zone that served as a buffer between North and South Korea ever since the armistice of the Korean War in 1953.

It was a dangerous place, since the North Korean military often sent raiding parties into the South or fired shells near the DMZ to harass the U.S. and South Korean troops who were stationed there to prevent another invasion. DMZ duty also meant primitive living conditions: often tents rather than permanent structures, inferior chow, meager recreational facilities, and extensive drills and alerts that significantly reduced free time. It was fully intended to be an unforgettable lesson for Yancy, and it was.

When he returned from the DMZ about two weeks after my inquiry, Yancy was no longer an easy-going and pleasant soldier. It was all work and no play as he went about putting the Fear of God – in the form of a seriously pissed-off and intolerant senior NCO – into his troops through his surprise visits in the middle of the night, unscheduled weekend inspections, and practice drills that stopped just short of loading live ammunition. Yancy made it absolutely crystal clear to his troops that he was not going back to the DMZ.

To celebrate his return and help him recover a bit of his former easygoing attitude, we dipped into the barrack lounge fund to throw a grilling party, even though the weather was not cooperating. Two of the guys volunteered to prepare a few dozen deviled eggs if Ms. Yun would assist in the shelling. On the day of the party, it was snowing lightly even though spring was about to begin, but that didn't stop us. With the help of Ms. Yun and her no longer shy daughter, we had the lounge set up with everything necessary for an indoor picnic. By six o'clock, everyone was chowing down on hamburgers, hot dogs, coleslaw, baked beans, deviled eggs, and any garnish that a guy could think of. In honor of the occasion, it was an open bar for all barracks residents. Yancy did lighten up somewhat, but the memory of his thirty days of hard time on the DMZ reminded him to stay on his toes.

As for Ms. Yun, it seemed that she had not given up her goal of getting her daughter prepared for attracting an American mate. After I had declined her shocking offer, she had finally convinced another barracks resident to school her daughter about the finer points of conjugal activity. Manny had accepted the challenge of educating Mrs. Yun's daughter. Nobody ever said anything, but it seemed more than a bit creepy and immoral that a man in his late-30s would deflower a very naïve 18 year old girl and proceed to instruct her in the ways of American sex, all so that she could snag some serviceman with her new skills and thus provide her mother with a comfortable old age. Holy conjugation!

The entire affair just reeked of – I couldn't put my thoughts into words, but it was just wrong with a capital "W"! The rest of us tended to avoid Manny when the now-coquettish Myŏng-tal was in his company. He probably realized that he was, in effect, being shunned, but the lure of attractive young Korean poon was too much for him to resist and he managed to draw out the "training" well into spring.

As the seasons changed to present us with better weather, one of the Skivvy-Niners also found himself in hot water with the brass. We were due for a visit from our headquarters in the States. The visiting team would include the two-star general commander who, despite his short stature, fancied himself as an accomplished tennis player, a Level 5. The squadron had been asked to find a suitable partner to play against the general. For anyone not brain-dead, a suitable player was one that would challenge the general a bit but would somehow manage to snatch defeat from the jaws of victory, so that the general would win, thus preserving the general's reputation as a ranked tennis player.

Ulrick was selected by virtue of his having achieved Level 7 a few years back. That fact alone should have been enough to make him an unsuitable opponent for the general, for as any true racket man knows, Level 7 players are world-class performers who don't like to lose. The match proceeded without incident until the general made an accidental save to break

Ulrick's service. That wasn't the problem, though; it was the gloating and the taunting that ensued. Ulrick was not known for having a great deal of patience, and after a couple of minutes of cheap talk from the general like, "Hey, how about that shot?" and "Gotcha, didn't I?" Ulrick had taken all he could take.

Ulrick moved to his best game, thrashing the general so soundly that there could be no doubt whatsoever that the gasping and over-the-hill officer was out of his league, despite his prideful boasting. After our colonel got an earful over the general's inglorious defeat, a tongue-lashing was later passed down with considerable wrath to Ulrick, who took the verbal dressing down without breaking a sweat. Afterward, Ulrick proudly proclaimed, "I stomped a mud hole up his two-star ass and made him walk it dry, the little bow-legged piss-ant Napoleon-complex sonuvabitch!" The next weekend in the Skivvy-Nine lounge, Ulrick drank whatever he wanted for free.

After that excitement died down in a couple of days, thoughts turned to the upcoming fundraising event carried over AFKN – American Forces Korean Network. I had been amused to learn some years back that some diplomatic fiction prevented American air bases in foreign countries from being called air force bases as they are in the states, and army forts had to be relabeled as camps. Oddly enough, in the beginning, the headquarters of all radio and television services for the military overseas was named the Armed Forces Radio and Television Service, but some politically correct ass-kissing politician changed the word "Armed" to "American" so as not to create any ill will. Somehow, they overlooked the word "Forces" in AFRTS or AFKN. When the subject ever came up, most of us simply thought it was a pointless attempt at renaming what was obvious to any observer. Evidently, no diplomat ever realized that putting a smiley face on a bomb did not change the fact that it still went fucking boom and killed people.

Regardless, the annual fundraising event carried mostly over radio was quite simple and very effective. At the appointed time, the on-air DJs would start off the fundraising by playing a song of extremely low appeal until some person or group made good on a pledge of more money than the DJ had initially put up. The higher pledgers got to choose a new song that would be played until yet another group came up with even more money to get it off the air. Skivvy-Nine had historically so dominated this event over the years that the rules had been modified so that no song could be played for more than a few hours, and then the process would begin anew. The new rules didn't matter, because Skivvy-Nine always came out on top.

The tradition had been started well before I ever made my first visit to Osan. Some Skivvy-Niner, whose name has been lost in the dust of history, had been impressed with the late Hollywood screen legend Robert Mitchum singing the song "Thunder Road" from the 1958 movie of the same name in which he starred. That Skivvy-Niner convinced all of his buddies to back him in pledging "Thunder Road" to play as long as possible. As soon as some other group paid more money to get a different song on the air, Skivvy-Niners would rally to get "Thunder Road" back on the air. In fact, after years of Skivvy-Nine domination, the name of the narrow lane leading from Broadway Boulevard on Osan Air Base up the hill to our Operations Center actually became known as Thunder Road. I always got a kick from the complaints about hearing "Thunder Road" without end. It signified that Skivvy-Niners had once again demonstrated their *esprit de corps* like no other unit, and that once again everyone knew that we were Number One –

Oom Ya Ya YA!

One day, shortly after "Thunder Road" had played its last at the end of its twenty-somethingth season, I walked into the main ballroom of the NCO Club to get some dinner and noticed a familiar-looking Korean woman in her thirties sitting with a guy along with a young boy, maybe twelve or so years old, evidently their son. I noticed her eyes following me as I went to a table several feet away. She continued to look in my direction until what I presumed was her husband caught her looking at me. As she broke eye contact when her husband turned to look in my direction, I focused on my menu, for I certainly did not want to be the cause of some disturbance with a jealous or otherwise insecure husband. I did, however, not fail to note that the woman was both attractive and stylishly dressed. While I was certainly not disfigured, I was equally aware that I wasn't any movie star. Either this woman remembered me or she had somehow divined my dazzling personality. We must have crossed paths in the Ville at some point in the past.

As I was ordering, I saw Ruthie stop to talk with the woman while completely ignoring the husband, although she did seem to speak briefly with the young lad sitting with the couple. I made a note to myself ask Ruthie what she could tell about this woman, since she and Ruthie seemed to know one another. The family got up to leave just as my food arrived, and the woman looked at me again with a fleeting smile on her face. I quickly nodded my head to acknowledge her greeting but refocused my gaze upon my plate as the three of them walked right past me on their way out.

Ruthie had not been the one to wait on me, so after the woman and her family had left, I intended to call her over to see what I could get out of her. Most of the time, Ruthie would not talk about other customers, and I knew that it was a good practice to stay out of other people's business. But I was intrigued. Why would this woman stare at me while with someone else? It was an unwritten rule in Korea that, if a guy and a business woman who had enjoyed a relationship with each other in the past were ever seen in the company of someone else, every effort would be made by each person to avoid having to acknowledge the presence of the other. It was the only way to prevent serious domestic disturbances, so I had to find out from Ruthie what was going on with that woman. Geezus, she had actually *gawked* at me.

When Ruthie was not busy with other diners in the club, I beckoned for her to come over. I told her what I had seen and then asked her straight out – me being an uncivilized American and not a subtle Korean – how well she knew the woman. Ruthie got a serious look on her face before she replied that she would tell me everything that I wanted to know because the woman had told her that it was fitting to do so if I ever asked about her. Now I was really curious. "Why would I have any interest in a married woman that I don't know in the first place?" I wondered out loud.

Ruthie was quite patient with me, a significant departure from her standard operating procedure. She asked me quietly if I knew the woman, to which I said that she seemed familiar but that I could not place her. Ruthie provided the woman's Korean name, the one she used before her marriage to the guy with whom she had been sitting. I shook my head to indicate that her name did not register with me. Ruthie softly said, "You knew her as 'Lucy' a long time ago." Holy history lesson! My jaw dropped in amazement and I probably looked like someone who had been struck by a hammer to the head.

Ruthie took in my look and paused before she asked me what I remembered of my relationship with Lucy. I told her about how Lucy and I had become friends as a result of her helping me improve my Korean back when my unit had first been deployed almost constantly to Korea more than a dozen years ago. I also mentioned that she had invited me to attend her son's 100-day celebration and that another airman and I had taken up a collection afterwards to help with her medical bills. I then revealed how she had collected me up off the streets and got me sober one day before we had been – and here I struggled with how to say it delicately – lovers the one time. Ruthie touched me on the shoulder, saying that she understood fully, for that was very close to how Lucy had explained her interest in me.

Again the hammer to my head! Lucy had an interest in me? I concluded my story to Ruthie by saying that Lucy had located me in the barracks one day much later because she had wanted to say a proper good-bye. I omitted my belief that Lucy had also wanted an opportunity for the two of us to be together one more time. Ruthie confirmed my unspoken thought by her very perceptive response, "You should have taken advantage of the opportunity; no woman likes to be turned down."

I explained to Ruthie that I thought Lucy was married at the time, but even if she hadn't yet tied the knot, I don't like getting between domestic partners, as that can be a recipe for somebody getting hurt. Ruthie challenged me, "What, you didn't like her any longer?"

"No, no, no!" I quickly replied as I searched for a good way to put it. "It would have been like only one breath of air to a drowning man," I finally explained, even if it was an exaggeration. "Besides, what would we have done afterward?

What would that have changed?" I asked. However, I did admit that I often wished that I had invited Lucy into my barracks room for a last special good-bye, and to hell with any consequences. Ruthie relented a bit, saying that she agreed with my take on the situation, but that she always liked to see love win out in the end.

To get the focus of our conversation away from me, I asked Ruthie, if she was such a sucker for romance, why she had never married. She looked at me with a wistful expression as she replied, "I am no cherry girl, you understand? I am careful, but marrying an American – Ha! How would that turn out? We could not put up with each other for long."

Ruthie was partly right, for she was a very strong and willful woman – she would have to be in order to survive in Korea. But I also thought that the right man, knowing how to deal with her fiery temperament, would have captured one helluva partner and had a greatly enriched life with Ruthie. Instead of telling her that, I did concur with her about Korean-American marriages often not being of long duration.

Consequently, I wasn't surprised when Ruthie told me that Lucy's marriage was not going well. Ruthie said that Lucy had become a U.S. citizen when she and her husband had been stationed in the States for a few years. Now that they were back in Korea, Lucy was taking courses to finish her college degree, and that was part of the trouble with her husband. He was against a woman being more educated than he was, and he saw a woman's place as being only in the kitchen – or the bedroom. Lucy, on the other hand, had goals now that she realized all of the opportunities open to her. I thought, "How cool is that! Good for her," and I said so to Ruthie.

I concluded that if Lucy ever broke free from her dumb ass

of a husband, I would certainly appreciate a chance with her. Since Ruthie had already informed me that Lucy had at least some lingering interest in me, why not, I figured. I asked Ruthie for a piece of paper and explained that I was going to give her my permanent home address in the States, where my parents lived. If anyone ever wanted to contact me, no matter where I was in the world, my parents could get word to me. I folded the paper over once and gave it to Ruthie with the request that she give it to Lucy – but only if Lucy revealed that she was getting divorced. I still did not want to be in the middle as the "other man."

Ruthie smiled at me as she said with a bit of sass, "Well, maybe I'll just use this address myself."

I looked straight into her eyes before boldly looking her up and down in a frank appraisal of her womanliness. I finally said, "You do that, Ruthie, you just do that."

Her smile disappeared to be replaced by a look of uncertainty, the only time I ever saw Ruthie unsure of herself. She didn't know whether I was serious or just putting her on. To be honest, I didn't know myself at the time. After some seconds of locked eyes, Ruthie glanced away before she returned to her old self to exclaim, "Ah, you give me the fits!" as she turned to walk away – but with an exaggerated sway of her nicely feminine hips.

I stayed away from the NCO Club during the evening hours when I thought that families would be most likely to be dining there. Instead, I either used the chow hall or the Snack Bar. Sometimes, delivered food was available without ever calling for it. One of the great things about Osan was that guys were always getting drunk and ordering food that would arrive after they either passed out or gotten too sick to eat. This food hardly ever went to waste and the Snack Bar delivery guys rarely got stuck for the tab.

Long ago, they had learned that what was rejected or unclaimed by one person would be gladly purchased by another, often in the same barracks or at least one nearby. In fact, I had learned from my Korean acquaintances on base that the various Skivvy-Nine barracks were considered choice locations regarding food orders in need of a buyer. The combination of intended and unintended deliveries of grub worked out well since it allowed me to avoid running into Lucy and her husband. If things were to work out for the two of them, then my presence would serve only to muddy the waters. If things didn't and they divorced, then Lucy knew how to reach me. I tried not to think of her.

There certainly were other events to occupy my thoughts, one of which was the rumor that the president of South Korea would visit Osan in the near future. This was a big deal, since the ROK – Republic of Korea – president was really a military dictator who had taken advantage of the electoral process to rise to that office and keep himself in that position. His immediate predecessor had been assassinated, and as a result, the incumbent president had an understandable concern about security.

Information about the upcoming visit was closely held and it wasn't until the actual day of the visit that details were released to the vast majority of airman at Osan. Everyone was told in all seriousness that the main gate of the base would be closed to all traffic shortly after the Day shift began. Briefings were held to disseminate the particulars of what to expect – and what to not do. One hour before the ROK president was to arrive in his escorted motorcade, all vehicular traffic on base would be stopped. No mention was made about vehicles such as fire trucks or military police vehicles, and I wondered about how the base would react to a bona-fide emergency.

But that was not all. One-half hour before arrival, all pedestrians would be forced inside, without exception. People were told not to look out windows for they ran the risk of being shot by the ROK bodyguard troops that would be lining the streets of Osan from the main gate to the flight line reviewing stand where the president would be treated to a pre-sale demonstration of the General Dynamics F-16 fighter aircraft's capabilities.

The Skivvy-Nine Operations Center was on Hill 170, which was about 500 feet above the rest of the base. Our building was roughly a mile away from the reviewing stand on the flight line apron, which was clearly visible from inside our security fence. Most of the Skivvy-Niners had never had an opportunity to see what an F-16 can do and were therefore quite willing to risk the threat of some South Korean rifleman from over 5,000 feet away.

The gate shack that controlled the entry and exit point for our compound had an excellent view of the east end of the runway, the very area from which the South Koreans had carted off chunks of newly laid asphalt so many years ago. The guard on duty agreed to notify us when the F-16 taxied toward the 9,000-foot runway in preparation for his demo flight.

We got the call letting us know that the fighter was on the move toward the end of the runway, and those of us who could be released from non-mission critical tasks ran to our compound perimeter fence to watch. That plane carried no external fuel tanks, no external munitions, and I would have bet, having seen a number of air shows myself, the aircraft had onboard only the amount of fuel necessary for this very specific mission. The plane had the least amount of drag and most likely carried the least amount of weight to deal with.

After juicing the throttle several time to create the ominous roar of a war bird impatiently waiting to get aloft, the pilot received the OK from the tower. When he started his takeoff roll, the plane was already 1,000 feet down the runway, having advanced that far from the times the pilot had goosed the throttle for noise effect. The reviewing stand was near the mid-point of the runway, only 3,500 feet away. With maximum afterburner thunderously providing more pounds of thrust than the aircraft weighed, the F-16 was airborne and already going vertical by the time it reached the reviewing stand. The pilot kept it accelerating straight up until the bird had climbed out of sight into the clouds high overhead within only a very few seconds.

The show was not over, for the pilot soon brought the jet back in at about 100 feet above the deck, with afterburner now off. The plane must have been just below sonic speed, so there was almost no auditory announcement of its approach. It shot past the reviewing stand – and us on the hill – in a blur and then it was out of sight over the horizon, again within just a few seconds. When the pilot returned again, his speed was considerably less, but as he passed by the reviewing stand, he performed a complete inside loop starting from roughly 500 feet to an altitude of less than 3,000 feet. Upon completion of one full loop, the pilot climbed to a few hundred feet and turned the agile aircraft in a tight circle that did not exceed a half-mile in diameter. Mission complete, he kicked in the afterburner and shot out of sight before returning to land in less than half the runway length and then taxiing up to the review stand to park at an angle that showed off the clean line of one helluva aerial warfare machine.

Nobody had ever seen a performance like that and all of us illegal viewers yelled and jumped up and down in appreciation of what our pilots and aircraft could do. "Let the sonsabitching North Koreans fuck with that!" I proudly thought. That brief show was probably the single most important sales event in the history of South Korean purchases of U.S. fighter aircraft, and the pilot was subsequently awarded an Air Medal for his flawless mission. For the rest of the week, just about the only thing people talked about – at least those that had been able to observe it – was that event, a once in a lifetime air show, and I had been there to see it.

It was fitting that my time at Osan – my final tour of duty anywhere overseas – was coming to an end soon after the impressive F-16 demonstration. It is always good to leave on a high note. Altogether, I had spent nearly fifteen of my twenty military years overseas and I was looking forward to the last year of my career in the States. Korea was changing, becoming more modern, but I wanted to preserve my memories of the country as it was when I first arrived so many years ago. Although I had enjoyed my time in Korea more than anyone I knew, I was beginning to think that maybe it was time to return to being an American.

I didn't realize it at the time, but my hankering to get away was really not about any interest in my native culture. It was due more to a burgeoning dissatisfaction with some – but certainly not all – of the leadership in Skivvy-Nine with whom I now had closer association due to my being a senior NCO. For example, the harsh treatment of Lt. Underhill for having acquired an STD and thus becoming an embarrassment to our commanding officer, and the childlike behavior of our prideful headquarters general for being whipped in a tennis match, to say nothing of the cavalier disregard by many of the command staff for Mr. Lee having reached an important milestone in his career with Skivvy-Nine. All of these incidents left me with a diminished regard for certain aspects of military life. The truth was that I was ready to be done with the Air Force, ready to become a civilian again.

I made my preparations and signed out of all the support organizations on base. There was time for me to make my final good-byes to my co-workers and fellow barracks mates as well as other friends on base, exchanging addresses with a few in the process, each of us recognizing that we would probably never use them, but going through the ritual expression of camaraderie and good will nonetheless. It was a happy time and it was a sad time as I worked at closing out one of the most meaningful periods in my life.

I thought that I might have briefly seen Lucy one last time when I ate my final breakfast at the NCO Club in order to say good-bye to Ruthie. I wasn't sure because somehow some damned dust had gotten in my eyes and they were watering fiercely as I clambered into a taxi for the short ride to the air terminal.

That August 1981 flight back to the States for my final year in the Air Force was the longest and most restless plane ride I ever experienced.

Epilogue

I have been retired from the Air Force for more than three decades now, just another old married man, but even though I have left Korea, it has never left me. I carry it within me, in my mind and in my heart. I often have thoughts of going back in order to visit my old haunts and to look up any former friends that might still be around, but time has changed nearly everything – except my memories, which remain as vivid as they ever were.

It is distressing to look at recent photographs and satellite imagery of Korea, simply because they are in conflict with the pictures of Osan Air Base and the Ville still vibrantly alive in my mind. I understand that such nostalgic efforts to revisit the past are doomed to failure, for nothing remains as it was during the period from the mid 1960s to the early 1980s. I accept that change is inevitable – and that it has been good for Korea, for I have seen it progress from a war-ravaged Third World country to the powerful Asian Tiger that it is today, improving the lives of everyone there. And yet ....

Every once in a while, something reminds me of the old Korea and I will smile as I reminisce about the days long past when I was first seen as a "jeep" and a "green bean," and then later recognized as an "old hand" in my own right. And, invariably, my thoughts will turn to how I met Lucy, unknowingly fell in love with her, and then let her slip away. On the occasions when my wife notices my reveries, she invariably says in mock reproach, "Ah, you are reliving your wild Dragonfly days in Korea, aren't you?"

There is no reason to deny it, and so I freely admit that mentally I had been far away in another time and place for a few moments. Keeping the same manufactured tone of admonishment in her voice, my wife will continue, "Well, perhaps you should consider leaving all that Skivvy-Nine stuff buried in the past. You know that those are tales you wouldn't tell your mother." Then she always comes over to where I sit and kisses me on the top of my now-bald head.

"Yes, Lucy dear," I predictably reply as I reach out to fondle her still enticing spots, "I will – I swear by the three holy Hans."

Acknowledgements

First and foremost, I must express deep appreciation to Esther Dille-McCoy for her insistence that these are tales that needed to be told – and that I was the one to do it. To Steve Levine, who also gave me the encouragement necessary to overcome any qualms about writing such a work, I am deeply indebted. Both of these individuals contributed greatly to the readability of this book through their frequent comments and suggestions, and I owe the two of them more gratitude than can be written here.

Also worthy of recognition are the flight crews assigned to the 6988th Security Squadron at Yokota Air Base in Japan who spent considerable time deployed with me to South Korea from early 1968 through early 1970. Not ever to be forgotten are the members – initially men only but later women too – of Skivvy-Nine (officially known as the 6929th – later changed to the 6903rd – Security Squadron) at Osan Air Base in South Korea from the mid 1960s to the early 1980s. As well, I want to acknowledge those airmen of the USAFSS Emergency Reaction Units from around the world who quickly became an integral part of Skivvy-Nine life in early 1968.

Of course, I cannot fail to call out for special appreciation the Koreans themselves that worked on Osan Air Base and in the Ville (now Songtan City) and who taught me more than any college professor or formal textbook possibly could about culture and language in non-metropolitan Korea. Many of them became good friends, thus greatly enriching my time in Korea – especially Pang Hyo-jŏng, truly my brother.

A heartfelt thank-you to all.

Robert E. McCoy
September 2015

CPSIA information can be obtained
at www.ICGtesting.com
Printed in the USA
FSOW02n0117101115
13090FS